ESCAPE TO MEXICO

Escape To Mexico
An Anthology of Great Fiction

Edited by Sara Nicklès

CHRONICLE BOOKS

SAN FRANCISCO

For Mary Strom, with love and *besitos.*

Page 259 constitutes a continuation of the copyright page.

Every effort has been made to trace the ownership of all copyrighted
material included in this volume. Any errors that may have occurred are
inadvertent and will be corrected in subsequent editions, provided notifi-
cation is sent to the publisher.

To maintain the authentic style of each writer included herein, quirks of
spelling and grammar remain unchanged from their original state.

Library of Congress Cataloging-in-Publication Data available.

ISBN 0-8118-3393-3

Manufactured in the United States of America.

Designed by elbow
This book was set in Tarocco, Eidetic™ Modern, and RETABLO™ ANTIGUO

Distributed in Canada by Raincoast Books
9050 Shaughnessy Street
Vancouver, British Columbia V6P 6E5

10 9 8 7 6 5 4 3 2 1

Chronicle Books LLC
85 Second Street
San Francisco, California 94105

www.chroniclebooks.com

We lay still for a time, looking at the tiny guavas and the per-fect, soft, high blue sky overhead, where the hawks and the ragged-winged zopilotes *sway and diminish. A long, hot way home. But* manana es otro dia. *Tomorrow is another day. And even the next five minutes are far enough away, in Mexico, on a Sunday afternoon.*

—D.H. Lawrence
Mornings in Mexico

ESCAPE TO MEXICO
An Anthology of Great Fiction

INTRODUCTION

"COME WITH ME TO MEXICO," says a character in Anaïs Nin's short story. "I want to wander about a little and find out who I am. . . ."

Mexico has long been viewed not only as a place but also as a state of mind. It is a land of possibilities and extremes, of passion and intrigue, a land where you can find yourself or lose yourself, depending upon what you desire. For a variety of reasons, the North American and British writers in this anthology sought out Mexico for themselves, some for years, others for shorter periods, and then chose it as a setting for their fiction.

The characters in these tales are both seeking something special in Mexico and leaving something behind. A couple starts a business, another couple resumes an affair. A man runs from the law, a woman flees with a gangster's money. Tourists look for bargains; an adventurer hunts for exotic plants; an anthropologist, a dissipated CIA agent, a gentleman hopes for complete idleness. Some are trying to forget sadness, while others are pursuing an endless fiesta.

They all escaped to Mexico.

What happens to them once they get there is often not

what they expect, however, and therein lies the heart of these tales. It is not travel in general that alters their perceptions and expectations and understandings, but rather the particulars of Mexico: the country is more than the location for each story — it is a character.

Fortunately, neither the insights into the country nor the selections from the great writers in this volume can be reduced to a simple formula. They are gathered here so that we can join in the varieties of experience, so that we can compare them with our own fantasies of flight, so that we can escape vicariously.

Or we can carry this book with us when we go.

Stones for Ibarra
Harriet Doerr

Here they are, two North Americans, a man and a woman just over and just under forty, come to spend their lives in Mexico and already lost as they travel cross-country over the central plateau. The driver of the station wagon is Richard Everton, a blue-eyed, black-haired stubborn man who will die thirty years sooner than he now imagines. On the seat beside him is his wife, Sara, who imagines neither his death nor her own, imminent or remote as they may be. Instead she sees, in one of its previous incarnations, the adobe house where they intend to sleep tonight. It is a mile and a half high on the outskirts of Ibarra, a declining village of one thousand souls. Tunneled into the mountain whose shadow falls on the house an hour before sunset is the copper mine Richard's grandfather abandoned fifty years ago during the Revolution of 1910.

Dark is coming on among the high hills and, unless they find a road, night will trap at this desolate spot both the future operator of the Malagueña mine and the fair-haired, unsuspecting future mistress of the adobe house. Sara Everton is anticipating their arrival at a place curtained and warm, though she knows the house has neither electricity nor furniture and, least of all, kindling beside the hearth. There is some doubt about running water in the pipes. The Malagueña mine, on the other hand, is flooded up to the second level.

Richard and Sara Everton will be the only foreigners in the village and they will depart in order, first Richard, then his wife. When Sara drives away for the last time, taking a studded leather chest, a painted religious figure, and a few flower pots, there will be no North American left in Ibarra.

~

For an hour the Evertons have followed footpaths and wagon trails that begin with no purpose and end with no destination. Although they can see their goal, a steep range of mountains lifting abruptly from the plain, they have found no direct way to approach it. The distant slopes rise first on their right, then on their left, and occasionally behind them.

"Let's stop and ask the way," says Sara, "while there is still daylight." And, as they take a diagonal course across a cleared space of land, she and her husband notice how the flat, pale rays from the west have lengthened the shadows of a row of tattered cornstalks, stunned survivors of the autumn harvest.

But the owner of this field, the crooked fig tree, and the bent plowshare dulled by weeds and weather is nowhere in sight.

Richard points to a drifting haze. "There's some smoke from a cooking fire." But it turns out to be only a spiral of dust whirling behind an empty dam.

"We won't get to Ibarra before dark," says Sara. "Do you think we'll recognize the house?"

"Yes," he says, and without speaking they separately recall a faded photograph of a wide, low structure with a long veranda in front. On the veranda is a hammock woven of white string, and in the hammock is Richard's grandmother, dressed in eyelet embroidery and holding a fluted fan. Beyond is a tennis court and a rose garden.

~

Five days ago the Evertons left San Francisco and their house with a narrow view of the bay in order to extend the family's Mexican history and patch the present onto the past. To find out if there was still copper underground and how much of the rest of it was true, the width of sky, the depth of stars, the air like new wine, the harsh noons and long, slow dusks. To weave chance and hope into a fabric that would clothe them as long as they lived.

Even their closest friends have failed to understand. "Call us when you get there," they said. "Send a telegram." But Ibarra lacks these services. "How close is the airport?" and to avoid having to answer, the Evertons promised to send maps. "What will you do for light?" they were asked. And, "How long since someone lived in the house?" But this question collapsed of its own weight before a reply could be composed.

Every day for a month Richard has reminded Sara, "We mustn't expect too much." And each time his wife has answered, "No." But the Evertons expect too much. They have experienced the terrible persuasion of a great-aunt's recollections and adopted them as their own. They have not considered that memories are like corks left out of bottles. They swell. They no longer fit.

~

Now here, lost in the Mexican interior under a January sun withering toward the horizon, Richard and Sara remember the photographs that turned first yellow, then sepia, in family albums. They remember the packets of letters marked *Mexico* and divided into years by dry rubber bands. They remember the rock pick Richard's grandfather gave him when he was six. His grandfather had used the pick himself to chip away copper ore from extrusions that coursed like exposed arteries down the slope of one mountain and webbed out into smaller veins up the slope of the next.

Richard, without stopping the car, gropes under the seat for the rock pick, touches it, then heads across a field of stubble toward a few stripped trees in the west.

Halfway to the trees, behind a clump of mesquite, a posted sign confronts the Evertons. According to the federal power commission, the community of El Portal is about to be electrified. A moment later, beyond a broken arch, they come to El Portal, a cluster of nine adobe houses and a colonial chapel so small, perfectly proportioned, and vividly domed that it might have been designed to be attached to the nursery of a princess in Córdoba or Seville.

"Only a very short priest could enter to say mass and only children worship there," says Sara. As if summoned, a boy and a girl with the half-formed bones and oversized front teeth of seven-year-olds materialize, staring, in a doorway.

Richard lowers the window. "Which is the way to Ibarra?" he asks, and the children, unable to reconcile the Spanish words with the aspect of the stranger, turn rigid as stone.

"Ibarra," the American says again. "In those mountains."

And he points in the direction of three peaks, skirted all around by a somber border of foothills. "Where the mines are," he says.

~

"What does he know about mining?" Richard's friends have asked one another. "What does she know about gasoline stoves and charcoal irons? In case of burns, where will they find a doctor?" The friends learn that the Evertons are taking a first aid manual, antibiotics for dysentery, and a snakebite kit. There are other questions, relating to symphony season tickets, Christmas, golf, sailing. To these, the answers are evasive.

Heedless of criticism and disbelief, the Evertons have gone ahead, mortgaged their house, borrowed on their insurance, applied for bank loans against dwindling collateral, and invested the total proceeds in rusty machinery apparently racked beyond repair.

"It's supposed to be a concentrating mill," one of the friends told the others. "Who's going to assemble it?"

But the Evertons neither notice the rust nor seem concerned about finding mechanical engineers in a village where only the youngest generation has graduated from the fifth grade. They indeed propose to operate the family mine and occupy the family house, and they see no reason why their project should not succeed.

~

The two seven-year-olds in the doorway, as if they had never heard of mines, remain fixed and speechless in their places. Suddenly a farmer, leading a lame burro, approaches the car from behind.

He regards the two Americans. "You are not on the road

to Ibarra," he says. "Permit me a moment." And he gazes first at his feet, then at the mountains, then at their luggage. "You must drive north on that dry arroyo for two kilometers and turn left when you reach a road. You will recognize it by the tire tracks of the morning bus unless there have been too many goats. Or unless rain has fallen. But this is the dry season."

He does not ask why the Americans are going to Ibarra, where they are sure to be conspicuous because of their car, their textbook Spanish, and their four suitcases, which he imagines to be full of woolens, silks, and lace.

He merely points and says, "The arroyo is beyond that tree." Together they look at the six remaining top branches of a leafless cottonwood whose destiny it has become to cook the beans and toast the tortillas of the nine families of El Portal until it is reduced to a stump. Then that other cotton-wood, farther down the arroyo, will in its turn perish gradually by the ax.

Before going on, the Evertons look around them at El Portal.

"You have a beautiful chapel," they say.

At these words, the man and the burro and the two children in the doorway turn their heads to regard the miniature structure with its carved stone lintel and filigree cross as if it had been built today, Saturday the twenty-seventh of January, between noon and four o'clock. But they don't reply. They cannot decide so quickly if the chapel is beautiful.

The Evertons drive toward the last of the houses, where a rooster stalks the flat roof, pecking angrily at crumbs of plaster.

"Probably, in a high wind, cornhusks fly up there, or acorns, or wild berries," says Sara, imagining a meal for the rooster, who now leans in the attitude of a vulture from the roof's edge and assesses them through hooded eyes. But there is not a gust of wind to carry husk or seed aloft.

"Without a tail wind we won't be bothered by the dust," says Richard, and turns north.

He is mistaken. They arroyo is smooth and soft with dust that, even in still air, spins from the car's wheels and sifts through sealed surfaces, the flooring, the dashboard, the factory-tested weather stripping. It etches black lines on their palms, sands their skin, powders their lashes, and deposits a bitter taste on their tongues.

"This must be the wrong way," says Sara, from under the sweater she has pulled over her head.

Richard says nothing. He knows it is the right way, as right as a way to Ibarra can be, as right as his decision to reopen an idle mine and bring his wife to a house built half of nostalgia and half of clay.

When they have gone two kilometers, they stop and look for the road to Ibarra. But it is as the man in El Portal half suspected. There have been too many goats. While the Evertons search the trampled ground, they notice that all around them the winter afternoon is folding in on itself. Toward the west, in the direction they must turn, are only random boulders, nopal cactus, and the shadows strung out behind.

But from the east, where a moment ago there was nothing, runs a boy, and, for the first time, the Evertons witness a recurring Mexican phenomenon: the abrupt appearance of human life in an empty landscape. Later it would become a commonplace experience. They had only to turn their backs momentarily on a deserted plain and a man on a mule would have ridden up behind them or a woman with a child settled on a nearby rock.

Now, out of a vast unpopulated panorama, here, close at hand, is a boy with a satchel. He observes the two North Americans without astonishment through quick eyes that are wide apart and expectant. The Evertons realize immediately that he is a person wholly committed to what is going to happen next. Within a minute he has offered to show them the way to Ibarra. It is the village where he lives.

"Then ride with us and be our guide," says Richard, and the boy climbs into the rear and accommodates himself between the suitcases and cartons.

"What is your name?" Sara asks in careful Spanish.

"Domingo García," says the boy. "At your orders." He smiles with white, even teeth.

"To the left of that big rock," he tells Richard. "Between those two huisache trees. Across that bridge."

The bridge is two parallel planks set about five feet apart over a canyon, and Richard has trouble aligning his wheels with the boards. He walks to the bridge and notices the depth of the gorge.

Domingo joins him and steps on a plank to try it. "You drive," he says, "and I will show you." Balanced on the brink, his back to the abyss, he extends his hands, palms facing. They move an inch to the right and half an inch to the left. When he is satisfied that the wheels are aimed at the boards, he runs back to insert himself again among the luggage.

"Straight ahead," says Domingo, and the Evertons are introduced to a second national peculiarity, one they will soon recognize on the streets of Ibarra and in towns and cities beyond. It is something they will see everywhere—a disregard for danger, a companionship with death. By the end of a year they will know it well: the antic bravado, the fatal games, the coffin shop beside the cantina, the sugar skulls on the frosted cake.

There are two more bridges, but Richard refuses further help. Sara shuts her eyes and sits still as a stone image while they cross. When it is over, she turns to the passenger behind.

"Did you walk far today?"

Domingo says he missed the bus this morning, so he had to walk all the way from La Gloria. La Gloria is where he has been enrolled in preparatory school by his older brother, Basilio, who does not permit him to miss even one class. But, thanks to this ride, he will arrive in Ibarra in time for the fiesta tomorrow, on the saint's day of the town. He asks if it is the annual visit of the bishop of the state or the carnival itself that is bringing the Americans to Ibarra. There is no hotel, he tells them, only Chayo Durán's *mesón*, and the four rooms may already be occupied.

"We are not visiting Ibarra. We are going to live there," says Richard. "In the house my grandfather built."

Domingo, now in possession of a clue, falls silent.

～

In the last century Richard Everton's grandfather built an adobe house in Ibarra for his wife. He took a stick and drew the shape of the house in the dirt while his mason observed the plan. First he drew a square around a patio, then one wing and then another, and then a veranda around it all.

～

The Evertons follow the invisible track pointed out by Domingo for half an hour until it abruptly mounts an embankment and they find themselves on a scraped dirt road.

They have traveled smoothly along it for ten minutes and are already in the foothills when a careening carnival truck overtakes them. Behind the cab, the wooden legs and tails of horses and the wooden necks of swans protrude from the splitting canvas that secures them.

"Did that truck have to cross the plank bridges?" asks Richard.

"No," says Domingo. "It came by this road which has been cleared as far as Ibarra. If you had remained on the highway from the capital, from Concepción, instead of turning toward El Portal, you would have seen the sign and the arrow. But the way you chose is five kilometers shorter."

Sara, reminded, lowers her window to shake dust from her sweater. Richard makes no comment.

~

They are climbing into the mountains now and negotiating a series of sharp blind curves. Ahead of them the truck shifts in and out of low gear, each time threatening to roll back and bury them under a carousel.

Now Domingo resumes the conversation he left off earlier. "Then you will live in the big white house and work the Malagueña mine," he says. "Like your grandfather."

Richard glances back at his passenger. "How do you know about my grandfather?"

"From the old men of Ibarra." And Domingo takes this opportunity to apply for a job. He says he is fifteen and strong, and has completed the ninth grade.

"Listen to your brother Basilio and stay in school." In the mirror Richard's clouded blue eyes meet Domingo's unshadowed black ones. "Later on you can start your career as a miner."

~

"Where is it?" the Evertons' friends had asked, and were shown Richard's map. On a blank space north of Concepción he had printed the name, Ibarra.

"It's on the outside edge of nowhere," said the friends. "You can't mean to spend the rest of your lives down there."

But it is indeed the Evertons' intention to spend the rest of their lives down here. They will not know until July that in Richard's case this will amount to six years.

"Count on at least six active years," they will be told by the doctor who diagnoses an irregularity or, put more clearly, a malignancy, in Richard's blood the summer after their arrival in Ibarra.

But by then they are already whitewashing the old house and pumping water from the third level of the Malagueña mine; the concentrating mill has already been installed and blessed. By then they will have planted the bougainvillea and the rose. By then the noon whistle at La Malagueña, silent for fifty years, will divide the day again, and in the plaza of Ibarra the sacristan, hurrying back to the church with a new broom, will notice that the clock in the tower is eleven minutes slow.

But they will not meet this doctor, a hematologist, until July.

"You have plenty of time," Richard says to Domingo. As the incline becomes steeper, he allows his car to drop farther behind the listing truck.

Now Domingo starts to identify the roofless sheds and rotting headframes that slant against the hillsides. He begins to pronounce in sequence the rich names of abandoned mines. "El Indio Gordo, El Paradiso," he tells the Evertons. "La Bonanza, La Purísima, La Lulu."

"I wonder," Sara suddenly says, but she does not disclose what it is she wonders. Looking at Richard's profile, she sees the thin scar on his cheek turn white and knows he has preoccupations of his own.

Halfway up this mountain, in the increasing chill and gloom of the winter evening, he has assumed, as he might assume a yoke that could break him, the awful responsibility of apportioning jobs. As though he were a seer, he envisions a group of men who will already have been standing at his gate for an hour when he opens it tomorrow. They will squat on their heels or lean against the wall or sit on rocks until he comes. Then each man will stand to introduce himself and shake hands. Their grandfathers knew his grandfather. Their fathers caught rabbits and killed snakes with his father when they were boys. They have survived by the thinnest margin since the mines shut down, one by one, after the Revolution.

When the truck and the car have passed the summit, descended a hundred meters on the other side, and started to accelerate along the level approach to the village, Richard is still composing what he will have to say.

"This will be a small operation. At first I can only employ a few. Everything depends on the grade of ore. We must install the machinery and find out how things go." He foresees the men looking at his face and then at the ground. They will not believe him. They have already heard about the car and the suitcases and the ham-and-cheese sandwiches the Americans divided with Domingo.

Then the Evertons, still caught in the wake of the truck,

turn abruptly to the right, find themselves on a cobbled street dropping down to a plaza, and here it is, Ibarra.

An immense stillness fills the square. Somewhere in it sound and motion lie suspended. Eyes, under the brims of hats or over the folds of shawls, follow them from park benches, deep-set doorways, and the lighted interiors of the grocer's shop and the pool hall. Even the driver of the carnival truck, already entering the cantina, stands fixed at the swinging door.

We have come to live among specters, Sara tells herself. They are not people, but silhouettes sketched on a backdrop to deceive us into thinking that the stage is crowded. She searches for an expression, any expression, in their eyes— the eyes of that man on the corner whose raised hand holds a cigarette he is allowing to burn to his fingers; the eyes of that woman who has lifted a dripping jar of water halfway to her head. They will never speak to me, she thinks. I will never know their names.

On the far side of town the Evertons leave Domingo at his house. Even in the dark it seems to sag. In front of it a fat woman sits on an overturned pail.

"My mother," says Domingo, and gives them final instructions. "Follow those pepper trees up the hill to the high stone wall and push open the gate," he says. "You will see your house in front of you."

~

So it is night when they arrive and too dark to examine the interior. They eat bananas in an empty room that smells of mice and weathered wood and, by the beam of a flashlight, set up camp cots on the veranda which, after tonight, they will call the porch. Rolled in blankets that still exude dust, they find they can see each other's faces by the stars. They are asleep almost at once, too tired to hear the quick, light feet of possums and raccoons as they approach and then retreat. Nor does a coyote, crying the night apart beyond the town, disturb them.

But at two o'clock in the morning, when the brittle leaves of the ash tree at the corner of the house cease to stir, Sara sits up in her cot. "I think I hear frost," she says to her sleeping husband.

Four hours later they awake shivering to a sudden dawn that floods up behind the eastern mesa and stains half the sky coral.

Now the house is revealed, and the garden.

But where is it all, the splendid past? The roof of imported cedar shingles, the wallpaper from France? The chandelier that held three dozen tapers? The floors that took so high a polish they seemed designed for dancing? Where is the clay tennis court that was rolled and chalked twice a week by the coachman, while the gardener, an expert with roses, tied back the profusion that threatened to overwhelm it? Where is the fountain, the gazebo, the hedge?

They might as well ask, where are the people in the photographs? Where the gentlemen in white flannels who lobbed slow balls to ladies running in shoes with French heels and silk laces to lob them back? Were they really here, the girls who rode sidesaddle from one parched hillside to another, the young men who came to house parties and said, "May I?"

"May I carry your camera?" they said. "May I fetch your watercolors?" Or at night, "May I show you Orion from the orchard?"

Now, in the uncompromising light of a new day, the Evertons, avoiding a column of red ants, stand on the cracked tile of their doorstep and stare across the expanse of naked earth that extends before them. On the balustrade of the porch three lizards, touched by the first rays of the sun, begin to puff out their throats. Hornets swarm in and out of a mud nest in the eaves.

"I wonder," says Sara, completing her unstated thought of last evening, "if we have gone out of our minds."

At this moment, which is six-thirty, Domingo García walks up the driveway whistling to himself. He has come to ask how they slept and to report that eighteen men are waiting at the gate.

"Is this a convenient hour?"

"I will talk to them now," says Richard, and, as if to celebrate these words, the jukebox on the plaza inaugurates the day with a mariachi song. A fanfare of trumpets spears the sky. Then a church bell rings, and dogs, burros, and cows confuse the thin morning air with their complaints.

Domingo, to let in this outburst all at once, pulls the gate wide. Sara watches her husband walk through, watches the small crowd rise and wait. Then she sees the men come forward, one by one, to shake his hand.

Across the Bridge
Graham Greene

'They say he's worth a million,' Lucia said. He sat there in the little hot damp Mexican square, a dog at his feet, with an air of immense and forlorn patience. The dog attracted your attention at once; for it was very nearly an English setter, only something had gone wrong with the tail and the feathering. Palms wilted over his head, it was all shade and stuffiness round the bandstand, radios talked loudly in Spanish from the little wooden sheds where they changed your pesos into dollars at a loss. I could tell he didn't understand a word from the way he read his newspaper—as I did myself picking out the words which were like English ones, 'He's been here a month,' Lucia said, 'they turned him out of Guatemala and Honduras.'

You couldn't keep any secrets for five hours in this border town. Lucia had only been twenty-four hours in the place, but she knew all about Mr Joseph Calloway. The only reason I didn't know about him (and I'd been in the place two weeks) was because I couldn't talk the language any more than Mr Calloway could. There wasn't another soul in the place who didn't know the story—the whole story of Halling Investment Trust and the proceedings for extradition. Any man doing dusty business in any of the wooden booths in the town is better fitted by long observation to tell Mr Calloway's tale than I am, except that I was in—literally— at the finish. They all watched the drama proceed with immense interest, sympathy and respect. For, after all, he had a million. Every once in a while through the long steamy day, a boy came and cleaned Mr Calloway's shoes: he hadn't the right words to resist them—they pretended not to know his English. He must have had his shoes cleaned the day Lucia and I watched him at least half a dozen times. At midday he took a stroll across the square to the Antonio Bar and had a bottle of beer, the setter sticking to heel as if they were out for a country walk in England (he had, you may remember, one of the biggest estates in Norfolk). After his bottle of beer, he would walk down between the money-changers' huts to the Rio Grande and look across the bridge into the United States: people came and went constantly in cars. Then back to the square till lunch-time. He was staying in the best hotel, but you don't get good hotels in this border town: nobody stays in them more than a night. The good hotels were on the other side of the bridge; you could see their electric signs twenty storeys high from the little square at night, like light-houses marking the United States.

You may ask what I'd been doing in so drab a spot for a fortnight. There was no interest in the place for anyone; it was just damp and dust and poverty, a kind of shabby replica of the town across the river. Both had squares in the same spots; both had the same number of cinemas. One was cleaner than the other, that was all, and more expensive, much more expensive. I'd stayed across there a couple of nights waiting for a man a tourist bureau said was driving down from Detroit to Yucatan and would sell a place in his car for some fantastically small figure—twenty dollars, I think it was. I don't know if he existed or was invented by the optimistic half-caste in the agency; anyway, he never turned up and so I waited, not much caring, on the cheap side of the river. It didn't much matter; I was living. One day I meant to give up the man from Detroit and go home or go south, but it was easier not to decide anything in a hurry. Lucia was just waiting for a car the other way, but she didn't have to wait so long. We waited together and watched Mr Calloway waiting—for God knows what.

I don't know how to treat this story—it was a tragedy for Mr Calloway, it was poetic retribution, I suppose, in the eyes of the shareholders whom he'd ruined with his bogus transactions, and to Lucia and me, at this stage, it was comedy—except when he kicked the dog. I'm not a sentimentalist about dogs, I prefer people to be cruel to animals rather than to human beings, but I couldn't help being revolted at the way he'd kick that animal—with a hint of cold-blooded venom, not in anger but as if he were getting even for some trick it had played him a long while ago. That generally happened when he returned from the bridge: it was the only sign of anything resembling emotion he showed. Otherwise he looked a small, set, gentle creature with silver hair and a silver moustache and gold-rimmed glasses, and one gold tooth like a flaw in character.

Lucia hadn't been accurate when she said he'd been turned out of Guatemala and Honduras; he'd left voluntarily when the extradition proceedings seemed likely to go through and moved north. Mexico is still not a very centralized state, and it is possible to get around governors as you can't get round cabinet ministers or judges. And so he waited there on the border for the next move. That earlier part of the story was, I suppose, dramatic, but I didn't watch it and I can't invent what I haven't seen—the long waiting in ante-rooms, the bribes taken and refused, the growing fear of arrest, and then the flight—in gold-rimmed glasses—covering his tracks as well as he could, but this wasn't finance and he was an amateur at escape. And so he'd washed up here, under my eyes and Lucia's eyes, sitting all day under the bandstand, nothing to read but a Mexican paper, nothing to do but look across the river at the United States, quite unaware, I suppose, that everyone knew everything about him, once a day kicking his dog. Perhaps in its semi-setter way it reminded him too much of the Norfolk estate—though that, too, I suppose, was the reason he kept it.

And the next act again was pure comedy. I hesitated to think what this man worth a million was costing his country as they edged him out from this land and that. Perhaps somebody was getting tired of the business, and careless; anyway, they sent across two detectives, with an old photo-graph. He'd grown his silvery moustache since that had been taken, and he'd aged a lot, and they couldn't catch sight of him. They hadn't been across the bridge two hours when everybody knew that there were two foreign detectives in town looking for Mr Calloway—everybody knew, that is to say, except Mr Calloway, who couldn't talk Spanish. There were plenty of people who could have told him in English, but they didn't. It wasn't cruelty, it was a sort of awe and respect: like a bull, he was on show, sitting there mournfully in the plaza with his dog, a magnificent spectacle for which we all had ring-side seats.

I ran into one of the policemen in the Bar Antonio. He was disgusted; he had had some idea that when he crossed the bridge life was going to be different, so much more colour and sun, and—I suspect—love, and all he found were wide mud streets where the nocturnal rain lay in pools, and mangy dogs, smells and cockroaches in his bedroom, and the nearest to love, the open door of the Academia Comercial, where pretty mestizo girls sat all morning learning to typewrite. Tip-tap-tip-tap-tip—perhaps they had a dream too—jobs on the other side of the bridge, where life was going to be so much more luxurious, refined and amusing.

We got into conversation; he seemed surprised that I knew who they both were and what they wanted. He said, 'We've got information this man Calloway's in town.'

'He's knocking around somewhere,' I said.

'Could you point him out?'

'Oh, I don't know him by sight,' I said.

He drank his beer and thought a while. 'I'll go out and sit in the plaza. He's sure to pass sometime.'

I finished my beer and went quickly off and found Lucia. I said, 'Hurry, we're going to see an arrest.' We didn't care a thing about Mr Calloway, he was just an elderly man who kicked his dog and swindled the poor, and deserved anything he got. So we made for the plaza; we knew Calloway would be there, but it had never occurred to either of us that the detectives wouldn't recognize him. There was quite a surge of people round the place; all the fruit-sellers and boot-blacks in town seemed to have arrived together; we had to force our way through, and there in the little green stuffy centre of the place, sitting on adjoining seats, were the two plainclothes men and Mr Calloway. I've never known the place so silent; everybody was on tiptoe, and the plain-clothes men were staring at the crowd for Mr. Calloway, and Mr Calloway sat on his usual seat staring out over the money-changing booths at the United States.

'It can't go on. It just can't,' Lucia said. But it did. It got more fantastic still. Somebody ought to write a play about it. We sat as close as we dared. We were afraid all the time we were going to laugh. The semi-setter scratched for fleas and Mr Calloway watched the U.S.A. The two detectives watched the crowd, and the crowd watched the show with solemn sat-isfaction. Then one of the detectives got up and went over to Mr Calloway. That's the end, I thought. But it wasn't, it was the beginning. For some reason they had eliminated him from their list of suspects. I shall never know why. The man said:

'You speak English?'

'I *am* English,' Mr Calloway said.

Even that didn't tear it, and the strangest thing of all was the way Mr Calloway came alive. I don't think anybody had spoken to him like that for weeks. The Mexicans were too respectful—he was a man with a million—and it had never occurred to Lucia and me to treat him casually like a human being; even in our eyes he had been magnified by the colos-sal theft and the world-wide pursuit.

He said, 'This is rather a dreadful place, don't you think?'

'It is,' the policeman said.

'I can't think what brings anybody across the bridge.'

'Duty,' the policeman said gloomily. 'I suppose you are passing through.'

'Yes,' Mr Calloway said.

'I'd have expected over here there'd have been—you know what I mean—life. You read things about Mexico.'

'Oh, life,' Mr Calloway said. He spoke firmly and precisely, as if to a committee of shareholders. 'That begins on the other side.'

'You don't appreciate your own country until you leave it.'

'That's very true,' Mr Calloway said. 'Very true.'

At first it was difficult not to laugh, and then after a while there didn't seem to be much to laugh at: an old man imagining all the fine things going on beyond the international bridge. I think he thought of the town opposite as a combination of London and Norfolk—theatres and cocktail bars, a little shooting and a walk round the field at evening with the dog—that miserable imitation of a setter—poking the ditches. He'd never been across, he couldn't know it was just the same thing over again—even the same layout; only the streets were paved and the hotels had ten more storeys, and life was more expensive, and everything was a little bit cleaner. There wasn't anything Mr Calloway would have called living—no galleries, no book-shops, just *Film Fun* and the local paper, and *Click* and *Focus* and the tabloids.

'Well,' said Mr Calloway, 'I think I'll take a stroll before lunch. You need an appetite to swallow the food here. I generally go down and look at the bridge about now. Care to come, too?'

The detective shook his head. 'No,' he said, 'I'm on duty. I'm looking for a fellow.' And that, of course, gave *him* away. As far as Mr Calloway could understand, there was only one 'fellow' in the world anyone was looking for—his brain had eliminated friends who were seeking their friends, husbands who might be waiting for their wives, all objectives of any search but just the one. The power of elimination was what had made him a financier—he could forget the people behind the shares.

That was the last we saw of him for a while. We didn't see him going into the Botica Paris to get his aspirin, or walking back from the bridge with his dog. He simply disappeared, and when he disappeared, people began to talk and the detectives heard the talk. They looked silly enough, and they got busy after the very man they'd been sitting next to in the garden. Then they, too, disappeared. They, as well as Mr Calloway, had gone to the state capital to see the Governor and the Chief of Police, and it must have been an amusing sight there, too, as they bumped into Mr Calloway and sat with him in the waiting-rooms. I suspect Mr Calloway was generally shown in first, for everyone knew he was worth a million. Only in Europe is it possible for a man to be a criminal as well as a rich man.

Anyway, after about a week the whole pack of them returned by the same train. Mr Calloway travelled Pullman, and the two policemen travelled in the day coach. It was evident that they hadn't got their extradition order.

Lucia had left by that time. The car came and went across the bridge. I stood in Mexico and watched her get out at the United States Customs. She wasn't anything in particular, but she looked beautiful at a distance as she gave me a wave out of the United States and got back into the car. And I suddenly felt sympathy for Mr Calloway, as if there were something over there which you couldn't find here, and turning round I saw him back on his old beat, with the dog at his heels.

I said, 'Good afternoon,' as if it had been all along our habit to greet each other. He looked tired and ill and dusty, and I felt sorry for him—to think of the kind of victory he'd been winning, with so much expenditure of cash and care—the prize this dirty and dreary town, the booths of the money-changers, the awful little beauty parlours with their wicker chairs and sofas looking like the reception rooms of brothels, that hot and stuffy garden by the bandstand.

He replied gloomily, 'Good afternoon,' and the dog started to sniff at some ordure and he turned and kicked it with fury, with depression, with despair.

And at that moment a taxi with the two policemen in it passed us on its way to the bridge. They must have seen that kick; perhaps they were cleverer than I had given them credit for, perhaps they were just sentimental about animals, and thought they'd do a good deed, and the rest happened by accident. But the fact remains—those two pillars of the law set about the stealing of Mr Calloway's dog.

He watched them go by. Then he said, 'Why don't you go across?'

'It's cheaper here,' I said.

'I mean just for an evening. Have a meal at that place we can see at night in the sky. Go to the theatre.'

'There isn't one.'

He said angrily, sucking his gold tooth, 'Well, anyway, get away from here.' He stared down the hill and up the other side. He couldn't see that the street climbing up from the bridge contained only the same money-changers' booths as this one.

I said, 'Why don't *you* go?'

He said evasively, 'Oh—business.'

I said, 'It's only a question of money. You don't *have* to pass by the bridge.'

He said with faint interest, 'I don't talk Spanish.'

'There isn't a soul here,' I said, 'who doesn't talk English.'

He looked at me with surprise. 'Is that so?' he said. 'Is that so?'

It's as I have said; he'd never tried to talk to anyone, and they respected him too much to talk to him—he was worth a million. I don't know whether I'm glad or sorry that I told him that. If I hadn't, he might be there now, sitting by the bandstand having his shoes cleaned—alive and suffering.

Three days later his dog disappeared. I found him looking for it calling softly and shamefacedly between the palms of the garden. He looked embarrassed. He said in a low angry voice, 'I *hate* that dog. The beastly mongrel,' and called 'Rover, Rover' in a voice which didn't carry five yards. He said, 'I bred setters once. I'd have shot a dog like that.' It reminded him, I *was* right, of Norfolk, and he lived in the memory, and he hated it for its imperfection. He was a man without a family and without friends, and his only enemy was that dog. You couldn't call the law an enemy; you have to be intimate with an enemy.

Late that afternoon someone told him they'd seen the dog walking across the bridge. It wasn't true, of course, but we didn't know that then—they'd paid a Mexican five pesos to smuggle it across. So all that afternoon and the next Mr Calloway sat in the garden having his shoes cleaned over and over again, and thinking how a dog could just walk across like that, and a human being, an immortal soul, was bound here in the awful routine of the little walk and the unspeakable meals and the aspirin at the botica. That dog was seeing things he couldn't see—that hateful dog. It made him mad—I think literally mad. You must remember the man had been going on for months. He had a million and he was living on two pounds a week, with nothing to spend his money on. He sat there and brooded on the hideous injustice of it. I think he'd have crossed over one day in any case, but the dog was the last straw.

Next day when he wasn't to be seen, I guessed he'd gone across and I went too. The American town is as small as the Mexican. I knew I couldn't miss him if he was there, and I was still curious. A little sorry for him, but not too much.

I caught sight of him first in the only drug-store, having a coca-cola, and then once outside a cinema looking at the posters; he had dressed with extreme neatness, as if for a party, but there was no party. On my third time round, I came on the detectives—they were having coca-colas in the drug-store, and they must have missed Mr Calloway by inches. I went in and sat down at the bar.

'Hello,' I said, 'you still about.' I suddenly felt anxious for Mr Calloway. I didn't want them to meet.

One of them said, 'Where's Calloway?'

'Oh,' I said, 'he's hanging on.'

'But not his dog,' he said and laughed. The other looked a little shocked, he didn't like anyone to *talk* cynically about a dog. Then they got up—they had a car outside.

'Have another?' I said.

'No thanks. We've got to keep moving.'

The men bent close and confided to me, 'Calloway's on this side.'

'No!' I said.

'And his dog.'

'He's looking for it,' the other said.

'I'm damned if he is,' I said, and again one of them looked a little shocked, as if I'd insulted the dog.

I don't think Mr Calloway was looking for his dog, but his dog certainly found him. There was a sudden hilarious yapping from the car and out plunged the semi-setter and gambolled furiously down the street. One of the detectives— the sentimental one—was into the car before we got to the door and was off after the dog. Near the bottom of the long road to the bridge was Mr Calloway—I do believe he'd come down to look at the Mexican side when he found there was nothing but the drug-store and the cinemas and the paper shops on the American. He saw the dog coming and yelled at it to go home—'home, home, home,' as if they were in Norfolk—it took no notice at all, pelting towards him. Then he saw the police car coming, and ran. After that, everything happened too quickly, but I think the order of events was this—the dog started across the road right in front of the car, and Mr Calloway yelled, at the dog or the car, I don't know which. Anyway, the detective swerved—he said later, weakly, at the inquiry, that he couldn't run over a dog, and down went Mr Calloway, in a mess of broken glass and gold rims and silver hair, and blood. The dog was on to him before any of us could reach him licking and whimpering and licking. I saw Mr Calloway put up his hand, and down it went across the dog's neck and the whimper rose to a stupid bark of triumph, but Mr Calloway was dead—shock and a weak heart.

'Poor old geezer,' the detective said, 'I bet he really loved that dog,' and it's true that the attitude in which he lay looked more like a caress than a blow. I thought it was meant to be a blow, but the detective may have been right. It all seemed to me a little too touching to be true as the old crook lay there with his arm over the dog's neck, dead with his million between the money-changers' huts, but it's as well to be humble in the face of human nature. He had come across the river for something, and it may, after all, have been the dog he was looking for. It sat there, baying its stupid and mongrel triumph across his body, like a piece of sentimental statuary: the nearest he could get to the fields, the ditches, the horizon of his home. It was comic and it was pitiable, but it wasn't less comic because the man was dead. Death doesn't change comedy to tragedy, and if that last gesture was one of affection, I suppose it was only one more indication of a human being's capacity for self-deception, our baseless optimism that is so much more appalling than our despair.

A Chance to See Egypt
Sandra Scofield

THE FIRST THING RILEY DID when he arrived in Tapalpa was to look for a hotel and make a reservation for that night. He could have made it back to Lago de Luz, but this town had a lovely plaza, with a bandstand and high, graceful trees. In the evening, the townspeople would be out. He would enjoy seeing the families with their children dressed up, and young sweethearts feigning indifference.

He ate lunch at the hotel across from the plaza, then made his way to the museum. The rock carvings mentioned in the guidebook were photographs; the originals, the placard said, were inaccessible mountain sites. *Well, yes,* he thought. What was he expecting? It would be terrible to tear up a cliff, a mountain, an outcrop of rock, even if you could. Still, he would like to see some petroglyphs. He would check the guidebook again, he would ask around at the Lakeside Society, to find out where it was possible to view some. If he couldn't make it this trip, he would go the next time.

He was standing before photographs of little stick conquistadors on horses. What a surprise they must have been to the Indians. He'd heard somewhere—it must have been in Santa Fe, when he and Eva went to an arts fair there—that the natives of the Americas had thought that each Spaniard and his horse was a single being, with six legs.

In Tapalpa, the guidebook said, there were pre-Hispanic carvings. So much to see. The realization that he could come back to the region—that the intention to return had already been forming in him—that was a six-legged surprise, too. Why not? Eva had taught him how easy it is to go from one place to another. She said once, "Boston, Paris, Cairo. The difference in travel is just a matter of hours on a plane. An itinerary is just a wish list made practical. We can go anywhere we want. Eastern Europe, Russia. See how it has all opened up."

He read in his book about the town and its church. There had been an earthquake 150 years earlier. The chapel was spared damage, and the next day, as the townspeople celebrated in the plaza, a cloud appeared in the sky, a vision of Christ on the cross. All of this was captured in paintings on the walls of the newer church next door. He lingered a long while before the paintings. A line of half a dozen people formed in the back, along the last pew by the confessional. A priest came in and entered the booth, and the line moved.

He found a shaded bench in the square and sat down to rest.

He could not help addressing Eva; it was a habit he had never really abandoned. He leaned back against the bench and closed his eyes. "I liked the paintings. They are very fine. Do you believe there was a real vision in the sky? Or was it all an accident of condensation? You would know such a thing where you are. So tell me, Eva, do you believe in miracles now?"

He opened his eyes. The real miracle would be Eva, here

with him. An itinerary, he knew now, was an act of faith. You believed you would live to see it.

A band of schoolboys in blue uniforms ran in front of him, shouting and tagging one another. An elderly man in a business suit, with a cane, sat on a bench to Riley's right, crossed his hands on the top of the cane, and turned to look at Riley with open curiosity.

Across the square, small clanking buses pulled up, paused a few moments, then pulled away. Riley looked up and saw "Mary of Tears" on one. The driver stepped down to have a smoke. He looked dapper, with a trim mustache, in a crisp white shirt and slim-fitting checked knit trousers. He called out a greeting to a taxi driver, waved at a bus pulling in behind, and stretched. Riley went to ask him about the village.

~

It was eight miles. The fare was a few centavos. Several passengers got on at the square, peddlers with mostly empty bags and sacks. There were more stops on the way through town, and at each, another rider or two climbed aboard. Outside of town the landscape was brush and rock and dry land. One by one the passengers went to stand by the door and motion toward the side of the road. At places with no apparent landmark, the bus halted and Riley watched through the window as the bus left the passengers behind. They trudged off across the land, toward their ranchos in the distance. From the bus there was no visible sign of population out there. The last four miles were on rough road and took most of the time of the trip. Near the village, Riley saw small tilled fields, plots of corn, and orchards no bigger than the floor plan of his sister's suburban house. Eventually, in the last mile or so, Riley was accompanied only by two women, one carrying a small squealing pig, the other swathed in rebozo and skirts, and hugely pregnant. The pregnant woman got off as the village came into sight and walked toward the slope of a hillside and the wisp of a fire in the distance.

Once the bus entered the village, it seemed impossible that it could navigate the broken and buckled stone street. At one point, Riley was thrown from his seat to the floor, and the woman burst into hoarse laughter, joined by the driver and, in some manner, by the pig. There was nothing for Riley to do but pull himself back to his seat with good humor. The driver parked the bus on a bare—and flat—dirt patch in what appeared to be the center of the village, though there was no plaza in sight. Riley asked the driver when the bus would return to the town. "Six and a half," the driver said. Time enough to look around.

The village was a dusty, unremarkable place, except for the chapel and the ruins of what had been a monastery, built at least two hundred years before. Probably it had been abandoned in the Revolution. The graceful arched door of the chapel was shaded by tall trees. In front was a large courtyard framed by a carved stone railing. On the far side of the chapel, a long stone wall ran one way for what might have been a city block; all Riley could see behind it was the broken roofline of a building. At the chapel steps a vendor was selling souvenirs from an old ice cream cart. He was an old man, missing many teeth, wearing a dark serape and white trousers. His wares were spread out across the top of the cart: laminated holy cards, plastic flowers, wooden rosaries, and curious lengths of crude rope knotted in several places. Riley asked about the ropes.

"For discipline," the old man said.

"How's that?" Riley asked.

The old man laughed, showing his gums. He took one of the ropes and hit himself lightly on one shoulder. "For the penitents," he said. He held one out toward Riley. "For your sins."

Riley declined the little whips and bought a holy card instead. The card was crammed with images: the Virgin, her baby son, angels, several saints and apostles, a pulsing heart in the upper right corner. He tucked it into his wallet. The vendor said, "You have come to see the Virgin, no?" When Riley said he had come for that, the old man said, "They enter close to the earth," and when he again saw Riley's lack of understanding, he fell abruptly to his knees and crawled around from the back of the cart toward the chapel, making his way back and forth like a crippled crab.

Riley intercepted his path and entered the chapel—on his feet.

~

The statue of the Virgin was unimpressive—two feet tall, a typical Guadalupe, with bruised gilt along the folds of her gown. She stood in a recessed alcove in the back of the chapel. The alcove was festooned with unlit Christmas lights, and in front of the statue were several banks of votive candles and a metal container with a slot for offerings. Riley dropped in a peso.

There was little light in the chapel, and none near the statue, and Riley could not see the Virgin's face very well. Certainly she did not appear to be shedding tears. But who could say? If so many said they had seen them, then surely they had seen something. It was good to think that Mary cried for you. That someone did. It eased the heart, to think that.

He took a taper and lit a candle and said a Hail Mary for his mother, then another for Eva, and another for her dull daughter Bernadette. He bent his head and closed his eyes for a moment to pray. As he opened his eyes again, the Christmas lights suddenly twinkled. In his peripheral vision he caught a glimpse of someone stepping away.

He slid another coin into the offering box. He thought of the señora who had sent him here, and lit yet another candle. Finally, he stuffed some bills into the offering box and lit all the candles, at least a dozen.

He stepped back into a pew to survey the sight of his candles burning. Now he could see that in the front, two women in black rebozos were kneeling on the floor between the pews. They held their arms up and out in front of them; they were saying the rosary together. He could hear the mutter of their voices and the slightest click of the rosary beads as they passed them through their hands.

He felt nostalgic, though he could not think for what.

He thought of the señora's description of the Virgin. "I have no heart's wishes anymore," he whispered. "Please give the nice woman from your village hers."

Back at the vendor's cart, he bought a rosary carved from a rose-colored wood, for his sister, who kept a Mary altar in a cleft under the stairs, off the kitchen; who prayed there every morning before the household woke; who mourned the loss of the Latin Mass, and the hairstyles of her children. She wanted Riley to move to the suburb. Children there needed pets too, she said. They had to drive fifteen miles to find a shop. Everyone spoke English.

The vendor thanked him and said, "How did you like the lights?" When Riley said he had been enchanted, the old man put his hand out and grinned, showing his gums. Riley pressed a coin into his palm.

～

The hot afternoon light had waned, and there were shadows on the wall that ran up the narrow street away from the chapel. On the other side, a building had been partly demolished, and the rubble lay in heaps in front of it. A long building of brick and stucco, with a single concrete step running its length, had three door openings. The building had once been red and white, with painted signs, but it was sunbleached and crumbling now. Riley could see men inside; one leaned against the doorway, drinking from a long-necked bottle. Outside, several more lounged against the wall, their hats pushed back, smoking and drinking. Riley realized he was very thirsty, and started toward the men, but he had taken only a few steps when two of the men stepped back inside, and the third went around the corner and out of sight. He lost his courage. Inside, there would be men at the end of a hard day, men who knew one another and would be suspicious of a gringo. What would he say to any of them? What would there be to drink?

He decided to wait by the bus. He leaned against it and looked off across the dirt at the squat buildings opposite, and the alleyway. The air was still and hot, though it would be cool in a little while. He smelled the smoke of cooking fires. Several women entered one of the buildings and came back out in a few minutes, carrying something wrapped in cloth. Suddenly the doughy hot smell of tortillas hit him, like exhaust from a truck, and he realized they were fetching food, and that he was hungry.

"Señor, Señor." A small boy approached him. "You want a beer?"

"Oh yes, I do." Riley said. The boy said he would bring it to him. He took Riley's coin. In a few moments he appeared again, slightly out of breath from his hurry, carrying a small plastic bag twisted shut, with a straw sticking out. He presented it to Riley.

It was his beer.

It wasn't cold, and it wasn't good beer, less so for having been poured into a Baggie, but it slaked his thirst, and he was happy to drink it. The child, maybe six years old, squatted on the ground nearby and watched him drink. He ran over as soon as Riley was done, to ask if he wanted another, and when he said he did not, took the little Baggie and the straw and ran away.

Riley tested the door of the bus and found it pushed open. He climbed the steps and sat a few rows back to wait. He closed his eyes for a moment.

He woke to the rumbling of his stomach, and glanced at his watch. It was seven-thirty. There was no sign of the driver. He looked out the window. There were several children, maybe ten to twelve years old, standing below, staring up at him. When they saw him looking, they laughed and looked at the ground, then up again.

There was nothing to do but go into the bar and ask after the driver. He stepped up and through one of the doors into darkness. *"Perdón, perdón,"* he said. The long narrow room was full of smoke and the acrid smell of sweat. A radio was playing loud cantina music. A fat man wearing a round straw hat asked him how he could help. Riley said he was looking for the driver of the bus. Several men guffawed.

"Already he's drunk," one of them said.

"Gone to his woman," said another.

Riley's stomach turned over. "But the bus—" he stammered. "He said, six-thirty."

"Oh yes, Señor," they told him. "Bright and early in the morning, the driver will be there in his clean shirt."

They turned away again. He half-stumbled back outside. For a moment he felt sick to his stomach, but he made himself take a long, slow breath. So what! he told himself. He misunderstood the time—though what was the driver thinking, to bring him to the village, knowing he could not leave till morning?

He looked around again. There had to be a phone. He would call a taxi to come for him from town. Maybe it would cost him ten dollars, so what? He saw one of the boys sitting in the dirt over by the bus and went to him. As he approached, the youngster jumped up. "Yes sir!" he said.

"I need a taxi." Riley said.

The boy grinned. "No taxi, Señor." Riley glanced around. There were no cars in sight. Far down the street past the chapel, a man walked slowly, bent over beneath the burden of a wooden table.

"From the town," Riley said. "I need to make a call." He put his hand to his ear. "There is a phone office, no?"

"For certain!" the boy said. "Sure, I can take you there."

Riley followed him down the alley between the bar and the tortilla shop, and around one more corner, to the entrance to a tiny room. There were two phones on the wall, with a piece of wood nailed in between them, and at a table, a young woman sat reading a comic book. She wore a white blouse with a deep starched ruffle, and a crucifix that fell partway behind the first button.

"A taxi will come from the town?" Riley asked her.

She glanced up, shrugged, then went back to reading.

"Please, you will call a taxi for me?"

"No, Señor," she said. "I regret it."

"But the phones—" He pointed to the wall.

She shrugged again. "They have not worked since Christmas," she said. "Such a pity."

When he stepped outside again, he looked for the boy and did not see him. A weary man pushed past him, carrying heavy lengths of rope on both shoulders. There was no sign of a place that would let a room.

He made his way back toward the bus. The boy was there with a man. The man held his hat in his hand.

"Señor," he said. "My son has told me you wish to return to the town."

"I do!" Riley said. "Can you help?" He did not think the man looked like someone with an automobile, but you could not know these things.

"Not I, no one, until morning. But you will come with us to my home. It is nothing, Señor, but it is yours tonight, and it is our honor."

"I thought—perhaps—the priest—" Riley said. He pointed toward the chapel.

"There is no priest, Señor," the man said. "The priest comes once a week to say Mass and hear our confessions. He comes from a neighboring village."

Riley said, "I can sleep on the bus."

The man inched his fingers around his hat a quarter turn. "My wife would not sleep all night if you had no supper, Señor. Soon it will be night, and cold, and you will hear the coyotes and feel you are alone." He stepped forward. "Please, honor us with your presence. I am Cayetano, the barber. This is my son Miguelito. My wife is waiting for us. You will stay the night."

Riley followed the child, and the man followed him. He tried not to think of the bed in the hotel, his pajamas, bottled water, a shower. Everything would be there in the morning, when the driver, in his clean shirt, delivered him.

~

They walked through the village—it did not take long—and beyond it a short distance, past a few skinny chickens and a small pig, to Cayetano's house. It was a low, tin-roofed two-room house. Outside, there were many tin cans attached to the wall and planted with small bright flowers. Inside, the rooms were separated only by a length of fabric, now pulled back to reveal a bed and table, a window with no pane, and a large poster of Jesus with the Sacred Heart. The first room, too, had a bed, a couple of chairs, and a crude cabinet with jars of canned fruit. There were many gilt-framed holy cards—Jesus ascending, a couple of Madonnas, baby Jesus, someone in medieval garb on a draped horse. The front door looked straight through a back door out into the cooking area, where the señora was bustling over a steaming pot, and a grill where tortillas were warming. There seemed to be children everywhere. Cayetano called them to him and lined them up—there were, in fact, seven—and named them. Only two were girls. Each child in turn tucked his or her head and smiled, then looked to the father for permission to run back to the patio and the skirts of their mother, or the freedom of the yard.

Cayetano practiced "Riley" many times to satisfy himself that he was saying it properly. He moved a chair to the center of the room, facing the patio, and bade Riley to sit, then pulled a stool up to sit beside him. Riley could see his wife at her cooking, and the younger girl, seven or eight, helping. Beyond the patio, a boy was practicing with a slingshot, aiming at small bottles and cans lined up on rocks. His father saw him too, and sat taller.

"Your children are handsome," Riley said. "Are they in school?"

Cayetano said, "They are strong children. Already the boys work in the field with their mother." He pointed to the child working on the patio. "The girl works in the house of the mayor, whose wife is sick. Her sister here watches the babies."

A child approached Riley slowly, carrying a toy. He looked to his father, who nodded, and then showed Riley that he had a plastic water pistol. He gave it to Riley to hold. He didn't seem to want anything of Riley, who simply patted the yellow toy and let it lie on his thigh. Cayetano said, "Beto is seven. He is in school. He is very smart, the teacher says. He says Beto could be anything." Cayetano smiled ruefully. "What would that be, do you think? Where would he have to go, and how would he live while he studied?"

Before Riley could respond, the señora called them to eat. Cayetano called for Miguelito to join them. The boy had washed his face and wetted his black hair, smoothed it back from his forehead. "Miguelito works in an orchard," his father said. "He keeps the ground clear. He knows already how to cut the branches back. This is useful, no?"

They sat at a rough table on the patio. By now it was dark,

and they ate by the light that spilled from the ceiling bulb inside the house, and candles set in Fanta bottles on the table. The woman and her daughter served them a plate of rice and beans and tortillas, and a plate of fried plantains. The tortillas had been folded and laid out, fanlike, on a plate, sprinkled with cheese and slices of hot pepper. Riley scraped the peppers aside as unobtrusively as he could, but the tortillas were hot where the peppers had lain, and soon he was teary-eyed. In a moment, the daughter brought a bottle of guava soda to the table. *Natural and artificial,* it read. It was crusted with dust. She brought a wet rag and wiped it carefully, then opened it for Riley. It was warm and sticky and unbelievably sweet, but he drank it and thanked her profusely, while Cayetano smiled at him and stuffed his own mouth with more peppers than Riley dreamed possible to eat. The children had gathered at the edge of the patio, but they waited until the men and Miguelito had eaten. Riley wanted to speak: Couldn't they all eat now? Couldn't the señora join them? But he knew it was not for him to say.

They drank coffee that was dipped from a clay jar on the grill. Cayetano offered him a cigarette, and he took it, though he had not smoked a cigarette since he was a boy. It was very strong, and he could not help coughing, which made the other man laugh companionably. Miguelito took a single drag from his father's cigarette, and did not cough at all.

The señora was filling tortillas with rice and beans for the other children, who sat away from the table, on the edge of the patio, or in the dirt.

The two men strolled in the yard for a few moments. Riley could hear loud voices some distance away, a shout, and then laughter. Somewhere a baby was crying. There were radios playing. They stood away from the house, and Cayetano said, "I will show you where to go," and took Riley to an outhouse. He waited for him and then walked with him back through the dark to the house.

Already the supper was cleared. The children were chattering in the house. The curtain between the rooms was drawn. Cayetano's wife and two of the older children arranged a mat on the floor where the chairs had been, and over it threw two rough blankets and a large shawl.

They gave Riley the bed in the front room, though he protested. The two girls slept on the floor. Miguelito and Beto took blankets out onto the patio. The little ones were taken into the other space with their parents. Riley lay down. He heard night insects, something rustling at the edge of the house, then everything quieted. There were murmurs from the other room. Cayetano's wife was praying aloud. He heard Cayetano say, finally, "Amen," and they were quiet. "Listen, Eva," he barely whispered. "Hear where I am."

~

In the night, something woke him, frightened him. There was a shuffling in the room, the moan of a child. He sat up and looked into the darkness. The moon was a mere sliver, and the light through the door, which was ajar, barely illuminated the sleeping figures. He decided he had been dreaming, and lay back down. He did dream. There were children swimming in a river. They were looking at him. He could see only the top half of their heads; below their noses, they were submerged. The water was murky, still. He couldn't see if the children were happy.

He woke to the sounds of the señora patting tortillas on the patio. It was barely dawn. Cayetano passed through and outside. In the night, the boys had moved inside near their sisters. They all lay in a mound under the shawl.

The two toddlers lay curled alongside Riley, their heads against his hip. Like kittens they were, their closed fists tucked under their chins or the curve of his thigh. He could feel his heart pounding, like that of a man in love. He lay perfectly still, not to disturb the children until the rest of the household rose. He watched until they waked and saw him and blinked in astonishment. One of them gurgled happily and this woke the other. The second child howled.

The strangeness of it. The older girl came and scooped up the child. The other children gathered around and stared at Riley solemnly. When he said, "Good morning, little ones," they scattered, screeching and laughing. A chicken ran through the room, and somewhere, in someone else's yard, a cock crowed.

ANGLE OF REPOSE
Wallace Stegner

MY FATHER, DESPITE HIS IDAHO governess, had gone to St. Paul's badly prepared, an inferior Western child. Grandmother was determined that I should not, and being past her working years, and with time to spare, she saw to my education personally. She read me poetry, she read me Scott and Kipling and Cooper, she read me Emerson, she read me Thomas Hudson. She listened to my practise recitations and helped me write my themes and do my numbers. My homework went in bound in neat blue legal covers, moreover, and a lot of it was illustrated by Susan Burling Ward. The quick little vignettes that ornamented the margins of themes and arithmetic papers looked as if they had been made by the brush of a bird's wing. They delighted my teachers, who pinned them up on blackboards and told the class how fortunate Lyman was to have so talented a grandmother.

I accepted her help willingly, because it brought me praise, but I had no clear idea of who she was or what she had done. The bindings of her books in the library were not inviting, and I can't recall ever reading one of her novels when I was young. I didn't know her writings, apart from a few children's stories, until years after her death, nor much

of her art either, since most of that is buried in the magazines that published her. I would have been surprised to hear
that some people considered her famous.

But I remember a day when I came home from school
and told her I had to write a report on Mexico—how
Mexicans live, or something about Mexican heroes, or some
incident from Cortez and Montezuma or the Mexican War.

She put aside the letter she was writing and turned in her
chair. "Mexico! Is thee studying Mexico?"

Yes, and I had to write this report. I was thinking
Chapultepec, maybe, where all the young cadets held off the
U. S. Army. Where were all those old *National Geographics*?

"I had Alice take them up to the attic." Her hand reached
up and unhooked her spectacles, disentangling the earpieces
from her side hair. I thought her eyes swam oddly; she
smiled and smiled. "Did thee know thee might have *been*
Mexican?"

It didn't seem likely. What did she mean?

"Long ago we thought of living there. In Michoacán. If
we had, thee's father would probably have grown up and
married a Mexican girl, and thee would be Mexican, or half."

I had trouble interpreting her smile; I could feel her
yearning toward some instructive conclusion. She took her
eyes off me and looked out into the hall, where the light lay
clean and elegant across the shining dark floor.

"How different it would all be!" she said, and closed her
light-sensitive eyes a moment, and opened them again, still
smiling. "I would have stayed. I loved it, I was crazy to stay. I
had been married five years and lived most of that time in
mining camps. Mexico was my Paris and my Rome."

I asked why she hadn't stayed, then, and got a vague

answer. Things hadn't worked out. But she continued to look at me as if I had suddenly become of great interest. "And now *thee* is studying Mexico. Would thee like to see what I wrote, and the pictures I drew, when I was studying it? It started out to be one article, but became three."

So she led me up here to this room, and from her old wooden file brought out three issues of *Century* from the year 1881. There they are on the desk. I have just been rereading them.

As a boy I never came into this studio without the respectful sense of being among things that were old, precious, and very personal to Grandmother. She flavored her room the way her rose-petal sachet bags flavored her handkerchiefs. The room has not changed much. The revolver, spurs, and bowie hung then where they hang now, the light wavered through the dormer, broken by pines and wistaria, in the same way. Then, there was usually an easel with a watercolor clothespinned to it, and the pensive, downcast oil portrait of Susan Burling Ward that I have moved up from the library is no proper substitute for Grandmother's living face; but reading her articles this morning I might have been back there, aged twelve or so, conspiring with her to write a paper called "My Grandmother's Trip to Mexico in 1880," illustrated with her woodcuts scissored from old copies of *Century Magazine*.

Her traveler's prose is better than I expected—lively, perceptive, full of pictures. The wood engravings are really fine, as good as anything she ever did. Our scissors left holes in both text and pictures, but from what remains I get a strong impression of the excitement with which she did them.

I remember excitement in her face, too, or think I do, and

in her leaning figure, and her fine old hands, when we resurrected those drawings forty years after she had drawn them. She chattered to me, explaining things. She excited herself just by talking, she remembered Spanish words forgotten for decades, she laughed the giggly laugh she usually reserved for safe old friends. Her agitation was too violent for her, it was close to hysteria and not far from pain. She got the giggles; she ended by bursting into tears.

Her Paris and her Rome, her best time, the lost opportunity that she may have regretted more than any of the other lost opportunities of her life. She would never have admitted it, she would have denied it with vehemence, she kept up all her life the pretense that Augusta was a superior Genius, but Grandmother was a much better artist than her friend, and she would have profited from, and certainly couldn't help envying a little, Augusta's opportunities for travel and study. Probably she nursed a secret conviction, which she would have suppressed as Unworthy, that in marrying Oliver Ward she had given up her chance to be anything more than the commercial illustrator she pretended she was. That sort of feeling would have grown as she felt her powers growing.

She came before the emancipation of women, and she herself was emancipated only partly. There were plenty of women who could have provided her the models for a literary career, but hardly a one, unless Mary Cassatt, whom she apparently never met, who could have shown her how to be a woman artist. The impulse and the talent were there, without either inspiring models or full opportunity. A sort of Isabel Archer existed half-acknowledged in Grandmother, a spirit fresh, independent, adventurous, not really prudish in spite of the gentility. There was an ambitious woman under the Quaker modesty and the genteel conventions. The light foot was for more than dancing, the bright eye for more than flirtations, the womanliness for more than mute submission to husband and hearth.

> Casa Walkenhorst
> Morelia, Michoacán
> September 12, 1880

Dearest Augusta—

It is now over a week since Oliver went off with the owners and the engineer of the prospective buyers to inspect the mine. They departed like a Crusade—but I shall save that for when I see you. It seems too good to be true that this letter can be mailed to the dear old studio address, and that when we return next month you and Thomas will be back in New York. After how many?—four long years when I have been deprived of the sight of you! My darling, we shall have more than Oliver's Crusade to talk about.

I am settled as happy as a worm in an apple at the Casa Walkenhorst, the home of Morelia's Prussian banker. With my *norteamericana* habits I am probably almost as disconcerting as a worm, or half a worm as Bessie would say, giggling—to Emelita, the sister-in-law who keeps Don Gustavo's house. But she is such a sweet and gentle nature, and such a model of consideration, that she would never let me know, no matter how much I disrupted her household. I could go around on stilts, and wearing a bearskin, and she would keep her countenance and her sweetness, convinced that these were the whims and eccentricities, or perhaps the native customs, of an American woman artist. For I am an artist here—my reputation is greatly enlarged by their inability to consult any of my work. But once when I made my own bed (having been brought up my mother's helper and having been maid of all work in a log cabin on a ditch) I heard her afterward scolding the maid for not being prompt, and so I have subsided not unwillingly into luxury, laziness, and daily drawing.

I have a double reason for soaking myself in this walled, protected domestic life. It provides me many sketches, and it gives me a model for what may become my own future. Oliver told me before he left that there is a good chance, providing the mine turns out well, that he will be asked to come back and run it. I will then have the problem of making a home here that we can live in according to our own habits, but that will not offend against Mexican conventions, which have little *give* in them.

You can imagine how such a house as Emelita's, beautifully run and hypnotically comfortable, affects my thwarted home-making instincts. I love the peace of this house, which was once a priests' college and retains its cloistered air. In the mornings there is a most satisfying sense of women's work going on, the hum of voices in far rooms, the chuckling of doves on their high ledges, old Ascención's broom scratching down the *corredor,* and from the rear court the slap and flop of clothes being washed, and whiffs of woodsmoke, strong soap, and steam. The other morning, coming past the work room off the kitchen, I stopped still, smitten by such a lovely smell of fresh ironing that I was instantly melted into a housewife. I make Emelita write me out the receipt for every unusual dish we eat—whether we stay or go, such things are beyond price.

I am as intimate here as a sister, as privileged as a guest, and I tag around after Emelita on her morning rounds, carrying my sketch pad and stool. The *salas* are uninteresting—overdecorated, with too much crystal and heavy furniture, but the kitchen is a treasure, hung with copper pots above its charcoal fires, and a thin, peevish cook who would be dismissed in a minute if she were not capable of such mouthwatering food. So we all praise and placate her instead, and she takes our praise and turns it instantly sour, and I draw her in her sourness and get a picture that I think Thomas and even you will like.

I draw everything—Ascención watering his flower pots, Soledad making up one of the great *lit du roi* beds, Concepción sweeping, crouching over her short-handled broom, the Indian women sousing their washing in the copper tubs that are sunk in stone furnaces in the back court, across from a fountain that plays with a cool tinkle into a stone horse trough under bamboos. I envy those washerwomen the place in which they labor, but my *norteamericana* instincts led me to suggest to Emelita that scrub boards might ease their backs, as a longer-handled broom might ease Concepcións. Ah no, she said. It would confuse them. They are used to doing it the old way.

Next day. I have seen the house—white stucco around a central patio, with a white wall around it all, and a bougainvillea swarming over the wall. Very definitely it will do. The rooms are good, and the arrangement of square within square, a wall around the house and the house around a court, will let us live as we please. It is very near the park, so that the three of us could ride there together, assuming that I can ride without shocking the citizens. Oliver will not mind, I know. He has a way of walking through conventions of that kind as if they did not exist, and being so much himself that pretty soon people begin adapting themselves to *him*.

Even when he is at the mine, which he will surely have to be half the time, Ollie and I might ride, accompanied by some Rubio or Bonifacio, once we had accustomed people to our irregularities. It gives me a delightful sense of wickedness to contemplate it, though I wouldn't think of being so cavalier with the proprieties at home.

I think it will do, I honestly think it will. You and Thomas can visit us here, instead of at that lighthouse on the Pacific to which I once confidently invited you. Morelia isn't Paris, but it is gorgeously picturesque. Much of it is made of a soft pink stone that in certain lights, or when wetted by a shower, glows almost rose. I think you would find subjects for your brush, as I find them for my pencil, on every corner.

Today, as we were returning from looking at the house, we passed the market, which I had never seen. It was thronging with Indians, the men in white pyjamas, the women with their heads and infants wrapped in *rebozos,* the children often in nothing at all except a little shirt. And the things spread out there on the ground, under the matting roofs! Oranges, lemons, watermelons, little baby bananas, *camotes* (sweet potatoes), ears of their funny particolored corn, strange fruits, strange vegetables, chickens hanging by the legs like so many bouquets of Everlasting drying in an attic. Turkeys, pigs, beans, onions, vast fields of pottery and baskets, booths where were sold tortillas and pulque and mysterious sweets and coarse sugar like cracked corn. Such a colorful jumble, such a hum of life, such bright hand-woven cottons and embroidered chemises! Over one side soared the arches of the aqueduct, and in the center was a fountain from which girls were drawing water, gathered around its bright splashing as bright as flowers. (In this place, the poor look like flowers, the rich like mourners—at least the women.)

I cried out at once that I must come and draw it in the morning, when the sun would be on the other side of the aqueduct and would throw its looped shadow across the market, and give me a chance to hold down the boil of all that human activity with some architectural weight. I asked Emelita if I could be spared Soledad or Concepción, to accompany me for a couple of hours. She never quivered. Of course. ¿Como no?

To her, I am sure it seemed a reckless and dangerous and improper request, for in the streets of this fascinating city no respectable woman walks, even accompanied by a maid. My stilts and bearskins were showing, but no one would have known from Emelita's face that I had asked anything at all out of the ordinary.

Later. What day? I lose track of time. I have been keeping back this letter for the post that leaves tomorrow for Mexico City. Every day is like the day before, but every day there is something that to me is new, too.

When I spoke to you last, I was planning to go and draw the market. I went. In the morning Emelita came to me, dressed in her black silk, while I was drawing Enriqueta at her lessons with Fräulein Eberl, and said that Soledad was free to go with me whenever I was ready. I was ready very soon, for I didn't want to miss the proper light, and went into the courtyard to find an expedition prepared that rivaled Oliver's Crusade. There was Ysabel with the carriage and the white mules. There was Soledad with a French gilt chair and a black umbrella. There was Emelita in her black silk. I had come down in my usual morning dress, and for once Emelita's resolution to notice none of my improprieties was not up to the occasion. Her look told me that I would embarrass her. Of course I made an excuse and went back and changed. But even when I was in proper costume, you cannot possibly imagine the consternation I caused—I on my gilt chair with pad and pencil, Soledad standing and holding the umbrella over me, Emelita bravely out of the carriage, but not *too* far, and looking as if every moment were not only mortal sin, but its punishment. It was all Ysabel could do to keep back the curious.

I could not bear to stay more than twenty minutes, keeping Emelita there in the sun scorning even to lift her hem from the dust, and my sketch was very sketchy. But the morning taught me two things. One is that it is perfectly *safe* to do most of the things that propriety frowns on, the other is that I won't again embarrass my Mexican friends by making them share my indiscretions.

Today one of the *mozos* returned from the Crusade, reporting that all were well and that they would be back as scheduled. He came for a fresh supply of wine, one of the mules having fallen and crushed his hamper. Don Pedro is not the sort to make his guests do without their luxuries, though it means sending a servant on a two-hundred-mile round trip.

In a week, therefore, I shall be seeing Oliver, and we shall be planning the shape of our future. My darling, I wish I could tell you now, but I must await Oliver's news. I shall have to tell you in New York—and how can we get around to the future, with all that past to catch up on?

Good night, darling Augusta. I have just been out in the *corredor* prowling up and down. The house is black and still. The starlight doesn't penetrate the shadows under the arcade, and does only a little to lighten the sunken court. It seemed profoundly peaceful and undangerous, strange but at the same time familiar, and I thought of summer nights at Milton, everyone else asleep, when we used to creep out in our night dresses and run barefoot on the wet grass. I fear I am a strange creature, my two great loves are of such different kinds. When Oliver is away from me I miss him and am restless until he returns, but isn't it strange, his absence makes me think so much more acutely of *you.*

Will you visit us in our white house with the bougainvillea, away down here in Michoacán? I mean to keep tempting you with my little exotic sweetmeats until you fall. But first I shall see you in that loved studio where we were girls and art students together a thousand years ago. Even if we are to stay here, as I now truly hope we will, we shall have to be in New York for a considerable time getting prepared.

Good night, good night. The church bells are solemn across the Plaza of the Martyrs. I feel smothered, lonely, eager, I don't know what. The future is as dark as the *corredor* out there, but might be every bit as charming once light comes on it. One thing I do know—it must have you in it, somehow, somewhere.

> Your own
> Sue

Night of the Iguana
Tennessee Williams

OPENING ONTO THE LONG SOUTH verandah of the Costa Verde hotel near Acapulco were ten sleeping-rooms, each with a hammock slung outside its screen door. Only three of these rooms were occupied at the present time, for it was between the seasons at Acapulco. The winter season when the resort was more popular with the cosmopolitan type of foreign tourists had been over for a couple of months and the summer season when ordinary Mexican and American vacationists thronged there had not yet started. The three remaining guests of the Costa Verde were from the States, and they included two men who were writers and a Miss Edith Jelkes who had been an instructor in art at an Episcopalian girls' school in Mississippi until she had suffered a sort of nervous breakdown and had given up her teaching position for a life of refined vagrancy, made possible by an inherited income of about two hundred dollars a month.

Miss Jelkes was a spinster of thirty with a wistful blond prettiness and a somewhat archaic quality of refinement. She belonged to an historical Southern family of great but now moribund vitality whose latter generations had tended to split into two antithetical types, one in which the libido was pathologically distended and another in which it would seem to be all but dried up. The households were turbulently split and so, fairly often, were the personalities of their inmates. There had been an efflorescence among them of nervous talents and sickness, of drunkards and poets, gifted artists and sexual degenerates, together with fanatically proper and squeamish old ladies of both sexes who were condemned to live beneath the same roof with relatives whom they could only regard as monsters. Edith Jelkes was not strictly one or the other of the two basic types, which made it all the more difficult for her to cultivate any interior poise. She had been lucky enough to channel her somewhat morbid energy into a gift for painting. She painted canvases of an originality that might some day be noted, and in the meantime, since her retirement from teaching, she was combining her painting with travel and trying to evade her neurasthenia through the distraction of making new friends in new places. Perhaps some day she would come out on a kind of triumphant plateau as an artist or as a person or even perhaps as both. There might be a period of five or ten years in her life when she would serenely climb over the lightning-shot clouds of her immaturity and the waiting murk of decline. But perhaps is the right word to use. It would all depend on the next two years or so. For this reason she was particularly needful of sympathetic companionship, and the growing lack of it at the Costa Verde was really dangerous for her.

Miss Jelkes was outwardly such a dainty tea-pot that no one would guess that she could actually boil. She was so delicately made that rings and bracelets were never quite small enough originally to fit her but sections would have to be removed and the bands welded smaller. With her great translucent grey eyes and cloudy blond hair and perpetual look of slightly hurt confusion, she could not pass unnoticed through any group of strangers, and she knew how to dress in accord with her unearthly type. The cloudy blond hair was never without its flower and the throat of her cool white dresses would be set off by some vivid brooch of esoteric design. She loved the dramatic contrast of hot and cold color, the splash of scarlet on snow, which was like a flag of her own unsettled components. Whenever she came into a restaurant or theatre or exhibition gallery, she could hear or imagine that she could hear a little murmurous wave of appreciation. This was important to her, it had come to be one of her necessary comforts. But now that the guests of the Costa Verde had dwindled to herself and the two young writers—no matter how cool and yet vivid her appearance, there was little to comfort her in the way of murmured appreciation. The two young writers were bafflingly indifferent to Miss Jelkes. They barely turned their heads when she strolled onto the front or back verandah where they were lying in hammocks or seated at a table always carrying on a curiously intimate-sounding conversation in tones never loud enough to be satisfactorily overheard by Miss Jelkes, and their responses to her friendly nods and Spanish phrases of greeting were barely distinct enough to pass for politeness.

Miss Jelkes was not at all inured to such off-hand treatment. What had made travel so agreeable to her was the remarkable facility with which she had struck up acquaintances wherever she had gone. She was a good talker, she had a fresh and witty way of observing things. The many places she had been in the last six years had supplied her with a great reservoir of descriptive comment and humorous anecdote, and of course there was always the endless and epic chronicle of the Jelkes to regale people with. Since she had just about the right amount of income to take her to the sort of hotels and *pensions* that are frequented by professional people such as painters and writers or professors on Sabbatical leave, she had never before felt the lack of an appreciative audience. Things being as they were, she realized that the sensible action would be to simply withdraw to the Mexican capital where she had formed so many casual but nice connections among the American colony. Why she did not do this but remained on at the Costa Verde was not altogether clear to herself. Besides the lack of society there were other draw-backs to a continued stay. The food had begun to disagree with her, the Patrona of the hotel was becoming insolent and the service slovenly and her painting was showing signs of nervous distraction. There was every reason to leave, and yet she stayed on.

Miss Jelkes could not help knowing that she was actually conducting a siege of the two young writers, even though the reason for it was still entirely obscure.

She had set up her painting studio on the South verandah of the hotel where the writers worked in the mornings at their portable typewriters with their portable radio going off and on during pauses in their labor, but the comradeship of creation which she had hoped to establish was not forthcoming. Her eyes formed a habit of darting toward the two men as frequently as they did toward what she was painting, but her glances were not returned and her painting went into an irritating decline. She took to using her fingers more than her brushes, smearing and slapping on pigment with an impatient energy that defeated itself. Once in a while she would get up and wander as if absent-mindedly down toward the writers' end of the long verandah, but when she did so, they would stop writing and stare blankly at their papers or into space until she had removed herself from their proximity, and once the younger writer had been so rude as to snatch his paper from the typewriter and turn it face down on the table as if he suspected her of trying to read it over his shoulder.

She had retaliated that evening by complaining to the Patrona that their portable radio was being played too loudly and too long, that it was keeping her awake at night, which she partially believed to be true, but the transmission of this complaint was not evidenced by any reduction in the volume or duration of the annoyance but by the writers' choice of a table at breakfast, the next morning, at the furthest possible distance from her own.

That day Miss Jelkes packed her luggage, thinking that she would surely withdraw the next morning, but her curiosity about the two writers, especially the older of the two, had now become so obsessive that not only her good sense but her strong natural dignity was being discarded.

Directly below the cliff on which the Costa Verde was planted there was a small private beach for the hotel guests. Because of her extremely fair skin it had been Miss Jelkes' practice to bathe only in the early morning or late afternoon when the glare was diminished. These hours did not coincide with those of the writers who usually swam and sunbathed between two and six in the afternoon. Miss Jelkes now began to go down to the beach much earlier without admitting to herself that it was for the purpose of espionage.

She would now go down to the beach about four o'clock in the afternoon and she would situate herself as close to the two young men as she could manage without being downright brazen. Bits of their background and history had begun to filter through this unsatisfactory contact. It became apparent that the younger of the men, who was about twenty-five, had been married and recently separated from a wife he called Kitty. More from the inflection of voices than the fragmentary sentences that she caught, Miss Jelkes received the impression that he was terribly concerned over some problem which the older man was trying to iron out for him. The younger one's voice would sometimes rise in agitation loudly enough to be overheard quite plainly. He would cry out phrases such as *For God's sake* or *What the Hell are you talking about!* Sometimes his language was so strong that Miss Jelkes winced with embarrassment and he would sometimes pound the wet sand with his palm and hammer it with his heels like a child in a tantrum. The older man's voice would also be lifted briefly. Don't be a fool, he would shout. Then his voice would drop to a low and placating tone. The conversation would fall below the level of audibility once more. It seemed that some argument was going on almost interminably between them. Once Miss Jelkes was astonished to see the younger one jump to his feet with an incoherent outcry and start kicking sand directly into the face of his older companion. He did it quite violently and hatefully, but the older man only laughed and grabbed the younger one's feet and restrained them until the youth dropped back beside him, and then they had surprised Miss Jelkes even further by locking their hands together and lying in silence until the incoming tide was lapping over their bodies. Then they had both jumped up, apparently in good humor, and made racing dives in the water.

Because of this troubled youth and wise counsellor air of their conversations it had at first struck Miss Jelkes, in the beginning of her preoccupation with them, that the younger man might be a war-veteran suffering from shock and that the older one might be a doctor who had brought him down to the Pacific resort while conducting a psychiatric treatment. This was before she discovered the name of the older man, on mail addressed to him. She had instantly recognized the name as one that she had seen time and again on the covers of literary magazines and as the author of a novel that had caused a good deal of controversy a few years ago. It was a novel that dealt with some sensational subject. She had not read it and could not remember what the subject was but the name was associated in her mind with a strongly social kind of writing which had been more in vogue about five years past than it was since the beginning of the war. However the writer was still not more than thirty. He was not good-looking but his face had distinction. There was something a little monkey-like in his face as there frequently is in the faces of serious young writers, a look that reminded Miss Jelkes of a small chimpanzee she had once seen in the corner of his cage at a zoo, just sitting there staring between the bars, while all his fellows were hopping and spinning about on their noisy iron trapeze. She remembered how she had been touched by his solitary position and lack-lustre eyes. She had wanted to give him some peanuts but the elephants had devoured all she had. She had returned to the vendor to buy some more but when she brought them to the chimpanzee's cage, he had evidently succumbed to the general impulse, for now every man Jack of them was hopping and spinning about on the clanking trapeze and not a one of them seemed a bit different from the others. Looking at this writer she felt almost an identical urge to share something with him, but the wish was thwarted again, in this instance by a studious will to ignore her. It was not accidental, the way that he kept his eyes off her. It was the same on the beach as it was on the hotel verandahs.

On the beach he wore next to nothing, a sort of brilliant diaper of printed cotton, twisted about his loins in a fashion that sometimes failed to even approximate decency, but he had a slight and graceful physique and an unconscious ease of movement which made the immodesty less offensive to Miss Jelkes than it was in the case of his friend. The younger man had been an athlete at college and he was massively constructed. His torso was burned the color of an old penny and its emphatic gender still further exclaimed by luxuriant patterns of hair, sunbleached till it shone like masses of crisped and frizzed golden wire. Moreover his regard for propriety was so slight that he would get in and out of his colorful napkin as if he were standing in a private cabana. Miss Jelkes had to acknowledge that he owned a certain sculptural grandeur but the spinsterish side of her nature was still too strong to permit her to feel anything but a squeamish distaste. This reaction of Miss Jelkes was so strong on one occasion that when she had returned to the hotel she went directly to the Patrona to enquire if the younger gentleman could not be persuaded to change clothes in his room or, if this was too much to ask of him, that he might at least keep the dorsal side of his nudity toward the beach. The Patrona was very much interested in the complaint but not in a way that Miss Jelkes had hoped she would be. She laughed immoderately, translating phrases of Miss Jelkes' complaint into idiomatic Spanish, shouted to the waiters and the cook. All of them joined in the laughter and the noise was still going on when Miss Jelkes standing confused and indignant saw the two young men climbing up the hill. She retired quickly to her room on the hammock-verandah but she knew by the reverberating merriment on the other side that the writers were being told, and that all of the Costa Verde was holding her up to undisguised ridicule. She started packing at once, this time not even bothering to fold things neatly into her steamer trunk, and she was badly frightened, so much disturbed that it affected her stomach and the following day she was not well enough to undertake a journey.

It was this following day that the Iguana was caught.

The Iguana is a lizard, two or three feet in length, which the Mexicans regard as suitable for the table. They are not always eaten right after they are caught but being creatures that can survive for quite a while without food or drink, they are often held in captivity for some time before execution. Miss Jelkes had been told that they tasted rather like chicken, which opinion she ascribed to a typically Mexican way of glossing over an unappetizing fact. What bothered her about the Iguana was the inhumanity of its treatment during its interval of captivity. She had seen them outside the huts of villagers, usually hitched to a short pole near the doorway and continually and hopelessly clawing at the dry earth within the orbit of the rope-length, while naked children squatted around it, poking it with sticks in the eyes and mouth.

Now the Patrona's adolescent son had captured one of these Iguanas and had fastened it to the base of a column under the hammock-verandah. Miss Jelkes was not aware of its presence until late the night of the capture. Then she had been disturbed by the scuffling sound it made and had slipped on her dressing-gown and had gone out in the bright moonlight to discover what the sound was caused by. She looked over the rail of the verandah and she saw the Iguana hitched to the base of the column nearest her doorway and making the most pitiful effort to scramble into the bushes just beyond the taut length of its rope. She uttered a little cry of horror as she made this discovery.

The two young writers were lying in hammocks at the other end of the verandah and as usual were carrying on a desultory conversation in tones not loud enough to carry to her bedroom.

Without stopping to think, and with a curious thrill of exultation, Miss Jelkes rushed down to their end of the verandah. As she drew near them she discovered that the two writers were engaged in drinking rum-coco, which is a drink prepared in the shell of a coconut by knocking a cap off it with a machete and pouring into the nut a mixture of rum, lemon, sugar and cracked ice. The drinking had been going on since supper and the floor beneath their two hammocks was littered with bits of white pulp and hairy brown fibre and was so slippery that Miss Jelkes barely kept her footing. The liquid had spilt over their faces, bare throats and chests, giving them an oily lustre, and about their hammocks was hanging a cloud of moist and heavy sweetness. Each had a leg thrown over the edge of the hammock with which he pushed himself lazily back and forth. If Miss Jelkes had been seeing them for the first time, the gross details of the spectacle would have been more than association with a few dissolute members of the Jelkes family had prepared her to stomach, and she would have scrupulously avoided a second glance at them. But Miss Jelkes had been changing more than she was aware of during this period of preoccupation with the two writers, her scruples were more undermined than she suspected, so that if the word *pigs* flashed through her mind for a moment, it failed to distract her even momentarily from what she was bent on doing. It was a form of hysteria that had taken hold of her, her action and her speech were without volition.

"Do you know what has happened!" she gasped as she came toward them. She came nearer than she would have consciously dared, so that she was standing directly over the young writer's prone figure. "That horrible boy, the son of the Patrona, has tied up an Iguana beneath my bedroom. I heard him tying it up but I didn't know what it was. I've been listening to it for hours, ever since supper, and didn't know what it was. Just now I got up to investigate, I looked over the edge of the verandah and there it was, scuffling around at the end of its little rope!"

Neither of the writers said anything for a moment, but the older one had propped himself up a little to stare at Miss Jelkes.

"There *what* was?" he enquired.

"She is talking about the Iguana," said the younger.

"Oh! Well, what about it?"

"How can I sleep?" cried Miss Jelkes. "How could anyone sleep with that example of Indian savagery right underneath my door!"

"You have an aversion to lizards?" suggested the older writer.

"I have an aversion to brutality!" corrected Miss Jelkes.

"But the lizard is a very low grade of animal life. Isn't it a very low grade of animal life?" he asked his companion.

"Not as low as some," said the younger writer. He was grinning maliciously at Miss Jelkes, but she did not notice him at all, her attention was fixed upon the older writer.

"At any rate," said the writer, "I don't believe it is capable of feeling half as badly over its misfortune as you seem to be feeling for it."

"I don't agree with you," said Miss Jelkes. "I don't agree with you at all! We like to think that we are the only ones that are capable of suffering but that is just human conceit. We are not the only ones that are capable of suffering. Why, even plants have sensory impressions. I have seen some that closed their leaves when you touched them!"

She held out her hand and drew her slender fingers into a chalice that closed. As she did this she drew a deep, tortured breath with her lips pursed and nostrils flaring and her eyes rolled heavenwards so that she looked like a female Saint on the rack.

The younger man chuckled but the older one continued to stare at her gravely.

"I am sure," she went on, "that the Iguana has very definite feelings, and you would be, too, if you had been listening to it, scuffling around out there in that awful dry dust, trying to reach the bushes with that rope twisted about its neck, making it almost impossible for it to breathe!"

She clutched her throat as she spoke and with the other hand made a clawing gesture in the air. The younger writer broke into a laugh, the older one smiled at Miss Jelkes.

"You have a real gift," he said, "for vicarious experience."

"Well, I just can't stand to witness suffering," said Miss Jelkes. "I can endure it myself but I just can't stand to witness it in others, no matter whether it's human suffering or animal suffering. And there is so much suffering in the world, so much that is necessary suffering, such as illnesses and accidents which cannot be avoided. But there is so much unnecessary suffering, too, so much that is inflicted simply because some people have a callous disregard for the feelings of others. Sometimes it almost seems as if the universe was designed by the Marquis de Sade!"

She threw back her head with an hysterical laugh.

"And I do not believe in the principle of atonement," she went on. "Isn't it awful, isn't it really preposterous that practically all our religions should be based on the principle of atonement when there is really and truly no such thing as guilt?"

"I am sorry," said the older writer. He rubbed his forehead. "I am not in any condition to talk about God."

"Oh, I'm not talking about God," said Miss Jelkes. "I'm talking about the Iguana!"

"She's trying to say that the Iguana is one of God's creatures," said the younger writer.

"But that one of God's creatures," said the older, "is now in the possession of the Patrona's son!"

"That one of God's creatures," Miss Jelkes exclaimed, "is now hitched to a post right underneath my door, and late as it is I have a very good notion to go and wake up the Patrona and tell her that they have got to turn it loose or at least to remove it some place where I can't hear it!"

The younger writer was now laughing with drunken vehemence. "What are you bellowing over?" the older one asked him.

"If she goes and wakes up the Patrona, anything can happen!"

"What?" asked Miss Jelkes. She glanced uncertainly at both of them.

"That's quite true," said the older. "One thing these Mexicans will not tolerate is the interruption of sleep!"

"But what can she do but apologize and remove it!" demanded Miss Jelkes. "Because after all, it's a pretty outrageous thing to hitch a lizard beneath a woman's door and expect her to sleep with that noise going on all night!"

"It might not go on all night," said the older writer.

"What's going to stop it?" asked Miss Jelkes.

"The Iguana might go to sleep."

"Never!" said Miss Jelkes. "The creature is frantic and what it is going through must be a nightmare!"

"You're bothered a good deal by noises?" asked the older writer. This was, of course, a dig at Miss Jelkes for her complaint about the radio. She recognized it as such and welcomed the chance it gave to defend and explain. In fact this struck her as being the golden moment for breaking all barriers down.

"That's true, I am!" she admitted breathlessly. "You see, I had a nervous breakdown a few years ago, and while I'm ever so much better than I was, sleep is more necessary to me than it is to people who haven't gone through a terrible thing like that. Why, for months and months I wasn't able to sleep without a sedative tablet, sometimes two of them a night!

Now I hate like anything to be a nuisance to people, to make unreasonable demands, because I am always so anxious to get along well with people, not only peaceably, but really *cordially* with them—even with strangers that I barely *speak* to—However it sometimes happens . . ."

She paused for a moment. A wonderful thought had struck her.

"I know what I'll do!" she cried out. She gave the older writer a radiant smile.

"What's that?" asked the younger. His tone was full of suspicion but Miss Jelkes smiled at him, too.

"Why, I'll just move!" she said.

"Out of the Costa Verde?" suggested the younger.

"Oh, no, no, no! No, indeed! It's the nicest resort hotel I've ever stopped at! I mean that I'll change my room."

"Where will you change it to?"

"Down here," said Miss Jelkes, "to this end of the verandah! I won't even wait till morning. I'll move right now. All these vacant rooms, there couldn't be any objection, and if there is, why, I'll just explain how totally impossible it was for me to sleep with that lizard's commotion all night!"

She turned quickly about on her heels, so quickly that she nearly toppled over on the slippery floor, caught her breath laughingly and rushed back to her bedroom. Blindly she swept up a few of her belongings in her arms and rushed back to the writers' end of the verandah where they were holding a whispered consultation.

"Which is your room?" she asked

"We have two rooms," said the younger writer coldly.

"Yes, one each," said the older.

"Oh, of course!" said Miss Jelkes. "But I don't want to make the embarrassing error of confiscating one of you gentlemen's beds!"

She laughed gaily at this. It was the sort of remark she would make to show new acquaintances how far from being formal and prudish she was. But the writers were not inclined to laugh with her, so she cleared her throat and started blindly toward the nearest door, dropping a comb and a mirror as she did so.

"Seven years bad luck!" said the younger man.

"It isn't broken!" she gasped.

"Will you help me?" she asked the older writer.

He got up unsteadily and put the dropped articles back on the disorderly pile in her arms.

"I'm sorry to be so much trouble!" she gasped pathetically. Then she turned again to the nearest doorway.

"Is this one vacant?"

"No, that's mine," said the younger.

"Then how about *this* one?"

"That one is mine," said the older.

"Sounds like the Three Bears and Goldilocks!" laughed Miss Jelkes. "Well, oh, dear—I guess I'll just have to take *this* one!"

She rushed to the screen door on the other side of the younger writer's room, excitingly aware as she did so that this would put her within close range of their nightly conversations, the mystery of which had tantalized her for weeks. Now she would be able to hear every word that passed between them unless they actually whispered in each other's ear!

She rushed into the bedroom and let the screen door slam.

She switched on the suspended light bulb and hastily plunged the articles borne with her about a room that was identical with the one that she had left and then plopped herself down upon an identical white iron bed.

There was silence on the verandah.

Without rising she reached above her to pull the cord of the light-bulb. Its watery yellow glow was replaced by the crisp white flood of moonlight through the gauze-netted window and through the screen of the door.

She lay flat on her back with her arms lying rigidly along her sides and every nerve tingling with excitement over the spontaneous execution of a piece of strategy carried out more expertly than it would have been after days of preparation.

For a while the silence outside her new room continued.

Then the voice of the younger writer pronounced the word "Goldilocks!"

Two shouts of laughter rose from the verandah. It continued without restraint till Miss Jelkes could feel her ears burning in the dark as if rays of intense light were concentrated on them.

There was no more talk that evening, but she heard their feet scraping as they got off the hammocks and walked across the verandah to the further steps and down them.

Miss Jelkes was badly hurt, worse than she had been hurt the previous afternoon, when she had complained about the young man's immodesty on the beach. As she lay there upon the severe white bed that smelled of ammonia she could feel coming toward her one of those annihilating spells of neurasthenia which had led to her breakdown six years ago. She was too weak to cope with it, it would have its way with her and bring her God knows how close to the verge of lunacy and even possibly over! What an intolerable burden, and why did she have to bear it, she who was so humane and gentle by nature that even the sufferings of a lizard could hurt her! She turned her face to the cold white pillow and wept. She wished that she were a writer. If she were a writer it would be possible to say things that only Picasso had ever put into paint. But if she said them, would anybody believe them? Was her sense of the enormous grotesquerie of the world communicable to any other person? And why should it be told if it could be? And why, most of all, did she make such a fool of herself in her frantic need to find some comfort in people!

She felt that the morning was going to be pitilessly hot and bright and she turned over in her mind the list of neuroses that might fasten upon her. Everything that is thoughtless and automatic in healthy organisms might take on for her an air of preposterous novelty. The act of breathing and the beat of her heart and the very process of thinking would be self-conscious if this worst-of-all neuroses should take hold of her—and take hold of her it would, because she was so afraid of it! The precarious balance of her nerves would be all overthrown. Her entire being would turn into a feverish little machine for the production of fears, fears that could not be put into words because of their all-encompassing immensity, and even supposing that they could be put into language and so be susceptible to the comfort of telling—who was there at the Costa Verde, this shadowless rock by the ocean, that she could turn to except the two young writers who seemed to despise her? How awful to be at the mercy of merciless people!

Now I'm indulging in self-pity, she thought.

She turned on her side and fished among articles on the bed-table for the little cardboard box of sedative tablets. They would get her through the night, but tomorrow—oh, tomorrow! She lay there senselessly crying, hearing even at this distance the efforts of the captive Iguana to break from its rope and scramble into the bushes. . . .

II

WHEN MISS JELKES AWOKE IT was still a while before morning. The moon, however, had disappeared from the sky and she was lying in blackness that would have been total except for tiny cracks of light that came through the wall of the adjoining bedroom, the one that was occupied by the younger writer.

It did not take her long to discover that the younger writer was not alone in his room. There was no speech but the quality of sounds that came at intervals through the partition made her certain the room had two people in it.

If she could have risen from bed and peered through one of the cracks without betraying herself she might have done so, but knowing that any move would be overheard, she remained on the bed and her mind was now alert with suspicions which had before been only a formless wonder.

At last she heard someone speak.

"You'd better turn out the light," said the voice of the younger writer.

"Why?"

"There are cracks in the wall."

"So much the better. I'm sure that's why she moved down here."

The younger one raised his voice.

"You don't think she moved because of the Iguana?"

"Hell, no, that was just an excuse. Didn't you notice how pleased she was with herself, as if she had pulled off something downright brilliant?"

"I bet she's eavesdropping on us right this minute," said the younger.

"Undoubtedly she is. But what can she do about it?"

"Go to the Patrona."

Both of them laughed.

"The Patrona wants to get rid of her," said the younger.

"Does she?"

"Yep. She's crazy to have her move out. She's even given the cook instructions to put too much salt in her food."

They both laughed.

Miss Jelkes discovered that she had risen from the bed. She was standing uncertainly on the cold floor for a moment and then she was rushing out of the screen door and up to the door of the younger writer's bedroom.

She knocked on the door, carefully keeping her eyes away from the lighted interior.

"Come in," said a voice.

"I'd rather not," said Miss Jelkes. "Will you come here for a minute?"

"Sure," said the younger writer. He stepped to the door, wearing only the trousers to his pyjamas.

"Oh," he said. "It's you!"

She stared at him without any idea of what she had come to say or had hoped to accomplish.

"Well?" he demanded brutally.

"I—I heard you!" she stammered.

"So?"

"I don't understand it!"

"What?"

"Cruelty! I never could understand it!"

"But you do understand spying, don't you?"

"I wasn't spying!" she cried.

He muttered a shocking word and shoved past her onto the porch.

The older writer called his name: "Mike!" But he only repeated the shocking word more loudly and walked away from them. Miss Jelkes and the older writer faced each other. The violence just past had calmed Miss Jelkes a little. She found herself uncoiling inside and comforting tears beginning to moisten her eyes. Outside the night was changing. A wind had sprung up and the surf that broke on the other side of the land-locked bay called Coleta could now be heard.

"It's going to storm," said the writer.

"Is it? I'm glad!" said Miss Jelkes.

"Won't you come in?"

"I'm not at all properly dressed."

"I'm not either."

"Oh, well—"

She came in. Under the naked light-bulb and without the dark glasses his face looked older and the eyes, which she had not seen before, had a look that often goes with incurable illness.

She noticed that he was looking about for something.

"Tablets," he muttered.

She caught sight of them first, among a litter of papers. She handed them to him.

"Thank you. Will you have one?"

"I've had one already."

"What kind are yours?"

"Seconal. Yours?"

"Barbital. Are yours good?"

"Wonderful."

"How do they make you feel? Like a water-lily?"

"Yes, like a water-lily on a Chinese lagoon!"

Miss Jelkes laughed with real gaiety but the writer responded only with a faint smile. His attention was drifting away from her again. He stood at the screen door like a worried child awaiting the return of a parent.

"Perhaps I should—"

Her voice faltered. She did not want to leave. She wanted to stay there. She felt herself upon the verge of saying incommunicable things to this man whose singularity was so like her own in many essential respects, but his turned back did not invite her to stay. He shouted the name of his friend. There was no response. The writer turned back from the door with a worried muttering but his attention did not return to Miss Jelkes.

"Your friend—" she faltered.

"Mike?"

"Is he the—right person for you?"

"Mike is helpless and I am always attracted by helpless people."

"But you," she said awkwardly. "How about you? Don't you need somebody's help?"

"The help of God!" said the writer. "Failing that, I have to depend on myself."

"But isn't it possible that with somebody else, somebody with more understanding, more like *yourself*—!"

"You mean *you*?" he asked bluntly.

Miss Jelkes was spared the necessity of answering one way or another, for at that moment a great violence was unleashed outside the screen door. The storm that had hovered uncertainly on the horizon was now plunging toward them. Not continually but in sudden thrusts and withdrawals, like a giant bird lunging up and down on its terrestrial quarry, a bird with immense white wings and beak of godlike fury, the attack was delivered against the jut of rock on which the Costa Verde was planted. Time and again the whole night blanched and trembled, but there was something frustrated in the attack of the storm. It seemed to be one that came from a thwarted will. Otherwise surely the frame structure would have been smashed. But the giant white bird did not know where it was striking. Its beak of fury was blind, or perhaps the beak—

It may have been that Miss Jelkes was right on the verge of divining more about God than a mortal ought to—when suddenly the writer leaned forward and thrust his knees between hers. She noticed that he had removed the towel about him and now was quite naked. She did not have time to wonder nor even to feel much surprise for in the next few moments, and for the first time in her thirty years of preordained spinsterhood, she was enacting a fierce little comedy of defense. He thrust at her like the bird of blind white fury. His one hand attempted to draw up the skirt of her robe while his other tore at the flimsy goods at her bosom. The upper cloth tore. She cried out with pain as the predatory fingers dug into her flesh. But she did not give in. Not she herself resisted but some demon of virginity that occupied her flesh fought off the assailant more furiously than he attacked her. And her demon won, for all at once the man let go of her gown and his fingers released her bruised bosom. A sobbing sound in his throat, he collapsed against her. She felt a wing-like throbbing against her belly, and then a scalding wetness. Then he let go of her altogether. She sank back into her chair which had remained demurely upright throughout the struggle, as unsuitably, as ridiculously, as she herself had maintained her upright position. The man was sobbing. And then the screen door opened and the younger writer came in. Automatically Miss Jelkes freed herself from the damp embrace of her unsuccessful assailant.

"What is it?" asked the younger writer.

He repeated his question several times, senselessly but angrily, while he shook his older friend who could not stop crying.

I don't belong here, thought Miss Jelkes, and suiting action to thought, she slipped quietly out the screen door. She did not turn back into the room immediately adjoining but ran down the verandah to the room she had occupied before. She threw herself onto the bed which was now as cool as if she had never lain on it. She was grateful for that and for the abrupt cessation of fury outside. The white bird had gone away and the Costa Verde had survived its assault. There was nothing but the rain now, pattering without much energy, and the far away sound of the ocean only a little more distinct than it had been before the giant bird struck. She remembered the Iguana.

Oh, yes, the Iguana! She lay there with ears pricked for the painful sound of its scuffling, but there was no sound but the effortless flowing of water. Miss Jelkes could not contain her curiosity so at last she got out of bed and looked over the edge of the verandah. She saw the rope. She saw the whole length of the rope lying there in a relaxed coil, but not the Iguana. Somehow or other the creature tied by the rope had gotten away. Was it an act of God that had effected this deliverance? Or was it not more reasonable to suppose that only Mike, the beautiful and helpless and cruel, had cut the Iguana loose? No matter. No matter who did it, the Iguana was gone, had scrambled back into its native bushes and, oh, how gratefully it must be breathing now! And she was grateful, too, for in some equally mysterious way the strangling rope of her loneliness had also been severed by what had happened tonight on this barren rock above the moaning waters.

Now she was sleepy. But just before falling asleep she remembered and felt again the spot of dampness, now turning cool but still adhering to the flesh of her belly as a light but persistent kiss. Her fingers approached it timidly. They expected to draw back with revulsion but were not so affected. They touched it curiously and even pityingly and did not draw back for a while. *Ah, Life,* she thought to herself and was about to smile at the originality of this thought when darkness lapped over the outward gaze of her mind.

Atticus
Ron Hansen

WENT NATIVE IN MEXICO FOR a while and made a friend of a shaman named Eduardo. Woke up coughing one morning in my shanty and found Eduardo inches away from my face and gently blowing cigar smoke at me. "Are you ready?" he asked in Spanish. And I looked out at three serious Mayans with wild black hair and filthy hand-sewn shirts that fell as far as their knees. Everything in them was saying how essential I was. So I walked behind them through a forest as green as Gauguin's Tahiti, honoring their habit of silence as we hooked off and onto paths seemingly without reason. We'd go ahead for half a mile and rest for five minutes, then hike for a hundred yards and rest for half an hour. It was impossible to predict when we'd stop, and harder still to tell how long the pause would be. I finally heard the boom and shush of the sea and held my hands up to shade my eyes from the flare of harsh sunshine and salt white sand. Finding the harbor was the whole point of the trip, but the Mayans halted again just inside the forest instead of going out to the water. I couldn't figure out their hesitation, and I asked Eduardo in Spanish why we were stopping. Eduardo looked at me like I was a toddler. And then he told me with infinite patience,

"We are waiting for our spirits to catch up."

~

I have a flat board on my knees for a desk, and on it my Scribe spiral notebook—*Hecho en Mexico por Kimberly Clark* in Naucalpan—is opened to the first page. My pen is an "EF uni-ball Micro," with a fine point and blue ink. I have no idea whom I'm writing this for. We are waiting for our spirits to catch up.

~

I first met Reinhardt Schmidt just after I got back from Colorado. I was sane as Atticus then. And cool. Wearing shades and waltzing through the great open-air market in Resurrección. It was a hot and crowded tent city that was as loud as a kindergarten playground and filled with hard-up people selling handicrafts, fabulous fruits and vegetables, plucked chickens with the heads still attached, items fresh from the trash. You did not see many *norteamericanos* there, but you did find bargains of the hijacked, five-finger discount, *What the hell do I do with this?* kind: Gillette razors, Goodyear snow tires still wrapped in tan paper, floppy discs that sold for a nickel apiece, a guy in head phones sitting on the trunk of a green Chevrolet that held nothing but Salem cigarettes. Reinhardt called it his duty-free shop.

I felt a hand fall faint as a butterfly on my forearm, and I looked down at a kid holding up a bottle of Jameson's Irish whiskey while his other hand waited like a tray for his pesos. *"Aquí,"* he said. Here. And he was surprised when I told him nah. *"¡Es para usted!"* It is for Your Grace. And then he tried English. "We gave you our special price."

And then I heard a voice just beside me say as he handed the kid his pesos, "We seem to be the same person."

Reinhardt Schmidt did, in fact, look like me but was far more the kind of handsome, fine-boned, fashion-model blonde that seems fit to be a flight steward for Lufthansa. His age was forty or younger—he never said—but he was an inch or two shorter, fifteen pounds lighter, a fast-twitch, friendly, full-of-energy type in fancy sunglasses, a formal white tuxedo shirt with its sleeves folded high as his elbows, green fatigue trousers from some foreign legion, and feet that were miserably without shoes but did have ankle bracelets. A hand-sized flash camera was hanging from a frayed cord around his neck.

The kid took a moment to look from face to face, as if he was flummoxed, and then to touch his own hair in explanation. *"Rubio,"* he said.

Reinhardt looked at me and I translated, "Blond." And then I told the kid, *"Mi gemelo malvado."* My evil twin.

The kid smiled and handed Reinhardt the whiskey and then hurried to his father's booth.

We introduced ourselves and we talked for five or ten minutes, no more. Reinhardt told me he was from Germany, but his English was the highly schooled kind that you hear all over Europe now and I figured that Germany was his geography of convenience, the origin of a passport he got by on. Even then I guessed he was lying, just another guy in Mexico on the lam; there was that wise-guy shiftiness, that hustle of flattery and fearing offense, of sizing you up for the squeeze while trying too hard to be friends. You saw his kind in all the American bars—hard-drinking, no-luck, full-time liars fleeing some trouble that was not all glamorous, financial reversals in the restaurant business or one too many wives, but who forced themselves to confide that they were in Mexico on an inheritance, here to write a novel that four or five editors were definitely interested in, or hiding out in a witness protection program, for Chrissake don't tell anybody. You heard them out if only to know what topics not to bring up again and the true story became a whiff of unpleasantness underneath all that perfume.

I have few other recollections of our first meeting but that he pronounced *have* like *haff* and *situation* without the *chu* sound of American English. Reinhardt told me if I needed a haircut—and his squinnying look said I did—he was the guy for me; he'd handled the heads of fabulously wealthy women in Hawaii—he hinted at a flair for other things, too—before he lost his work permit and took a galley job on Mick Jagger's yacht—a great guy, by the way—and happened onto a fabulously wealthy surgeon and his wife who needed Reinhardt to crew for them. A half year he was with them, sailing, playing backgammon, attending to their needs. Everything blew up a few weeks ago in Cuba—hot sex, discovery, gunplay—and he'd hightailed it here on the proceeds of the wife's Piaget watch, which he'd hocked for just such an emergency.

Well, he probably knew about the American expatriate's tolerance for bullshit and I, of course, have a further tolerance for madness, so I forgave his fabrications and when, hardly five hours later, Reinhardt bumped into me at The Scorpion ("Oh, hi!" he said. "Are you following me?"), we talked like friends in the making. I was fully medicated with gin and tonics by then and fell into a fraught stream of consciousness about Renata, an hour or more of she-done-me-wrong in forty variations, and Reinhardt took it all in oh-so-sympathetically, but fishing a little, too: Was she pretty? Did I have a picture of her? How often did I see her? Was she dating other men? Did she have a private income? And where did she live? I have forgotten my answers; I have not forgotten that I finally felt party to one of those *Strangers on a Train* routines; I half expected some unholy pact to follow when he halted his questions long enough to order a shot of José Cuervo and quaff it fast and peer resolutely into The Scorpion's mirror. But he just looked at me dully and said, "I have no money to pay for the tequila. Would you let me cut your hair?"

And so it was that Reinhardt arrived at my house one noon in the first week of January with his things in a kind of European saddlebag slung over his left shoulder. And I sat on a kitchen stool, a skirt of fabric under my chin, his silence behind me only increasing as his hands firmly held my hair and his scissors flashed, and I felt his tension for the first time and inferred that he was homosexual and hesitating over an invitation. But just as I was about to talk about what I fancied was not being said, Reinhardt filibustered about his jail time in Honolulu for hashish smuggling. A brutal year, but he made friends with a guy inside who got him a hairdresser's job with Universal Television. I forget all the ways in which he altered his first version of his life, forget even how he ended up with a film unit manager's job on four music videos, but a friend at Tri-Star liked his work so much that he was sent to Mexico to scout locations for a famous actress's next picture ("You haff heard of her, belief me") and then his boss went over to Paramount and the picture was put into turnaround and Reinhardt was left here high and dry. Which is why he carried a camera with him; he was always framing shots. Alan Pakula called him here just a few days ago and told him to sit tight, he was in preproduction on a film that would have a four-day shoot in Cancún and he wanted Reinhardt on his team. "And so I wait."

I was famished for English at the time and fairly indifferent to those florid tall tales, so I offered him feeble amens through all the foregoing ("Wow." "Too bad." "Amazing." "No!"), but as he put a gel on my hair, he turned his attention to me. Was I here on an inheritance? Was my father rich? Were my paintings selling well enough to afford a house like this? Oh, was I renting? Were the owners here often? Were the house and its contents fully insured? Reinhardt had seen a friend lose everything; he was just fantastically worried about me, he didn't know why. Well, he did. Don't be offended, but I seemed a wunderkind, even at forty. Which is why I ought to have worldly people to watch over my affairs. "You are so honest and trusting and others, I can tell you, are so . . . I have not the word: *schlau?*"

"Sly?"

"Yes! Sly. You do not realize. I have no talent myself, but I have *skills.* You know? You maybe need help with the finances? Business affairs? Finding things at the cheapest price? I have contacts. And abilities. Arranging things is my gift."

"Here. Hold my wallet for me," I said.

Reinhardt smiled and flicked off the hair dryer. "Excuse me?"

His scheming was so obvious, so insultingly free of finesse and bunco, that I fell into silence. And then he held a mirror up and held his face close to mine so that both of us were in the frame. "Great haircut," I said. And it was true; just like his.

ESCAPE TO MEXICO

"Look at us," he said. "We could be brothers."

"I have one already."

Reinhardt casually turned to put the mirror on the kitchen countertop. "Oh? And what is his name?"

"Frank."

"And is he living in Colorado?"

But I was heading upstairs by then. I got thirty dollars in pesos and heard him fool with the Sinatra CD on the dining room player until he found "Witchcraft." And when I got downstairs he was hunting through the full rack of discs.

"Are you casing the joint?"

Reinhardt smiled uneasily. "What does it mean, 'casing'?"

I handed him the pesos and he stuffed them in his front pocket with only a furtive count. "Was it expensive," he asked, "this stereo system?"

Weeks hence, I feared, I'd return from my night work in the jungle and everything in that house would be gone, presto chango, and Reinhardt would be showing his kindness to some other wunderkind. "I have something I'd like to give you," I said.

"Oh?" he asked, and there was a child's Christmas glimmer in his eyes as I went to the hallway closet and hauled out a fair painting I'd fired off of a hillside and rainstorm skies and the seething gray waters just below my studio. I was frankly surprised by the honest respect he offered that sketch, the fascination and honor and joy Reinhardt took in holding it up and fully appraising it. You'd have thought it was a Corot. "This is fantastic!" he said. "This is great!" And there was a faint gloss of tears in his eyes as he fetchingly grinned at me. "We Europeans take friendship seriously. I'll have to do something for you." . . .

~

On good days I painted in the jungle, faking it mostly, far too much hard-won technique and far too little imagination. Otherwise I hung out at the hotels, half-baked on hashish or the hard drugs I could score off college kids on their getaway flings, as goofy as that, cruising the *playa* in jams and sunglasses and a teal satin shirt, like the playboy of the Caribbean, hunting babes who were already high and inviting them home for an up-all-night, and then coming to in that *Oh, Jesus* chaos of emptied bottles and passed-out strangers and somebody softly sobbing upstairs. Anything to stay buzzed, to forget my obsession: self-prescribing Dexedrine, Percodan, Ritalin, and Valium at the *farmacia* and trying out fancy chemistry projects until I felt the attack of the thousand spiders. I was halfway through an imitation of Malcolm Lowry in Cuernavaca: fit and tanned in the afternoon, grinning for the camera in white shorts and huaraches, with Ovid's *Metamorphoses* in one hand and a full bottle of gin in the other; and far far gone by nighttime— feckless, sulking, furious, unshaved, in a fuddle of shame and neediness, failure becoming his full-time job.

But as skin-your-nose low as I was, there were a hundred others just like me down there, the formerly talented, the formerly with-it, hulking over shot glasses in the frown of drunkenness, not talking because we couldn't form words, having no company but fear, and pitifully tilting down for a taste because our hands weren't working quite right. You could find us haunting the *centro* at five A.M., walking car wrecks and homicides, waiting for the cantinas to open again and looking away from each other because we hated seeing that face in the mirror. You heard all kinds of reasons for being in the tropics: for their arthritis, their pensions, the fishing, the tranquil and easygoing ways, but the fact was a lot of us stayed because Mexico treated us like children, indulging our laziness, shrugging at our foolishness, and generally offering the silence and tolerance of a good butler helping the blotto Lord What-a-waste to his room. In high school my brother knowingly told me, as a kind of dire warning, "There are people who do on a regular basis things you have never even imagined!" I was now one of those people. Eventually it had become fairly ordinary for me to lose the handle and black out so far from home it might as well have been Cleveland, sitting there in a foul doorway in the *barrio*, fairly sure I'd had sex but not knowing with whom, blood on my shirt front, puke on my shoes, kids stealing the change from my pockets, and so little idea where my Volkswagen was that I used up an afternoon in a taxi just prowling the streets until I found it. And then, of course, there was a celebration and I fell into a wander again.

I have trouble putting a date to that particular spree, but it was late January, four months since I'd got off lithium, and for days I'd been floorboarding it into what Renata used to call "a heightened state of mental fragility." Whether it was insanity or the aftereffects of pharmacy, I felt brilliant, ebullient, invulnerable, full of gaiety and false good health and a giddy, *Wow, isn't this freaky?* excitement. Well-being for me, though, is often like the aura that precedes the seizures of epilepsy, and I was headed for doom even while I was heartily being in my prime, Captain Electric, happy-go-lucky Scott. Stuart tried abiding me at Printers Inc and found himself not up to the task, and when I showed up at his villa ("Hi, honey; I'm home!") Renata gave me that *Oh, you poor puppy* look. We finally went out to inflict ourselves upon Mexico and found our way onto a bus tour of Resurrección, one of those *You are here* jaunts put on by the grand resort hotels to lure their elderly out of their rooms. And by then I was falling into a funk of aloneness and loss and desolation, hunkered down inside those old, old feelings of lunacy and finding familiar faces in all the Americans on that air-conditioned tour bus ("We know each other!), as if I were part of some cosmic class reunion, déjà vu to the max—that old guy daubing sunblock fifteen on his nose and the hunch-backed woman holding her purse with both hands were as friendly to me as regulars at the truck stop café in Antelope, and wasn't that Aunt Clair? Were I still full of optimism and hail-fellow-well-met I would have been tempted to shout hel-los and harass the old people with my frantic happiness, but my fluky head chemistry was forcing me into a bleak house of paranoia, restlessness, even terror, and I was trying to hold back, quiet the hectic tattoo of my heartbeat, put the watchdog out on his chain in case things got too weird.

Which they did. We'd motored through the *centro*, found photo opportunities with the fishing boats and the fruit sell-ers, heard the chamber of commerce pitch about a sky's-the-limit real estate future, and halted in front of the Church of the Resurrection. We were going on a walking tour, the girl in charge said. She said we would "find inside the *parroquia* many furnishing from Espain that the padres are bringing to Mexico in the eighteen century."

I have no idea if it was intuition or if some psychic flood-waters were opened and feeding me insights into the past, but I felt superior to whatever that girl's presentation would be. I felt like a former inhabitant, like I knew that place when the paint was still fresh, as if the hallways, the hidden doors, the shellacked pictures on the walls were as familiar to me as my father's house, and I'd forsaken the right or possibility of going inside again. Call it superstition or just a bad trip, but it felt as heavy as shot-in-the-night reality, like I was a kid on the first porch step of a haunted house, and my first remedy of choice was to hide my head underneath the sheets. I have a hard time making these events obey anything but the horrible logic of nightmare. I just know that as the old people herded off the bus I was shaded by the wings of madness and just sat there in my place, heartsick, holes for eyes, frail as an invalid, and shaking like it was forty below.

I heard Renata ask, "Are you spooked?" And I realized that she and I were the only passengers still on the bus, and that the frustrated driver was fixing a hard squint on us in his rearview mirror.

I just said, "I'm not ready for this."

"You don't have to go in," she said.

"Are you sure?"

"I'll see if you can stay." Renata gallantly went forward to help out the crazy person.

I heard Spanish and hours seemed to pass as I hunched forward, my face hidden in my hands, and inhaled, exhaled, as if that would be my only job from then on. Then I heard Renata say it was not possible, it was break time and the bus was being shut down, I'd fry inside with the air off. She took hold of my wrist and led me like a child to the door and ever so tenderly onto the sidewalk.

You'd have thought I was a head-on collision the way the Americans lurked on the sidewalk, talking about me, retreating, *Don't get anything on me* in their looks as I was hurried across the street, my feeble shoes shuffling a sandpaper rasp from the cobbled paving, and was settled like an ill-wrapped package on a park bench in the *jardín*. She said, "You know, I'm not that healthy myself. We can't take care of each other." If I looked at Renata then it was fleetingly, but I followed her with a toys-in-the-attic stare as she waded back into that hushed crowd, and I fended off self-doubt by thinking that this helplessness and despair was her scene, not mine, I was *fine* until she took my hand. *I have to go now,* I thought. *I have to wash. I'll eat my food with a fork.*

A full day later in my house and I was fine again, honest, no fooling. Waking up and holding my hands out in front of my face in that *how-many-fingers* final exam of full consciousness and perspective. But one frightening leer from Mr. Hyde in the bathroom mirror told me that I ought to get out of town for a while. And so I hurried into a bleached shirt and chinos and hiking boots, filled a box with food, block-lettered a note for María, and headed out to Eduardo's to hie the lunatic into the hills.

We shared a past, Eduardo and I, that made his friends consider my visits to his shanty in the jungle a kind of jubilee of wild invention, so within the next few days all the families in the area found their way to his place to hear the holy fool. My first night there fourteen men and boys settled on their haunches around a fire, inhaling huge handmade cigars until they were wholly intoxicated, and fascinatedly watched the zoo animal in his own private *Weltschmerz*. Eduardo finally squatted next to me and whispered in Spanish, "We wait for a speech."

I gave it some thought and recited in English a high school lesson of the first paragraph from *Moby Dick:*

"'Whenever I find myself growing grim about the mouth; whenever it is a damp, drizzly November in my soul; whenever I find myself involuntarily pausing before coffin warehouses, and bringing up the rear of every funeral I meet, and especially whenever my hypos get such an upper hand of me that it requires a strong moral principle to prevent me from deliberately stepping into the street and methodically knocking people's hats off—then I account it high time to get to the sea as soon as I can.'"

I have no idea what my English sounded like to them, but when I finished, a few softly applauded me in their flat-palmed way and one at a time they got up and finally left, fully entertained.

Hectic that life was not. We fetched water from the hole and used posts to tamp kernels of corn in a field that was still hot with soot and ash, but otherwise the hours passed at half-speed in a whine of insects, Eduardo instructing his heedless wives in their work while the heat soaked the black-and-blues away. Each night Eduardo's oldest wife, Koh, offered me a hideous brew of *balche* and chewed roots and seed pods that I took in perfect obedience. And I'd sleep hard, hammered, until high noon, hearing nothing but pigs and chickens and the chinking noise of machetes hacking down great trees in the jungle, feeling nothing but the infrequent, faint, floating touch of children's hands on my face and hair.

And then Saturday afternoon Eduardo and three of his friends invited me fishing, and we hiked through the forest to a harbor where a high-sided skiff was lolling on the swells as a teenaged boy in a racing suit fiddled with a fifty-horsepower outboard motor terribly hitched to its transom. I looked north and found far off the shell gray of the pollution that tarnished Resurrección, but the shoreline was otherwise foreign to me.

We got naked and thrashed out to the skiff with our clothes held high overhead, and I heard only highly accented Mayan as they pulled themselves up over the gunwale and joshed about something having to do with the gringo. I played the fifth wheel, *Oh don't mind me,* and faced them stonily from the forward sailing thwart as the kid in the racing suit got the motor going and we surged a half-mile farther out to a barrier reef where the water was as tepid and clear as Perrier but from a distance had the turquoise color of kitchens in the fifties.

The kid killed the motor and hurled overboard three concrete blocks that were tied to the painter line. An old face mask half eaten with salt and fairly good fins were handed to me, and then a four-foot spear just like they had. Winking, I gave them the old thumbs-up—what a good sport, what a trouper. The first to jump over the side was me, and then I heard hoots and the four crashing in, handling the seawater without face masks or fins and twisting like otters around the white elkhorn coral and infant sponges as they hunted brilliant wrasse and groupers and rainbow parrotfish. I went up for air a full minute before one of them did—they held their breath like turtles—but finally they all did flutter up for air with a boxfish that trailed shreds of blood, and I skimmed down past colonies of intricate lavender and red coral through a school of glorious blue tang that shuddered and broke apart at my presence and then rejoined into one mind again, and then I stroked farther past a terrace of black brain coral and sea anemone to a floor of sand. And there I found a stingray almost fully hidden in the sand, its fake-seeming yellow eyes flashing uninteresting news until irritation or fright finally registered and with a fluff of its gorgeous iron gray wings the sand floated away like smoke and the stingray was suddenly in a flight that was fluent as ointment. The first surge took it twenty feet from me, and then in its sovereignty it glided into a stall and oh so gently rippled its wings until the floor settled over it again.

Either I read it somewhere or Eduardo told me, but in their religious ceremonies ages ago, pre-Cortez, the Mayan high priests used to stab the barb of the stingray's tail in their penises and the poison would kick them into head trips that seemed to offer hallucinatory interpretations of the future. You'll have a sense of how far gone I was then that I found the hurt and danger of that kind of rush crazily alluring. I got high on threat and foreboding; I was like those heroin addicts who find they can get off just with the needle. I ought to have flashed up to the surface for air, but I felt a strong and irrational need to touch that stingray, and I kicked down until I was just above the fish, watching it blankly watch me.

I have given up trying to be persuasive about this. You get these looks: *Oh sure, stingrays.* But in fact a flock or herd or plague of stingrays majestically soared in from nowhere, five or six of them wrestling up against me in a thrall of motion, their soft wings sheathing me, their tails frantically whipping, falling away only to flare up against my flesh, showing their white undersides as their toothless mouths seemed to foolishly smile. I have no idea what attracted them. I have never felt anything so much like pure muscle, that filled me with such loathing. It was like one of those Renaissance paintings of Saint Anthony being persecuted by demons. The stingrays jolted hard into me and held me under and one blunt head knocked my face mask off. And I was near fainting for lack of air when I heard the Mayans there with me, churning their legs and fighting the wings until a spear jarred into one and a pink orchid of blood seemed to grow from its skin and their hands took hold of its head and ventral gills. And as I shot upward, they gingerly followed, hauling the fish to the skiff.

The kid was kneeling by a gunwale with a gaff. Enormously pleased, he helped me up into the boat and patted my head and heaped Spanish praise on me until he could heave the stingray onto the flooring. But then the others got in and huddled far from me by the engine as if they were afraid of getting anything of me on them. Even Eduardo found nothing more to do than frown at my bad karma.

We went farther up the coast to an inlet and the pretty white skirt of beach that was near Eduardo's shanty. Women in five-dollar American dresses were there chanting songs as they husked corn around a fire, and Eduardo's wife Koh shyly handed me a jar of the fermented corn whiskey called *chicha*.

I frankly brought nothing to that party; I was an anchorite, *il penseroso*, off by himself on a rock, hearing their talk but not understanding, hearing the high whine of insects at sundown. I felt apart from humanity, as full of friction and self-pity as a fractious misfit feeding on his miseries. Koh filled my jar again as the stingray was flayed, and as our food was cooked Eduardo sat by me in four or five minutes of silence before hesitantly saying in Spanish, "We are afraid of you."

"Why?"

"Bad things happen," he said. "We fear for our children." Eduardo's secret name in Mayan was *Nicuachinel,* he who sees into the middle of things.

Elegant Spanish escaped me. I offered him something like, "Well, that's just stupid."

But Eduardo simply said, "You go home now, please."

So I gathered my few things, got into my Volkswagen, and headed back to Resurrección.

COLLAGES
Anaïs Nin

WHEN BRUCE FIRST CAME TO Vienna Renate noticed him because of his resemblance to one of the statues which smiled at her through her bedroom window. It was the statue with wings on its heels, the one she was convinced travelled during the night. She observed him every morning while eating her breakfast. She was certain she could detect signs of long journeys. His hair seemed more ruffled, there was mud on his winged feet.

She recognized in Bruce the long neck, the runner's legs, the lock of hair over the forehead.

But Bruce denied this relationship to Mercury. He thought of himself as Pan. He showed Renate how long the downy hair was at the tip of his ears.

Familiarity with the agile, restless statue put her at ease with Bruce. What added to the resemblance was that Bruce talked little. Or he talked with motions of his body and the gestures were more eloquent than the words. He entered into conversation with a forward thrust of his shoulders, as if he were going either to fly or swim into its current, and when he could not find the words he would shake his body as if he were executing a jazz dance which would shake them out like dice. His thoughts were still enclosed within his body and could only be transmitted through it. The words he was about to say first shook his body and one could follow their course in the vibrations running through it, in the shuffling rhythm of his feet. Gusts of words agitated every muscle, but finally converged into one, at the most two words: "Man, see, man, see here, man, oh man."

At other times they rushed out in rhythmic patterns like variations in jazz so swift one could barely catch them. He was looking for words equivalent to jazz rhythms. He was impatient with sequences, chronology, and construction. An interruption seemed to him more eloquent than a complete paragraph.

But Renate, having been trained for years to read the unmoving lips of statues, heard the words which came from the perfect modelling of Bruce's lips. The message she heard was: "What does one do when one is fourteen times removed from one's true self, not two, or three, but fourteen times away from the center?"

She would start with making a portrait of him. He would see himself as she saw him. That would be a beginning.

They worked together for many afternoons. What Bruce observed was compassion in her voice, what he saw under her heavy sensual eyelids was a diminutive image of himself swimming in the film of emotion which humidified her eyes.

"Come with me to Mexico," said Bruce. "I want to wander about a little until I find out who I am, what I am."

And so they started on a trip together. Bruce wanted to put space and time between the different cycles of his life.

It was during the long drives through hot deserts, the meals at small saffron-perfumed restaurants on the road, the walks through the prismatic markets to the tune of soft Mexican chants that he said, as Renate's father had said: "I love to hear you laughing, Renate."

If the heavy rains caught them in their finest clothes, on the way to a bullfight, Renate laughed as if the gods, Mexican or others, were playing pranks. If there were no more hotel rooms, and if by listening to the advice of the barman they ended in a whorehouse, Renate laughed. If they arrived late at night, and there was a sandstorm blowing, and no restaurants open, Renate laughed.

"I want to bring all this back with us," she said once.

"But what is this?" asked Bruce.

"I am not sure. I only know I want to bring it back with us and live according to it."

"I know what it is," said Bruce, spilling the contents of their valises over the beds, and searching for the alarm clock. Then he repacked negligently, and as they drove away, a few hours later, on a deserted road, he stopped, wound up the alarm clock, and left it standing on the middle of the road. As they drove away, it suddenly became unleashed like an angry child, the alarm bell rang like a tantrum, and it shook with fury and protest at neglect.

Sometimes they stopped late at night in a motel which looked like a hacienda. The gigantic old ovens, shaped like cones, had been turned into bedrooms. The *brasero* in the center of the tent-shaped room threw its smoke to the converging opening at the top. The cold stone was covered with red and black *serapes.* Renate would brush her long hair. Bruce would go out without a word. His exit was like a vanishing act, because he made no announcement, and was followed by silence. And this silence was not like an intermission. It was like a premonition of death. The image of his pale face vanishing gave her the feeling of someone seeking to be warmed by moonlight. The Mexican sun could not tan him. He had already been permanently tinted by the Norwegian midnight sun of his parents' native country.

From occasional vague descriptions, Renate had understood that his parents had brought him up in this impenetrable silence. They had a language they talked between themselves and had only a broken form of English to use with the child. They had left him in America at the age of eleven, without any words of explanation, returned to Norway, and let him be brought up by a distant relative.

"Distant he was," said Bruce once, laughing. "My first job was given to me by a neighbor who owned the candy machines in which kids put a penny and get candy and sometimes if they are lucky, a prize. The prizes were rings, small whistles, tin soldiers, a new penny, a tie pin. My job was to insert a little glue so the prizes would never come down the slot."

They laughed.

"When I met you in Vienna, I was on my way to see my parents. Then I thought: what's the use? I don't even remember their faces."

Before he had left the room, they had been drinking Mexican beer. He said looking at his glass and turning it in his hand: "When you are drunk an ordinary glass shines like a diamond."

Renate added: "When you are drunk an iron bed seems like the feather bed of sensual Sultans."

He rebelled against all ties, even the loving web of words, promises, compliments. He left without announcing his return, not even using the words most people uttered every day: "I'll be seeing you!"

Renate would fall asleep in her orange shawl, forgetting to undress. At first she slept, and then awakened and waited. But waiting in a Mexican hotel in the middle of the desert with only the baying of dogs, the flutter of palm trees by cadlelight, seemed ominous. And so one night she went in search of him.

The countryside was dark, filled with fireflies and the hum of cicadas. There was only one small café lit with orange oil lamps. Peasants in dirty white suits sat drinking. A guitarist was playing and singing slowly, as if sleep had half-hypnotized him. Bruce was not there.

Returning along the dark road she saw a shadow by a tree. A car passed by. Its headlight illumined the side of the road and two figures standing by a tree. A young Mexican boy stood leaning against the vast tree trunk, and Bruce was kneeling before him. The Mexican boy rested his dark hand on Bruce's blond hair and his face was raised towards the moon, his mouth open.

Weeping Renate ran back to the room, packed and drove away.

She drove to Puerta Maria by the sea where they were exhibiting her paintings. And the image of the night tree with its flowers of poison was replaced by her first sight of a coral tree in the glittering sunlight.

It eclipsed all the other trees with the intensity of its orange flowers growing in tight wide bouquets at the end of bare branches, so that there were no leaves or shadows of leaves to attenuate the explosion of colors. They had petals which seemed made of orange fur tipped with blood-red tendrils. It was the flower from the coral tree which should have been named the passion flower.

As soon as she saw it she wanted a dress of that color and that intensity. That was not difficult to find in a Mexican sea town. All their dresses took their colors from flowers. She bought the coral tree dress. The orange cotton had almost invisible blood-red threads running through it as if the Mexicans had concocted their dyes from the coral tree flower itself.

The coral tree would kill the memory of a black gnarled tree and of two figures sheltered under its grotesque branches.

The coral tree would carry her into a world of festivities. An orange world.

In Haiti the trees were said to walk at night. Many Haitians swore they had actually seen them move, or had found them in different places in the morning. So at first she felt as if the coral tree had moved from its birthplace and was walking through the spicy streets or the dazzling festive beach. Her own starched, flouncing skirt made her think of the coral tree flower that never wilted on the tree, but at death fell with a sudden stab to earth.

The coral tree dress did not fray or fade in the tropical humidity. But Renate did not, as she had expected, become suffused with its colors. She had hoped to be penetrated by the orange flames and that it would dye her mood to match the joyous life of the sea town. She had thought that steeped in its fire she would be able to laugh with the orange gaiety of the natives. She had expected to absorb its liveliness intravenously. But to the self that had sought to disguise her regrets the coral tree dress remained a costume.

Every day the dress became more brilliant, drenched in sunlight and matching its dazzling hypnosis. But Renate's inner landscape was not illumined by it. Inside her grew a gigantic, tortured black tree and two young men who had made a bed of it.

People stopped her as she passed, women to envy, children to touch, men to receive the magnetic rays. On the beach, people turned towards her as if the coral tree itself had come walking down the hill.

But inside the dress lay a black tree, the night. How people were taken in by symbolism! She felt like a fraud, drawing everyone into her circle of orange fire.

She attracted the attention of a man from Los Angeles who wore white sailor pants, a white T-shirt, and who was suntanned and smiling at her.

Is he truly happy, she wondered, or is he wearing a disguise too?

At the beach he had merely smiled. But here in the market, the one behind the bullring, he was lost, and he appealed to her. He did not know where he was. His arms were full of straw hats, straw donkeys, pottery, baskets and sandals.

He had strayed among the parrots, the sliced and odorous melons, the women's petticoats and ribbons. The petticoats swollen by the breeze caressed his hair and damp cheeks. The palm-leafed roofs were too low for him and the tips of the leaves tickled his ears.

"I must get back soon," he said. "I left my car alone for two hours now."

"They're not strict with tourists," she answered. "Don't worry."

"Oh, it's not in the street. I wouldn't leave it in the street. I tried every hotel in town, until I found one where I could park my car near my bedroom. Do you want to come and see it?"

He said this in the tone of a man offering a glimpse of an original Picasso.

They walked slowly in the sun. "It's such a beautiful car," he said, "the best they ever made. I raced it in Los Angeles. It's as sensitive as a human being. You don't know what an ordeal it was, the trip from Mexico City. They are repairing the road—it was full of detours."

"What happened to you?"

"Nothing happened to me, but my poor car! I could feel every bump on the road, every hole, the dust, the stones. It hurt me to see it struggle along that road, scraped by pebbles, stained with tar, covered with red dust, my beautiful car that I took such care of. It was as if my own body were walking on that road. I had to drive through a river. A little boy sat astride the hood, and guided me with a propeller-like gesture of his hand, indicating the best path through the water. But I never knew when we were going to get stuck there, my poor low-slung car in muddied waters, where the natives wash all their laundry, and bathe the cattle. I could feel the sand and grit in the motor. I could see the flies, mosquitoes, and other insects cluttering the air vent. I never want to put my car through such an experience again."

They had reached a low, wide rambling hotel surrounded by a vast jungle garden. There under a palm tree, among sun flowers and ferns, stood the car, sleek and shining, seemingly undamaged.

"Oh, it's in the sun," cried the man from Los Angeles and rushed to move it into shadows. "It's a good thing I came

back. Do you want to sit in it? I'll order drinks meanwhile."
He held the door open.

Renate said: "I would love to drive to the beach on the other side of the mountain. It's beautiful at this time of the day."

"I've heard of it, but it wouldn't be good for the car. They're building on that road. I hear them set off dynamite. I wouldn't trust Mexicans with dynamite."

"Have you been to the bullfight?"

"I can't take my car there, the boys steal tires and side mirrors, I hear."

"Have you been to the Black Pearl night club?"

"That's one place we can go to, they have a parking lot with an attendant. Yes, I'll take you there."

Later when they were having a drink, the sun descended like a meteorite of antique gold and sank into the sea.

"Ha," breathed the man smiling. "I'm glad it's cooler now. The sun is not good for my car."

Then he explained that for the return home he had made arrangements to get his car back without suffering anymore. "I booked passage on a freighter. It will take three weeks. But it will be easier on my car."

"Be sure and buy a big bottle of mineral water," said Renate.

"To wash the car?" asked the man from Los Angeles, frowning.

"No, for yourself. You might get dysentery."

She offered to speak to the captain of the freighter because she talked Spanish.

They drove to the docks together. The captain stood half-naked directing the loading of bananas and pineapples. He wore a handkerchief tied to his forehead to keep the perspiration from falling over his face. The orange dress attracted his eyes and he smiled.

Renate asked him if he would consent to share his cabin with the American, and take good care of him.

"Anything to please the señorita," he said.

"How will you fare on fish and black beans?" she asked the car worshipper.

"Let's buy some canned food, and a sponge to wash the salt off my car. It will be on the open deck."

The day of his departure the beach town displayed its most festive colors; the parrots whistled, the magnolia odors covered the smell of fish, and the flowers were as profuse as at a New Orleans Carnival.

Renate arrived in time to see the car being measured and found too big for the net in which they usually picked up the cargo. So they placed two narrow planks from the pier to the deck, and the man was asked to drive the car onto the freighter. One inch out of the way and both car and man would fall into the bay. But the owner of the car was a skilful driver, and an amorous one, so he finally maneuvered it on deck. Once there, it was found to be so near the edge that the sailors had to rope it tightly like a rebellious bronco. Lashed to the ship by many ropes it could no longer roll over the edge.

Then the man from Los Angeles moved into the only cabin with his big bottle of mineral water and a bag of canned soups.

As the freighter slowly tugged away he cried: "I'll let you know in what state my car gets there! Thanks for your help."

A month later she received a letter:

Dear Kind Friend: I will always remember you so gay and carefree in your orange dress. And how wise you were! If only I had listened to your warnings! I used the mineral water to wash the salty mist off my car, and so the first thing that happened was that I got the 'tourista' with a high fever. The captain kept his word to you and shared his cabin with me, but also with a barrel of fish, cans of gasoline, and hay for the animals. Then the sea got pretty rough and the car began to roll back and forth, and at each roll I thought it would plunge into the sea. I decided to sleep inside it, and if anything were to happen we would both go together. At the first town we stopped at, we took in a herd of cattle. They were crowded on deck, and they pushed against my car, dribbled on it, and even tried to gore it. At night they quarrelled and I don't need to describe the stench. The heat was as heavy as a blanket. At the second stop we took in a Madame and about twenty call girls who were being moved to another house. The captain gallantly offered his cabin. Tequila was free on board and so you can imagine how rowdy the nights were. After three weeks I arrived in Los Angeles a wreck, but my car is in fine shape. I had it lubricated and I wish you could hear it purr along the roads. Los Angeles has such wonderful roads.

MEXiCAN NiGHT
Sherwood Anderson

SINCE THEY HAVE BUILT THE new paved road from Laredo on the border down over the mountains to Mexico City, the tourists in their cars come always in greater and greater numbers. They come from the cities and from the small towns. Sometimes the cars come singly and sometimes in cavalcades. There is the fascination of being in a strange foreign place and of getting what seems such a lot of Mexican dollars for, say, a ten-dollar bill. We tourists buy guide books and dictionaries. Some of us . . . bring cameras and take thousands of shots of the straw-thatched huts in Mexican villages, of the little naked boy babies, of the arrieros, with their pack trains . . . the little shuffling burros with their half dance step under their great loads, followed by their Indian drivers, also shuffling softly, softly along.

We tourists are like an army in that we all seem to congregate in certain towns, in certain hotels. On the way down and back we stop at the same towns. We go to the Xochimilco, to Taxco, where we buy silver of Bill Spratling. We gather together in groups and, as it is in the army, strange and often unfounded rumors run about among us.

There is, for example, always the idea that a revolution

may start at any moment. That and the question of holdups, or people kidnapped, carried off by bandits into the hills. It all gives a thrill, adds a touch of spice. You'd really think there had never been such a thing as a kidnapping or a holdup in our own beloved land.

This or that happened to a man from Des Moines. "There was a man, one of the natives, came right up to him. I got this straight. He asked this man a question and because he couldn't answer, didn't know the lingo, the fellow drew a knife and stabbed him. Of course it wasn't in the papers. They don't let you know such things.

"And they say that the soldiers you see . . . they say they'll hold you up as quick as a bandit."

These and other stories, running among us tourists. I've an idea that most of us, the males among us, would much rather be at home or, if we have to take the wife for a trip, we'd much rather have gone to California, say to Hollywood. We tell each other so. "But, you see, there's the wife," we say. We explain to one another how it is, how, just because certain women from our towns have been down here and have brought home a lot of baskets and these serapes and things and maybe made talks before the Women's Clubs about Mexican art and this Diego Rivera, we have to be dragged down.

We had got into this little Mexican town, Fred and I and the two newspaper men. It was when the President of Mexico took over the oil companies, American and British, and the newspaper men were going down by train but, as we had space in the car, they said they would come with us.

So we were in this town off the big highway and it was night and, when we had been there for an hour or two, one of the newspaper men who spoke Spanish, having got us well fixed up in the town's one hotel, these other people arrived. They were like us in that they were in a town where few tourists stopped. They had got out of the main stream, had perhaps lost their way. There was a small, nervous man of, say, fifty-five, with two women, his wife and another . . . his wife's sister, Fred said. He said that the sister had been a schoolteacher and had retired on a pension. He said they were from North Dakota . . . he could have got that from their car license . . . and he went on, in a way he has, describing the lives of these three people after the first glance as though he had come from their town and had known them all his life. It is exasperating to hear Fred go on in this way about people he doesn't know at all, and what is most exasperating is that so often he is right.

Anyway there we were in this town and it was night, just after dark, and these people came. They drove up in front of the little hotel that had a patio into which, if you were skillful enough, you could drive your car through a very narrow driveway . . . you had to go down a steep stony side street to the driveway . . . and there we were, just loafing and looking, and, as we had all agreed it might be better not to drink water, we had been hitting the Scotch. We were on a little veranda above the patio and, when the man had unloaded his women, he tried to drive down the steep side street and into the patio and he jammed his car.

He got it caught in the narrow driveway and couldn't move it and, as always happens in a Mexican town, at least since we tourists have been coming down in such flocks, the car was literally covered with Mexican kids.

They were on the running boards of the car, they were

perched on the hood, they had run on ahead, they were giving directions in Spanish, they were grinning and waving
their arms, they were like a freight train crew making up a
train in a railroad terminal. One kid motioned for the man to
back the car, another to come ahead. They kept it up, grinning, dancing and waving arms until the car was hopelessly
jammed and the man, who Fred declared was a manufacturer
of washing machines . . . (you'd have thought, to hear Fred
talk later, that he had been in business with the man, or had
married into his family or something) . . . had got out of the
car. He had to crawl over one of the mudguards and he
slipped and fell. He was in the patio below us, his two
women having come out to join us. We were all standing and
looking down at him and, naturally, he was furious.

He was blaming Mexico. He was blaming his wife and
his wife's sister. He was there in the patio, as I have suggested, a somewhat small, obviously nervous man, bald and
with a little mustache. As he stood looking up at us and
scolding . . . he kept waving his arms and hopping about . . .
the ends of his mustache also seemed to be hopping up and
down.

And he had the Mexican kids on his hands. As he
hopped about, they hopped. They had begun a chant that all
we tourists in Mexico have come to know. There were many
pairs of small brown hands thrust out and, as the man
addressed us from above, telling us that it was the kids that
had got him into the trouble with the car, saying that, anyway,
he had never wanted to come to Mexico, blaming his wife
and his wife's sister, they carried on the chant. They made a
kind of chorus to his shrill sharp voice.

"Ten cents. Ten cents. Ten cents," they chanted. They had

made a circle about him and, as he grew more angry, shouting and scolding more and more shrilly, they, like all the kids in the world, began to enjoy the situation. They kept chanting the two words, the only English words they knew; they danced about him; they kept thrusting the little brown hands at him.

Then something else happened. The man below had appealed to us, asking if any of us could speak what he called their lingo, wanting us to tell the kids to vamoose, and the one of our party who might have helped, the newspaper man who spoke Spanish, had answered, saying, no, that we didn't know a word of Spanish . . . the particular newspaper man is named Lindsey . . . Jake Lindsey . . . and I had seen him, but a moment before, step aside and whisper something to the hotel proprietor, a Mexican with a big mustache, explaining, as I later found out, the situation, putting it up to him to help carry on the show, being thus as malicious as the kids. The hotel proprietor, like many Mexicans, was not averse to seeing an American in a ridiculous position . . . this thing always being carried on between peoples who do not speak the same language, do not live in the same sort of civilization . . .

All this going on, the Scotch, I dare say at work in us . . . it had come out of Jake Lindsey's bag and the hotel man had been in on it . . . the man's wife and his wife's sister begging him to come on up out of the patio, pleading that a man could be got to get the car out of the driveway, reminding him that every time he got excited he was sick afterwards, the man protesting, the kids dancing about him and carrying on their chant, the hotel proprietor grinning, the great racket going on attracting the attention of people in the street outside.

As suggested it was already night, and dark, but there was light in the patio and outside, in the village street, there were men coming home from their work in the fields. They were the sort of men we had been seeing all that day in the road. They were Mexican farmers, some afoot, some mounted on their little burros and, in the hand of each, the inevitable machete.

It is a long knife. It is the sort of knife used by the American farmer to cut corn but the Mexican, being a Mexican, has glorified it. Sometimes he has it in a leather sheath like a sword, sometimes it is curved at the end and sometimes straight. They all carry machetes. They wear them as they wear their shoes, when they have shoes. They carry them into town, into the fields. Fred says they sleep with the machetes in their hands.

The men were coming from the fields and, hearing the racket in the patio, they were curious. They began climbing over the car jammed in the driveway. They advanced toward the excited man and the circle of kids and, up above, the two women seeing them advancing so, the long knives in their hands . . . the truth was that they were all grinning . . . the two women began to scream and, turning and seeing the men with the knives, the man below fled up a flight of stairs to us.

"Ten cents. Ten cents. Ten cents."

They followed the man, now gone white, up the stairs to the veranda above but stopped there. The man had already engaged rooms and the hotel proprietor, thinking no doubt that the show had gone on long enough, went and threw open a door to one of the rooms. They ran in and the door was slammed and the newspaper man, that Jake Lindsey who might have helped the man and wouldn't, began to shower ten-cent pieces among the kids. He threw them into the patio below and the kids dashed down, the Mexican men with the long knives standing and laughing. They began waving the knives about.

"Viva America," they shouted. Laughing, they crawled away, over the jammed car that the two newspaper men later released and got back into the street of the town.

~

It was a night of sounds. It was a night of plots. I have an idea that I did not succeed, in spite of patient inquiry, in getting at the truth of it all. Fred says he wasn't in on it but I think he lied and I am sure that the two newspaper men and the Mexican hotel proprietor were in it up to their eyes.

As for myself, as I had been driving all day, I slept; but before sleeping I did get the feel, the sound, the smell of the Mexican village at night. For one thing, wanting to wear down the Scotch, I went for a walk, but how long and how far I walked I don't know. I was in many little dark streets. I was in a market crowded with people. The brown, barelegged Mexican kids kept calling to me. There were two or three words of English they had learned. "Allo! Good-by!" they said and laughed. Now and then one of the kids varied it a bit. "Allo! O.K.!" he said.

As I have said, it was a night of sounds, and it is everywhere the same on such a night. There are these nights when the world seems suddenly filled with strange and unnatural sounds. I have known them in America but in Mexican towns the night sounds are all so new. The border between the two countries is such an absolute border. There are these strange people . . . certainly to the American, strange . . . who do not seem to want our way of life, who are continually holding fiestas, who do not build skyscrapers in their cities, who hold dances in their churches, who use primitive wooden plows in their fields, who adore bull fights and passionately desire pistols with inlaid ivory handles. There are these Spaniards, Mestizos, Indians, Africanos, all seemingly living happily together.

There was all of this on this particular Mexican night, and there was the man in the room with the two women. As I learned later they did not come out to dine but they stayed in the room into which they had fled. Fred said that when the newspaper men were getting the car out of the driveway and were driving it into the patio, he did see the door to their room open a crack. He said that the man looked out, put his hand to his forehead, moaned and shut the door again.

And then the long night came with its sounds. Have you ever slept alone in a strange house when the wind blew, when windows rattled, when doors seemed to open and close mysteriously, when strange shadows ran across the floors?

There must have been a company of Mexican soldiers marching in a road. There was the steady rhythmic sound of marching feet and, somewhere in the distance, a drum began to beat. There was the distant sound of cheering.

These sounds for a time, and then others. Even in the heart of Mexico City the cocks crow all night. It must be that Mexican city men keep fighting cocks. They were crowing in the town, and men shod in the sort of soft leather sandals called "huarachos" were going up and down the street outside. They walk softly. Then they run a little, then walk again. There is a soft rhythm. Occasionally a group of them stopped in the street. They may have been farmers who had come into town. They carried machetes. I myself, awakening once in the night, saw a group under my window. I heard the soft footsteps of other men in the street and the continual crowing of the cocks. The men in the street, outside my window, spoke softly together. They kept looking up and down the street and as I stood watching and wondering, before I threw myself on my bed to sleep again, I heard, first a sudden outburst of the town cocks crowing, and then, in the silence, a voice. It was the voice of the man with the two women. "Look! Listen!" he moaned. "It is a signal. We will be murdered and robbed." He spoke of his car in the patio below. "It isn't locked. We'll lose our things," he said, and when he had stopped speaking there was the sound of low laughter. That, as I found out later, came from the Scotch. It had died in me but it was alive and at work in Fred, in the two newspaper men and in the man with the big mustache who ran the hotel.

It was, however, the crowing of the cocks that was to drive at least one American tourist out of Mexico, release him, free him from the necessity of visiting with his wife and his wife's sister innumerable Mexican churches, from going to the Xochimilco to ride in a boat, from seeing all of the Diego Rivera murals.

The man from North Dakota was in his room with the two women and they had not undressed. He had seen his car brought into the patio but it was not locked. He must have heard the marching of the soldiers and seen the men with the machetes standing under his window.

And then the cocks began crowing and Fred and the two newspaper men, who were in an adjoining room . . . they had got the hotel proprietor in there . . . they still were drinking the Scotch and when the cocks kept crowing, they also began to crow.

It began and they kept it up. There was this outburst of crowing. Fred said that one of the newspaper men, a little high, went down into the patio. There was a little old Mexican man, a kind of guard, on post in the patio, to watch the cars of such occasional tourists as came that way, and the newspaper man, that Jake Lindsey, the one who spoke Spanish, had got him into the plot. He may have taken him some of the Scotch.

He also began to crow. He stood in the patio and crowed. The two newspaper men and the hotel proprietor in the room above crowed and the Mexican cocks, scattered about over the town, crowed lustily.

It was a bedlam. It was too much for the man from North Dakota. It convinced his two women. No doubt it seemed to them that signals were being given for another Mexican revolution. It became connected in their minds with the men with the machetes under the window and the marching of the company of soldiers. Fred said that if he and the others hadn't been spiffed, they would presently have chucked the fun . . . they kept hearing the moans and the prayers of the three people in the adjoining room . . . but that, spiffed as they were, it had all seemed innocent enough.

They kept it up, Fred, the two newspaper men, the hotel proprietor and the guard, down in the patio, until the Mexican night was almost gone and the three tourists could stand it no longer. They made a dash for it. Fred said that he and the others came out of the room where they had been holding wassail and stood on the balcony above the patio. He said that the man from North Dakota had a pair of scissors in his hand. They were, he thought, a contribution of one of the women . . . and that he stood before the little old Mexican guard and waved them back and forth trying, Fred thought, to pass them off as a gun, and then, when the women had got into the car, he sprang in and made a dash for the driveway.

He made a dash for it and this time, there being no Mexican kids to confuse, he made it all right. He was in the street outside and there was a streak of morning light in the east. He was making for the border, and as he drove rapidly away the three Americans and the two Mexican men, the hotel proprietor and the little old guard from the patio—he with the serape about his old shoulders, ran into the street and stood together, sending up a chorus of crows. Fred, in telling of it, said that they were all a little ashamed but that on the other hand they all felt that in getting one male American tourist thus out of the country they were doing a rather high class favor to him.

Build My Gallows High
Geoffrey Homes

THE ANGRY WIND THREW SNOW against the windows of Whit Sterling's apartment on the seventeenth floor of a house on Fifty-Seventh Street. Out there in the mist was the East River and a tugboat complained mournfully as it headed north. Sterling lay under a tufted quilt and the pink silk made his cheeks pinker than ever. He had a fine head of black hair and a thin mustache. The mild young man who let Red and Fisher in went back to the chair beside the bed and sat down. He was holding a copy of *North of Boston* and his forefinger marked his place in the book of poems.

'Take your coats off and sit down,' Sterling said. 'Lou, break out the Scotch.'

'Too early,' said Red.

'Speak for yourself,' said Fisher. 'I could use a drink.'

Wearily the mild young man got up, put his book on the chair and went into the other room. Red indicated the book.

'Lou was reading to me,' Sterling said. 'How you been, Red?'

'Fair, Whit.'

'Business good?'

'Lousy. And yours?'

'Average.'

The man named Lou returned with Fisher's drink, gave it to him grudgingly and resumed his seat. 'Don't talk any more,' he told Sterling.

Sterling's head relaxed on the pillow. There were lines of bitterness around his mouth and his eyes were clouded with pain.

'Somebody has to talk,' Red observed. 'This is no social call.' Fisher shot a pained look at him.

'Mr. Sterling wants you to find a young woman for him,' Lou explained.

'I thought he might,' said Red. 'Mr. Sterling is not the forgiving type. Why did she shoot him?'

'That's unimportant,' Lou brushed the question aside.

'Except to Whitney,' grinned Red. 'Eh, Whit?'

Sterling's expression hardened. He wet his lips and his lids lowered over his eyes.

'Her name is Mumsie McGonigle,' Lou went on in his cool, precise voice. 'After the shooting she disappeared. So did fifty-six thousand dollars.'

Fisher looked up from his drink, whistled softly. Lou gave him a disapproving glance.

'A police case,' Red observed.

Sterling spoke without opening his eyes. 'No. Yours.'

'So that's how it was,' said Red.

'We're not asking you to think.' Lou took a wallet from his pocket, extracted five one-thousand-dollar bills and held them out to Red. 'Find her. Bring her back here and forget it.'

'You want her, or the dough?' Red asked, ignoring the proffered bills.

'Both.'

'And what happens to her?'

'Nothing.'

Red's look had disbelief in it. Lou smiled. 'She left under the impression she had killed Mr. Sterling,' said Lou. 'Naturally she was frightened.'

'And her conscience hurt her,' Red said.

Sterling opened his eyes. They were as warm as a cat's. 'My gut keeps me from laughing. Will you get busy?'

Through the smoke of his cigarette, Red grinned at the man under the pink quilt. 'Tell me more about Mumsie, Whitney.'

'He shouldn't be talking,' Lou protested.

Sterling ignored the protest, adjusted his pillow so that he could look across at Red, gingerly touched his stomach. 'I had it coming. She found me with another dame. I want her back.' He motioned to Lou. 'Show him her picture. Then maybe the bastard will believe me.'

Languidly Lou crossed to the dresser, opened the top drawer, took out a photograph and, returning, handed it to Red. He stood over the detective, holding the wad of money in his right hand.

Red stared at the lovely oval face. After a moment he turned his attention back to Sterling. 'I'd want her back too,' he admitted. 'But then, I'm a sentimentalist. I never suspected you of tender moments, Whit.'

Fisher spoke for the first time. 'For Christ's sake,' he said, 'don't you ever run down?'

'He's having fun.' Sterling offered Red a thin smile. 'Five thousand now and another five when you bring her back. Plus expenses.'

'And God help Mumsie.' Red flicked the picture with his forefinger.

Whit shook his head. 'I won't touch her.'

'Any idea where she went?'

'Mexico, probably. I took her there last year and she loved it. Anyway, that's where I'd suggest looking.'

Across the bed Red could see the windows. He could see the snow flaking down and could hear the wind petulantly rattling the glass. There would be sun in Mexico—sun and a warm wind, orchids in the jungle and a sky washed clean of clouds.

Reaching out, he took the money from Lou's hand and thrust it carelessly in a pocket. He stood above the bed, dribbling smoke from his thin nostrils.

'A deal, Whit. On one condition. You don't lay a hand on her and none of your boys lays a hand on her.'

'I said that already.'

'I'll see you after a while.' Red headed for the door, opened it, threw a bleak smile back at Sterling and went out. Fisher hurried after him.

At the elevator Fisher held out one hand. 'Come on— give!'

Red gave him two one-thousand-dollar bills. 'Wrap Gertude in mink,' he suggested. 'And start checking railroad stations.'

'What are you going to do?'

'Pack,' Red said.

The door creaked. He didn't look toward it, but he knew who was there. He knew Mumsie was looking at him. He kept his eyes on the window and pretended to be asleep. Beyond the barren, brown hills the Sierras were like ghosts of mountains.

There had been mountains in Mexico—great, towering cones of mountains. There had been plateaus patched crookedly with cane fields and there had been the lacy hem of the warm blue sea in Acapulco Bay. The lock clicked. Mumsie's soft footsteps went away. He closed his eyes, remembering:

There was a little cafe named La Mar Azul, half a block from La Marina Hotel in Acapulco. It faced the plaza and on Saturday nights it was a fine place to sit and drink beer and listen to the band. Then it was very crowded. But on other nights it had plenty of room. Red used to drop in and sit there, watching the domino players, listening to the click of the ivory pieces and the soft voices, hearing the loud speaker on the theater around the corner. Late at night, when he lay in his hot room on the sixth floor of the hotel, the brassy music of the speaker was bad. But he didn't mind it in the cafe.

The cafe was open to the world. Kids kept threading their way between the tables, trying to sell lottery tickets and post-cards, or offering to shine your shoes for ten centavos. They bothered Red a lot at first. After a while they took it for granted he was not a tourist. So they let him alone.

And after a while the little boys who wanted to show you the town for fifty centavos gave him up as a bad job too. That first week, when he wandered through the hot little town, they were always at his heels, pleading, smiling, tugging at his coat. But presently he could walk unmolested. He used to move slowly through the dusk, past the open-air markets where you could buy a pair of huaraches for a peso and a hat for ten centavos, where you could get a meal for a tostan from a woman squatting by her charcoal brazier.

It was very hot that time. In the afternoons Acapulco slept. On the long crescent of beach to the south the people drowsed under yellow and green umbrellas. A few brown kids paddled in the warm water. No one swam much. Red did.

He liked that water, so heavy with salt you could lie for hours on top of it, clean and blue and warm. You could lie and watch the odd cloud patterns on the bleached sky.

He had been there three weeks when he saw Mumsie. He was in La Mar Azul and she came along the street and stood in front of the place, staring in as though searching for someone. She flicked Red with a glance. Her gaze moved to the empty table near him and she walked slowly to it and sat down. She put her hands on the table and looked at them.

Red wasn't the only one there who saw her. Every man in the place relaxed his attention from the game he was playing and watched her. There was a good reason. She was a slim, lovely little thing with eyes too big for her face and the serene look often seen on nuns. She wore a white linen dress and a hat of fine straw, as pale as her hair. The players gave her more warm looks from their dark eyes, shrugged and went back to their games. A lone woman, but an American. So that made it all right. Americans were odd. In Acapulco you saw so many of them you got used to their peculiarities.

Red didn't speak to her that night. He wanted to. He wanted to smile at her and move to the chair across the table so that he could see the color of her eyes. He thought they must be blue—pale blue like the sky over the bay.

But they weren't blue. Red found that out the next night. The loud speaker on the front of the theater was braying and across the plaza some guy was keeping his hands on the horn of an automobile. The horn played three notes. The domino players didn't mind. One of them was a policeman but he didn't do anything about the horn.

She came along the sidewalk and this time she didn't look at anyone. She merely went to the same table and sat down. He heard her low, sweet voice asking the waiter for a brandy and plain water. He caught her eyes and grinned. A ghost of a smile crossed her face. He asked: 'May I?' She dropped her glance.

The waiter brought her drink. Red beckoned to him, asked for another beer and when it came watched her over the top of the tall glass. The dress she wore tonight was of some soft green stuff, but her hat was the same and her shoes and her bag matched the hat. She took a black note-book from her bag and began writing in it with a tiny gold pencil. As she wrote she pulled her eyebrows together and pursed her full lips. Her lips were very red and made her skin seem paler than it really was.

A ragged boy crossed from the plaza and headed straight for her table. His soft voice begged for just one little centavo—*please senorita, just one.* She smiled at the flat, dirty brown face. Surely, the boy continued in Spanish, the senorita could spare one tiny centavo.

She looked at Red then. She spoke. 'What does he say?'

'He wants a cent,' Red said. Red waved him away—told him to run along before he cut his ears off. The boy laughed and took some lottery tickets from his pocket.

'The senorita will win a fortune perhaps,' the boy suggested.

Red got up, moved to her table, gave him a fifty-centavo piece and took one of the tickets.

'*Gracias, senor,*' the boy said.

'*Por nada.*'

'Which means?' she asked.

'For nothing,' Red said, as the boy went away. 'May I sit down?'

'Yes.'

'Thank you.'

'*Por nada.*' She smiled and a light seemed to go on in her eyes. They were light brown, flecked with bits of gold, and her long lashes made shadows on her fine pale skin.

'I wanted to speak to you last night,' Red said.

'I know.'

'You looked lonely.'

'I'm not. Was that why you wanted to speak to me?'

'No. I wanted to ask you to walk along the beach in the moonlight. I wanted to sit beside you on a hill.'

'You're the lonely one.' She smiled again. Red wanted her to keep smiling—she was even lovelier then. 'I don't know your name.'

'Does that matter?' Red asked

'Yes.'

'They call me Red.'

'How odd,' the girl laughed softly. 'Red what?'

'Markham. And yours?'

She shook her head. 'You wouldn't believe it. Why are you in Acapulco?'

'I like it.'

'Tourist?'

'Indolent,' Red said. 'This is a fine place to be indolent in.'

'Even if you're lonely?'

'I'm not lonely any more.' He reached across the table and covered her hand with his own. 'They have a fine bar at the El Mirador. Shall we walk up the hill and have a drink?'

'Not tonight.'

'Tomorrow then?'

'Tomorrow afternoon. Say four.'

'You won't run away?'

'No.'

'Thank you.'

'*Por nada.*' She said the words as though she liked the sound and her voice did things to Red's stomach.

~

El Mirador made Red think of Carmel—the hotel hanging on the edge of the cliff, the rocks and the sea and the sky. They sat at a table, high above the water. On the cliff below two boys chased an iguana. After a while they caught him and came clambering up the rocks, one of them holding the ugly thing by the tail. The girl shuddered. She asked, 'Why?'

'To eat,' Red said. He was glad when they were gone. Then there were only the cliffs and the sea gnawing at the rocks far down and two buzzards riding an air current low over the blue-green water. 'This isn't Mexico,' Red said.

'Oh yes.' She sipped her daiquiri, leaned on the porch railing and nodded at the buzzards wheeling by. 'They're Mexico. I've seen them by the dozens roosting in the dead trees along the road. I've seen them everywhere. They're always with you, like—' She cut the sentence off and there was darkness in her eyes.

'Like what?'

'Death,' the girl said, staring across at him.

The shadows of the birds slid across the rocks. 'I know a place where there are only the cliffs and the sea,' Red said. 'White sand. White and clean. The rocks shut out everything but the sky and the sea. There's nothing to make you think of death.'

Mumsie rose. 'Show it to me,' she said softly.

～

Not far away the waves gnawed hungrily at the rocks. They lay in shadow on the warm sand and high above them hung one lost and lonely cloud. Mumsie sat up and watched the water running up the beach, stopping to push the smooth, white pebbles around a bit with cool white fingers, then drawing away. Presently she turned and stared down at Red. His head was pillowed in his hands.

'When do we go back, Red?' she asked suddenly.

Red's glance rested on her face. He took one of her hands. 'There's no hurry. He didn't die.'

'Oh.'

'He wants you back.'

'So you'll take me?'

'I've been thinking about things.'

With her free hand she made patterns in the sand. Red pulled himself up beside her, slid one arm around her shoulders.

'I could tell him you hopped a boat,' Red said. 'I could tell him you had lost yourself in Panama or Chile. Anywhere. That I'm not bloodhound enough to pick up your trail.'

'Would he believe you?'

'I'll chance it.'

'Then what?'

'You and I,' Red said softly.

'He'd find us. You don't know him like I do, Red.'

Red grinned. 'I don't want to. What about it?'

'I can't go back.'

'No. And maybe he doesn't want you back after all. Maybe he wants his fifty-six thousand bucks.'

She threw him a puzzled glance. 'Fifty-six thousand? Is that what he said?' Red nodded. 'So that's why you'll take a chance on me?'

'We'll give it back to him. I'll say I found you and talked you out of the dough but couldn't persuade you to come back.'

'I didn't take that much money,' Mumsie said. 'Not anywhere near that much. He lied to you. I took enough to get me here. There's very little left.'

'All the better, then.' His arm tightened about her. 'You can't accuse me of being greedy.'

'No. Only of being foolish.' She shrugged his arm away, stood up and moved down the sand. The waves swept up the beach and drove her back. Without turning she spoke. 'All you know about me is I lived with a gambler and when he got tired of me I shot him and ran away.'

Red rose to stand beside her. 'That's not all.'

'What else?'

'A moment.'

'Is that enough?'

'Yes.' He pulled her closer, tilted her face with one forefinger and kissed her. The waves reached out for them, drew back, reached out again. Far above, the tidy wind swept the lonely cloud away behind the hills.

You got over things like love and death. The thought was somehow frightening when you knew that one of these days Ann might get over you. But you couldn't deny it, couldn't say, 'Hell, it won't happen to us.'

Mumsie had come along the hall and had opened the door a while ago. There was a time when he would have been almost breathless waiting for her to come to him, waiting for her lips, her breasts and her body.

Yes, he had rid himself of desire but he had taken a beating doing it. Love for her was long since dead or, rather, love for the woman he had imagined was dead.

At first he hadn't loved her. Those weeks in Acapulco— the nights hot and still until a morning wind came along, the days bright with Mexican voices that were like cricket songs—he had wanted her as he had wanted no other woman in his life. But he saw the imperfections—a smallness, a stinginess, a tendency to give grudgingly or not at all of everything but her body.

It was on the boat wallowing amiably north that he had stopped seeing clearly. Mumsie became something he made up—not a beautiful woman who had put a lead slug in Whit Sterling's belly. It had taken a good kick in the teeth to bring the true picture into focus.

The night was hot, the sea an unruffled inland lake so smooth you could find stars in it. He lay back in his deck chair looking shoreward at the mountain wall that was Mexico's west coast. Someone ran along the narrow deck and then she was down on her knees beside him, clinging to him, pressing her face against his chest.

'Oh, Red!' she cried.

His fingers touched her neck, moved up through the soft mass of her hair. 'Yes, Mumsie.'

'I'm afraid.'

'Of what?'

'You won't come back. You'll leave me in Los Angeles and you won't come back.'

'Of course I'll come back.'

'You mustn't. I'm no good. I'll never be any good. Such a black soul, darling.'

'Black velvet,' Red said. 'Anyway, I like black souls.'

'Right now you do. After a while you'll start thinking.'

'Who named you Mumsie?'

'A man.'

'Your father?'

'He called me Harriet. Don't ask about the other.'

'I want to ask. I like to pry into your past. It excites me.'

'Someday it won't. Someday you'll start seeing ghosts. Oh, Red, I've a secret for you.'

'Say it.'

'I adore you.'

He found her lips and then the dream began.

In the night it rained and he heard the rain hitting the deck. Suddenly the tiny cabin was cool. Mumsie asked: 'Who wrote it?'

'Wrote what?'

'You know what. The poem I'm thinking.'

'I'm not a mind reader,' Red said sleepily. 'How do I know the poem you're thinking?'

'It goes, "When I am dead and over me bright April shakes down her rain-drenched hair."'

'Go back to sleep and stop being so cheerful,' Red said. He turned over away from her and lay there looking at the gray patch that was the window, listening to the rain drop down, listening to the thump of the engines and the slap of the waves against the rusty steel.

'Teasdale,' Mumsie said. 'That's who wrote it.'

She put her body tight against his back and he could feel her warm breath on his neck. 'I wouldn't like it. I wouldn't like being dead and having April let her rain-drenched hair down on me. Would you like it, Red?'

'Go to sleep.'

'I wouldn't have you with me. That's why I wouldn't like it.'

He turned and held her close. 'How did you happen to read Sarah Teasdale?'

'A man read it to me.'

'The same man who named you Mumsie?'

'No.'

'My God!' Red said. 'What do you do—collect men?'

'I told you not to pry. Anyway, they don't matter any more.'

'That's heartening.'

'Do I ask you about all your women?'

'Want to hear?'

'No.'

'Tell me about Whit Sterling.'

'No.'

'He read you the Teasdale poem.'

'Yes. How did you know?'

'The only time I saw him, a guy was reading *North of Boston* aloud to him. He was in bed with a stomach ache. When you get through with me, will you shoot me?'

'Red!' The name was a crying protest.

'I just wanted to make sure,' Red said. 'Now let's go to sleep.'

'Haven't we anything better to do?'

'Yes,' Red said.

~

He took bits of her life and put them together—bits whispered to him in the night. Yet there were not enough to round it out. So he made up the rest. He had time enough on that trip up the coast. The old ship didn't seem to give a damn if it ever rounded the San Pedro breakwater. Nor did he.

An unpleasant job confronted him—leaving Mumsie, heading east and trying to make Whit Sterling swallow a tall tale. Not that he worried much about it. He was too busy finding a soul for Mumsie to worry about anything. Yet, when they left the ship and rode by taxi into the hot, dispirited mediocrity that was Los Angeles he decided to put it off for a while.

There was a little house in Laurel Canyon with a creek in front of it. A footbridge crossed the creek and sometimes, when the boys at the reservoir opened the gates, water ran under the bridge. It was cool and quiet in the canyon. Behind the house a hill rose steeply. You could walk up the creek and then there were no houses—nothing but brown hills on which the Yucca candles were burning out. At night the coyotes howled on the ridge. Mumsie said she used to hate them. That was because they made her lonely. Mumsie said she had forgotten what loneliness was so she didn't hate them any more.

A week, and then Red started worrying. So she drove him to Pasadena in the car they had bought and cried a little while they waited for the train.

'I wish you wouldn't go,' Mumsie said.

'I have to,' Red said.

'Why?'

'I'm running out of money,' Red told her. 'I want to sell my business to my partner and start another here. And I can't do it unless I settle up with Sterling.'

Mumsie's eyes grew thoughtful. She started to speak. Watching her, he felt a sudden sharp distrust. Perhaps—he wouldn't finish the thought. Her speech went unsaid.

He kissed her and swung up on the steps as the train started moving. Seeing her so small and alone in the fading sun-light, his faith came back.

THE WISHING BOX
Dashka Slater

AT THE PYRAMIDS IN MITLA the anthropologists called my father Goose. His name was Angus, but it sounded like Goose when Mexicans said it, and he looked like a goose as he walked through the ancient city, his neck way ahead of his body. He was just out of college and everything excited him, every piece of chipped stone, every pot shard. He liked living cultures more than dead ones and stole down to the village below the site whenever he could, but the archaeologists were paying him to stay among the pyramids and help catalog the artifacts. He spent the mornings in front of a typewriter in a palapa office, logging identifying notes onto a stack of index cards. When the sun grew hot and the senior members of the dig retreated into the shade for their afternoon siesta, he left his typewriter and climbed among the ruins' giant rocks, his fair skin turning pink in the sun.

In the evenings, Indian girls came from the village to sell dinner to the men at the site. They were the sisters and daughters of the men who were hired to haul the fallen rocks back into position, small barefoot girls with wide hips and strong legs. At seven o'clock you could see them walking up the path toward the ruins, their crimson skirts and blue head scarves a bright spot of color in the dust. My mother, Irma, was one of those girls. She had a round face with a high curved forehead and wide, cinnamon-colored lips. She and her friends carried baskets of cooked food and fruit wrapped in leaves and corn husks. They weren't allowed into the city of their ancestors, so the men came down the path to meet them, wiping the ancient dust from their hands as they walked.

Angus was the tallest man she had ever seen, and she had seen plenty of Anglos since anthropologists began coming to Mitla. He was sitting on a rock, rolling a cigarette. He watched her carefully as she handed him an orange from her basket and put the coin he gave her into the pocket of her apron. Then he reached out and grabbed her wrist.

She didn't flinch, just stood looking at him with her other arm curved around the lip of the basket that was resting on her hip. Even though he was sitting and she was standing, they were nearly at eye level.

"What is this from?" he asked. His fingers stroked the long cut that traversed her left hand.

She looked down at his fingers and laughed.

"From cutting fruit." She mimed the motion of the knife slipping. Then she pulled her hand away and hoisted the basket back onto her head. He watched her as she walked toward the other men, one hand stabilizing the basket, her blouse pulled tight across her breasts.

After that he asked her a different question each time she came up to the site with a basket of food. First he asked her about the local markets, what food people ate, and where it came from. Later he asked her about Mitla. She told him that long ago, Mitla had been the center of the world of the dead, before the sun rose over the earth. In those days the heavy stones were soft and light, and even though the ancient ones were tiny as babies, they piled them into monuments. She told him about the souls of dead people, how they grow hungry from travel and angry if they aren't provided for. How sin makes the soul heavy and weighs down the bodies of the dead.

The truth was, she liked to talk. She couldn't linger for long or she wouldn't sell any fruit, but she blurted out the answers to his questions in one breathless sentence before turning to the next customer. Most of the time he only understood half of what she said; she spoke Spanish with a thick Indian accent, and Zapotec phrases kept sneaking into the torrent of words.

"Do you talk so much at home?" he asked her, and she told him that she didn't speak a word until she was two years old. Her parents were afraid she'd grow up mute, so they gave her water that hens had drunk from, which always loosens a stuck tongue. "Maybe they gave me too much," she said, laughing.

~

After a few weeks my father wasn't thinking as much about the dusty stones of Mitla as he was about Irma's dusty calves. Once she came up to the site with a jug of pineapple juice. As she poured it into a mug for him, a drop landed on her leg and a shiny streak of brown skin opened in its wake. Suddenly he wanted all of her revealed to him, not just that one wet streak.

He liked that Irma knew more than he did about something he was interested in, and for the first time what he was interested in was another person. He thought about her as he lay on the hard mattress in his hotel room overlooking the main square of the village. Her body was dense and round like the stone idols in the ruined city. There was a whole culture bundled up in that body, a whole history of tribal legends and customs. He stayed up all night reading about the ancient Zapotecs, finding questions to ask her on every page. He had never needed much sleep, or food either for that matter, but now the lack of it gave him a new awareness of his height. When he walked the ruins during siesta, he felt himself teetering, even on the flat grass field where the ancient Zapotecs played ball. He attributed his vertigo to the heat, and to love, and to exhaustion. But often when we are struck by the hand of Fate, the blow sends us reeling.

He wasn't the only one off-kilter. My mother, as she walked down the path that led from the ruins to her parents' house, felt her body fading into lightness. She weighed nothing. It was all the talking she had done. In truth, she didn't talk much at home. There wasn't time for it or room—her two older brothers and four older sisters did more than enough talking. And her sweetheart Eligio, whose family lived next door to hers, talked so much that she couldn't get a word in edgewise. Sometimes she nearly fell asleep to the sound of his voice droning on and on like the legs of a cricket. Only during those few minutes at Mitla could the words fall away from her. Later she told me she believed that talking was her mistake. Words kept inside were a ballast, steadying her. Without them she was knocked off course. She didn't understand that we are all on one course from the beginning, so she blamed herself instead of blaming Fate.

They got married. Why should I bother telling about the meetings between my father and her father, the disapproval of my father's colleagues, the excitement of my mother's parents, who could think only of American riches? What is there to say about Eligio, who was taken by surprise? Irma and Angus were married in the village church, with all the days of ceremony and feasting before and after, the blessings and the dancing and the gifts of turkeys and chocolate and cigarettes and the men getting drunk on tepache and mescal.

It was my father who insisted on the whole long rigmarole; he wanted to see how it was done. It was halfhearted, even the blessings. No one likes to have their customs on display, and my father's curiosity was embarrassing to everyone. Eligio got drunk and danced by himself, murmuring all the while about the fickleness of love. Of course, he promised to murder my father, but he had too gentle a spirit to carry it out.

My father's parents weren't invited to the wedding. He wrote them a letter afterward, knowing that they would be angry that he had married a peasant, and that his having done so in a Catholic church would nearly kill them.

～

He told Irma they would stay in Mexico. His idea was that he would study the Zapotecs, and she would be his translator and informant. He could teach her to read and then to type and she would type his notes for him. They moved into a hacienda-style house where she slept in a bed for the first time in her life. When they made love, the bed moved with them and the sensation made her laugh. She laughed the whole time he was inside her. Not because it was her first time; she had gone to meet Eligio in the fields more than once. But making love with Angus was different than it had been with Eligio. Eligio talked the whole time, commented on the smell of the bean leaves dying back into the fallow earth, the sound of the wind tumbling down the sides of the mountains, the feel of her hands pressed against his back. Angus was quiet when they made love, and she was so much shorter than him that her face was buried in his chest. He raised himself up on his elbows and looked down at her and she craned her neck back to find his eyes, but the distance was too far for their mouths to cross, and they made love without exchanging a single kiss.

~

Six months after he wrote them about his marriage, my father got a letter from his parents. He picked it up at the post office in town and brought it home without reading it. He was angry that they had taken so long to write and angry that they had written at all; he was always aggravated by the people who were close to him. Other people's desires slowed him down, tripped him up. He preferred to do exactly as he pleased and thought the world would be a better place if everyone else did the same.

"Why don't you read it?" Irma asked him when she found the letter on the dining room table.

He shrugged and let his eyes cloud over with preoccupation, as if he were too busy to give the question much thought. "I know what they have to say," he said without lifting his head from the book he was reading. "I've heard it my whole life."

Every morning my mother placed the envelope next to her husband's plate, and every day it lay there unopened, growing spotted with the fallout from his breakfast.

After a week went by, she opened up the letter. She didn't know the story of Pandora, or of Eve and the apple, or of Bluebeard's wife, but she knew that it is men who run away from Destiny, women who know they cannot run and so demand to know its name.

The handwriting was thin and spiky. Irma had only learned the fundamentals of reading and her command of English was sketchy at best. The evil in the world flew out of Pandora's box in a rush and a torrent, but it took all day for my mother to decipher her father-in-law's letter. I have it still, so I can tell it to you exactly. My mother saved it as a keepsake so she could always remember how things fell apart.

My Dear Boy,

There is no point in telling you our reaction to your letter. You knew what it would be when you made your decision and no doubt hurting us was your intention. If it was, you have succeeded. Your letter made no attempt to spare your mother pain and for her sake I have had no wish to answer it. But we have had news which requires me to swallow my disappointment and write to you.

Your mother is very ill and my opinion as a doctor is that she will not last the winter. She has cancer of the stomach and it is spreading quite quickly through her body. In spite of everything she would like to see you before she passes on. I cannot vouch that all will be forgiven; only the Lord can truly forgive. I can only tell you that if you come now you will be welcome in our home and your wife will be welcome also.

When Irma showed him the letter, my father knew he was trapped. There was nothing to do but go back and pay his respects to his dying mother. They left a week later, stopping in Mexico City long enough to buy my mother a pair of shoes and two wool dresses, a blue one for every day and a black one for the funeral.

The train ride to Boston took almost two weeks. Irma spent most of the trip with her nose pressed against the glass, watching the color fade from the landscape as the train hurtled north. First the green dwindled away from the edge of the tracks, and then the blue seeped from the sky. Finally even the brown was gone. By the time the train pulled into Boston's South Station, everything was white.

~

Do you see now? My mother was a fish, the letter was a dangling worm. She swallowed it and it wriggled from her belly to her chest and wrapped itself around her heart.

Three months they were supposed to stay in Cambridge, but that mother-in-law liked dying so much she didn't want to stop. She spent all winter dying and all spring and summer. My mother cared for her like an angel, not out of selflessness but out of habit. She had worked hard all her life. She didn't know that working hard would make her in-laws treat her like a servant.

In the fall, Irma discovered she was pregnant. As she emptied her mother-in-law's bedpans, she was thinking about the baby taking its first breath of air in her mother's house. Air that smelled of coffee and chickens and dust, not the air of ice and sickness that she was breathing now. In Mitla you clean the afterbirth, seal it in a clay jar, and bury it near the house; otherwise the baby will go blind, or worse. My mother dreamed she was in the garden behind her in-laws' tall Victorian, placenta oozing from between her legs. Sometimes she had her hands cupped between her thighs and the warm pulp spilled over them and fell into the snow.

Other nights she held the afterbirth in one hand and with the other she was digging, her fingernails clawing at the frozen earth and never denting it.

My father's mother died in February 1929. Irma was five months pregnant. When she found her mother-in-law sitting in a rocking chair by the window with a shawl over her knees and no life in her chest, she felt the weight of her dreams lift. She set a tray of food and water on the nightstand so that the dead woman's soul could gather provisions for the long journey to the world of the dead. She was happy then. She thought she was finally going home.

But first they had to wait for the funeral and the burial and for the will to be read. And then my father decided she was too far along, she shouldn't travel, and besides, it was better to have the baby there where there were doctors. And then the worm slid down into Irma's womb and wrapped itself around the baby's throat. She lost the child in her seventh month.

And then she was too sick to travel. After that my father was teaching for the summer at Harvard and had to wait until the fall to leave. By that time my mother was pregnant again. And then it was: You can't travel while you're pregnant, you've already miscarried once.

This time I was the baby in her womb. I looked up and saw the worm. The worm was the future: cold, coiled, and hard as clay. I saw the truth: She was never going home again.

The Lost Art of Desire
Robin Beeman

Now ALONE WITH SAM, the glass of rum in her hand, Jenna walks out to the narrow balcony onto which both their rooms open. Sam follows, bringing the candle with him. Setting it on the railing, he comes up so close beside her she can feel his breath in her hair. She lifts her glass. "*Salud!*"

He clinks his glass against it. "To adventure," he says, brushing back the strand of her hair falling over her eyes. Adventure is a word he loves. It's a word that gives Jenna a knot in the stomach. This is not the trip she would have chosen, but then she was the one to choose last year's trip and they agreed to take turns. He touches her forehead lightly with his lips. "We do deserve a little celebration."

She takes a sip of the rum, dark and sweet. He brings out a joint, lights it, inhales and offers it to her.

"They'll put your face in the toilet if they catch you with that here," Jenna says, only partly joking. The official country policy takes a dim view of drug use. She lifts the little cigarette to her lips and draws in the aromatic smoke.

"We'll be careful," he says, letting the smoke out slowly. "It's just so damn good to actually get here and have you with me. I don't want to travel alone anymore." She lets the smoke out in a quick breath. She can never hold it in for very long. He draws in once more, then holds the glowing stub toward her. She shakes her head. He licks his fingers and damps out the smoldering end. "There," he says. "Done with. We shall be circumspect again. God knows, I don't want my face in the toilet." He sits in one of the two metal chairs and places his feet up on the railing. She sits in the other. The jungle begins right on the other side of the balcony. From the kitchen below comes the sound of people talking, their voices spilling out with the thin nimbus of light from the window. In the sky, the moon hovers, a pale smudge in the humid air.

Even now after midnight, the heat lingers. It's cooler here at 2000 feet than in the town at sea level where they spent last night, but still hot. She sips the rum slowly, waiting for him to begin. They hadn't really talked yesterday. There was too much going on—her arrival and the wait for her baggage, misplaced by the airline, then the changes in their hotel accommodations at the last minute. She was so tired after all of it that she went to her room directly after dinner, leaving Sam to himself in the hotel bar. She's still tired. Getting away this time was harder than before.

"I'm thinking how curious it is that a change in location can cause such a huge change in perception," he says. "I mean, that seems to be one of the reasons that people travel, but it's surprising just how well it works." It's the kind of general statement he likes to make to begin a conversation, the sort of thing a teacher says to get a class going. They both teach high school, he history, she English, though in different towns. For the last two summers they've traveled together, both times to places with ruins.

~

They met on a tour of the pyramids of Teotihuacán outside Mexico City, a tour she hadn't intended to take but which the hotel by mistake booked for her. On the drive out of the city she caught herself casting quick glances at the man with sandy, rather curly, hair sitting beside her. He seemed abstracted at first, restless. His eyes were a dark hazel, almost olive with sun crinkles in their corners. She watched him talking to the driver, then look out of the window, his gaze pensive, but also curious. Her husband Hugh had shrewd blue eyes which took pleasure in the mischief of the world, a pleasure Jenna believed made it easy for him to be the successful lawyer he was. This man had a guidebook on his lap, and a notebook. He'd been here in Mexico years ago, he told her, but had forgotten so much. He was preparing to teach a class in ancient civilizations to an honors group.

Looking beyond him to watch the raw and dismal outskirts of the city pass by, Jenna decided she liked him. He was intelligent, but he wasn't weighed down by this fact as some men were—though there was something weighing him down. When their car veered sharply to take advantage of an opening in the traffic, she found herself thrown against him, the bare skin of her arm against the bare skin of his arm, tan with fine sun-bleached curling hairs. A current of electricity ran through her, jolted her, something she hadn't experienced in years. She didn't hurry to sit upright and neither did he, though he was jammed against the door. She caught him studying her, when she turned to him. She quickly looked away, then back, astonished by a flash of awareness passing between them. Something had happened. Just like that. She moved to sit up and he did too. The driver was telling them about an important building on their left, the noise of a passing truck rumbling over his words. It didn't matter that neither of them could hear what he had to say. Trembling, she tried to compose herself, looking at her hands, her narrow fingers, her clear polish, her wedding band. She then looked at his hands. Long fingers with blunt tips. Nice hands. No rings.

Dark clouds moving in from the east covered the sky as Jenna and Sam were midway up the Pyramid of the Sun. They were on the summit when the rain caught them. He kept his arm around her as they hurried down the narrow steps. In the car she had a sweater which she put on, sorry to have no excuse for him to hold her. That evening she had plans for dinner with people she'd met at the language school. They said good-bye in the hotel lobby. He had plans too.

The next day they went together to the museum of archaeology. "When you walked through those ruins yesterday, did you like to imagine them all bright and sparkly and full of people?" she asked as they stood looking at a diorama reconstructing life in the Valley of Mexico before it fell to the Spanish. "No," he said. "Then it would be just another busy city. I like to see what remains after time. I'm interested in aftermaths."

They walked out onto the sidewalk beside the Paseo de la Reforma and she recited "Ozymandias" for him. When she finished, he pulled her to him and kissed her. She put her arms around him, kissing him back, trying to take all of him in with her mouth. Cars spewing exhaust fumes raced by them. A convertible full of young men whistled approval. They pulled apart and looked at each other. He had a lovely full lower lip, a strong chin. She kissed him this time. The next day they flew together to Oaxaca to visit Mitla and Monte Alban. The next summer they went to Italy and Greece, her choice, strolling through temples and amphitheaters where occasionally only a few broken pillars remained.

~

"When we travel, we want things to be different, but not too different," she says, wondering whether she should have more rum. What she's drunk already combined with the pot and the beer at dinner are making it hard for her to keep her eyes open.

"That sounds about right." His voice has a woolly quality, a rough-textured warmth. Hearing his voice after being away from him is still strange. "We're hoping for an encounter with the unknown, but the not too unknown. Which is why we take guidebooks. But we do hope for a revelation or two.'

She laughs. He always lugs around so many guidebooks on a trip. She usually brings one guidebook, a bird book, and several novels. "We try to control as much as possible so we can be free to be amazed. Is that it?" She's rambling. They kissed at the airport and held each other in the taxi yesterday, but this morning he'd gone out to check on the plane before she woke. Then they spent hours in the consulate, a grimy place with a useless wheezy air-conditioner, where she was informed that the size of her photograph wasn't right for a visa. In fact, the man implied the photograph might not even be of Jenna. It *was* a terrible photo. She'd had her hair trimmed only a few days before it was taken and, shorn of her usual mass of dark curls, her cheekbones and chin became more prominent. Now her hair had grown out again. After the clerk agreed that the photograph was more than likely of Jenna, Sam explained how it could easily be cut to size, the man continuing to look dubious. Finally, Sam took a pair of scissors from the man's desk, trimming the photo there in front of him. Though the clerk refused to give up his skeptical scowl, he did glue on the photo and press the embossing seal over it—as if doing them a favor.

"It was hard to get away, wasn't it?" He puts his feet down and moves his chair closer to her.

"Dreadful." She closes her eyes. "I don't want to bore you with it, because it was tedious more than anything." She tilts her head against his shoulder, the cool cotton, the warm skin beneath, and feels a sharp pin prick on her arm—a mosquito, despite the smelly repellent. "I don't think I can keep my head up."

"It has been a long day. But I want to sit out here a while longer." After the excitement, he always comes down and his sadness sets in. There isn't a question of his trying to share his sadness with her or make her a part of it. She now knows it's better if she leaves him to be alone with it. In the morning he'll be up at dawn walking around these new ruins, making his way over rubble, inspecting stones, checking with his guidebook, setting up his camera, ready to become expansive again.

Her room smells of Raid too and there's no water in the tap. Lighting a candle, she uses water from the bottle by her bed to wash her face and brush her teeth. A shower is out of the question. She changes into a nightgown and lies on the bed with the sheet over her. From beyond the screened windows issues that other sound, that slow inhalation and exhalation of the jungle like a creature lying in wait. She paces her own breathing to it, listening in the intervals between breaths for signs of what it might want. In a room below music begins, a wailing love song in Spanish on a scratchy radio belonging to someone with the foresight to have batteries. It's odd listening to someone else's music, a little like spying.

~

She wakes when Sam knocks over one of the chairs on the balcony. The moon is high and the sky glows with a milky radiance. He stands in his shorts looking toward the jungle, listening to staccato explosions like a string of fire-crackers going off. "What is it?" she asks going to him.

"Someone shooting," he says. "It's far away."

She walks back into the room in a sleep daze, having heard a thrill in Sam's voice, a thrill at the thought that the rebels are not, after all, out of the area and that he's close enough to hear them. Both yesterday and this morning, they've been told alternately that the rebels were invented by the foreign press, that there are no rebels but only insignificant drug smugglers and bandits, or that there are rebels but only a few and they've moved farther north to the border, crossing from one side to the other, depending on the situation.

She drifts back into sleep and dreams not of Sam but of Hugh, dreaming that she and Hugh are driving along the coast to a cabin they rented outside of Mendocino. When they get to where the cabin should be, it's gone and a strange unpleasant town where people glare at them is in its place. She's confused and angry with Hugh for having gotten them into such a dreadful situation. Then she's alone, walking along the beach looking for something she's lost—a comb maybe. The sky is very dark with an ugly purple glow near the horizon.

Sam's lips on her shoulder wake her. She reaches up. At last he's here beside her, after so long. He smells so like Sam and no one else, a scent like sage in the sunlight, despite the rum on his breath and the insect repellent. After missing him desperately for a year, she wasn't able to run into his arms in the airport or bring him into her bed that first night. It takes time to move from one situation to another—from Hugh and the tension, but also the familiarity, of that relationship to Sam. It takes time to ease back into the intimacy they shared when they parted last summer.

He kisses her forehead, then her cheek, her throat. She's been difficult, she knows, making it hard for him to approach her. It isn't easy for her to fall back into step with him after so much time apart, to find herself once again in this life they share between them. She was exhausted and agitated all during the flight from California. She and Hugh had gotten the boys off to camp, which then gave Hugh time alone with her to try to dissuade her from leaving. But now Sam has her in his arms and is bringing her back to what she knows of him, of who they are together.

She pulls off her nightgown, wanting to feel every inch of him against her, to feel his heart pounding. She places her fingers on the hard muscles of his back, breathing upward to him, to the reality of him here with her. He draws away a little, moving his fingers over her, beginning with her breasts, her nipples, as if learning her once more, and giving her time to learn him once more too. Sam makes love as if he wants to know how it will turn out, as if it might be different each time—and it is.

Through the open window come more of the popping sounds, but they seem to be getting fainter.

The Recruiting Officer
David Lida

WHEN RICK SHOWED UP FOR work there was a message to report to the assistant deputy chief of station immediately. What a pain in the ass. Who did a little Yalie shitheel like Boggs think he was, ordering around Rick? He had a splitting headache, a runny nose, a sore throat, and hadn't had his coffee yet. He'd go to the cafeteria first and let the little prick wait.

On the other hand, it was already eleven. He was supposed to have turned up at the office at eight-forty-five. Rick decided to take care of his business with Boggs first.

Big mistake. Within minutes of arriving at Boggs's office, Rick felt blindsided, smacked upside the head, the legs kicked out from under him. It surfaced that the assistant deputy COS, twenty-six, chinless and balding with a blond fringe, had made the appointment to give Rick's ass a formal chewing-out. The throbbing in Rick's head was so severe that he only heard scattered pieces of Boggs's lengthy speech.

". . . your customary crap . . . failing to fill out your contact sheets and expense reports . . . you would have been sent a memo. . . . The Company doesn't come down on a guy for having a drink now and then or even more than that . . ."

Rick snorted emphatically to detain the snot dripping

from his nose, and searched his pockets for a Kleenex. He didn't have any. He ran a hand under his long, hooked smeller to wipe off any liquidy mucus residue from his hadlebar mustache. With his squared-off, bottle-thick, plastic-framed glasses, Rick looked a little like a Groucho Halloween mask.

" . . . you went too far . . . that shouting match with the Cuban at the embassy party. That was disgraceful."

Rick sat rigidly on the other side of the wood-paneled desk, a conceited smile exposing small, even, rodentlike teeth. "What?" he said. "Wait a second. I had a little spat. Who the fuck cares?"

"You were at a diplomatic function representing the State Department! Arguing with a Cuban attaché!" Boggs's voice went higher as he became agitated. The squeak grated on Rick's nerves.

"So the fuck what? He's just some little embassy pussy, in the cultural section."

"That's not the point, Rick! It's an embarrassment to everyone at the embassy. Need I remind you of the sensitivity of your diplomatic cover?"

"Oh, for shit's sake, Boggsy. What fucking cover? Half the people in this embassy are CIA and everybody in Mexico knows it." Rick's throat ached. He burrowed into his shirt pocket for a cigarette, removing one from the hole atop the packet. The harsh smoke would soothe the pain, and in the bargain irritate Boggs, who had asthma.

Boggs looked at Rick's dossier, spread open on his desk. "Your debacle of a few weeks ago doesn't exactly inspire confidence in your powers of judgment," he said, tapping his forefinger on a sheet of paper.

He referred to an incident in which a traffic cop had pulled Rick over for careening down Palmas at 120 kilometers an hour at two in the morning. At the police station, Rick had been too plastered to answer any questions, so drunk that he didn't even recognize the embassy's on-duty officer who'd come to fetch him.

Rick began to blow smoke rings toward the ceiling. "Boggsy," he asked, "did it ever occur to you that there's a method to my madness?"

A slight smile formed on Boggs's lips. "Frankly, no, Rick. But by all means, let's hear it."

Rick leaned forward in his chair and began to speak in a clipped singsong, as if to an obstinately sluggish child. "Okay, my friend," he said. "I am the Soviet Counterintelligence chief of the Mexico City branch of the CIA. Do you think I got this far by being a fuckup? By being a falling-down drunk? I'm in *Operations*. The Company pays me a nice buck to find KGB here in Mexico, turn them over and get them to work for us. That is my fucking *job*, my delightful and gratifying life's work." His nose itched, and his glasses slipped down as he twitched it.

"Now how do I go about achieving this *task*? I drink heavily in public, and make strange remarks, and even once in a while get into an embarrassing *altercation*, so that gossip will drift back to the fucking Russians that there is a loose cannon in the American Embassy. They will come to me, thinking they can recruit me. But here's the *rub*, Boggsy: instead, I recruit them.

"It's a simple process. That is how a guy in Operations works. That's *recruitment*. Okay? How a guy as young as you gets to be assistant deputy chief of station without knowing that is one of life's great mysteries. Whose cousin are you, anyway? In any case, there's your lesson for the day, free of charge." He snorted wet mucus up his nose again, and a puddle of it fell to his throat. He swallowed, and took another drag of his cigarette.

Boggs laughed, but due to the smoke in the room it emerged as a wheeze. "So you're claiming your drunkenness is just an act."

"Right, Sherlock."

Boggs looked for another sheet in Rick's dossier. "The four bulls at lunch. The multiple cuba libres at night. The seventeen-hour vodka sessions with Igor."

"It's part of my job! You know that! You drink with these bozos so you can cozy up to them and recruit them."

The words had begun to sound hollow even to Rick. In truth his record spoke for itself. He had been in Operations for fourteen years, since 1969. After his first posting in Ankara, his station chief had concluded that "he couldn't recruit his own mother." Then he'd been sent to work in New York. Although he'd run a few big fish there, he hadn't reeled any of them in. And here in Mexico City, he hadn't pulled a single Soviet plum. Nothing. *Nada.* A gold-plated goose egg.

Despite the fact that Mexico City in 1983 was crawling with KGB. They worked in the Soviet Embassy, and in the embassies of all their satellites. All those "foreign correspondents" so eager to report Mexican news to Albanian and Bulgarian press agencies: more KGB. Those jolly business travelers with their schemes to import chile peppers and tequila to Ukraine. Even some of the musicians with the long unpronounceable names in the symphony orchestras.

They were busy little beavers, too: they solicited moles in the American diplomatic corps. They met with their American agents in Mexico, because it was safer than in U.S. territory. Mexico was also a passageway for the guns and missiles going to the Sandinistas in Nicaragua, the FMLN in Salvador, and God only knew who else in which other banana republics.

And if they had come anywhere near Rick's fingers, they'd managed to waltz right through. Sweat began to appear in a patch atop Boggs's crown, the only spot where his hair still grew with any thickness. His breath came out in labored short spurts. "Thanks for the lesson," he said. "Maybe you should become a professor after you go home. You seem to be a lot better at theory than practice." He removed a gray metal canister from his jacket pocket, uncapped and shook it, and put it in his mouth, deeply inhaling two spritzes of its contents.

"Finished, Boggsy?"

"I won't even comment on your bold-faced denial of your drinking problem. Except to inform you that not only will it find its way into your evaluation, but that a cable has also been sent to headquarters recommending that you get counseling when you return to Virginia." Rick noted that, now that he could breathe freely again, the young bureaucrat seemed to have warmed to his task.

"Is that all?"

"There's one other thing. Your affair with our little Colombian access agent. You know that's against policy. Her apartment was used as a safe house by various agents. She was also passing on worthwhile intelligence. Your dalliance with her put the brakes on all of that."

Rick removed his glasses and rubbed his puffy eyes. "Boggsy, before you stick your foot in it any further. Anything you say about Rosario, you're talking about the woman who's going to be my wife."

"But I thought you were already married," Boggs stammered.

Rick looked out the window at the palm trees that lined the street in back of the embassy. "That's been finished for a long time."

"Well." Boggs rubbed his chinlessness with two fingers. "That's about it," he said. "So you know what you can expect from your evaluation. "I'm sorry I had to be the one to tell you about it." He closed the dossier on his desk.

"Don't be sorry," said Rick, taking a last drag from his cigarette and blowing the smoke directly at Boggs's head before stubbing it out in a black plastic ashtray on his desk. "Thanks for warning me. I'll be shitting in my pants all the way back to Virginia." He stood and straightened his necktie. "Now if you don't mind, I've got a message for your boss. Your boss who didn't have the balls to have this little chat with me himself. Who's probably not here because he's passed out or on a three-day bender himself. Would you tell him something for me, Boggsy?"

"Sure, Rick. What do you want me to say?"

Rick glanced at the folder in front of Boggs, with his full name printed on a label across its cover: ALDRICH HAZEN AMES. He'd never felt quite comfortable with those three pompous barrels, preferring plain Rick. "Tell him I said fuck you. With a Russian hard-on." He stood there for a moment, staring at Boggs with his triumphant rat-toothed smile.

∼

In the back of a yellow cab bolting down Reforma, Rick tried to settle his jangled nerves. Boggs was just a candyass pencil pusher. Their whole conference had been a joke. It was nearly impossible to get fired from the Company. Rick's own father, also CIA, had been a far worse drunk than he was; by the end of his career, he napped at his desk most afternoons. Yet he'd stayed on, forgotten but not gone, retiring with a full pension at age sixty.

The scathing evaluation would be skimmed over by brass at headquarters and then sent to the back of a bulging file cabinet, never to be examined again. Back in Virginia, Rick would probably drift in limbo awhile, in "strategy," on "committees," until one bigwig or another, likely someone with whom he'd been through junior officer training all those years ago, decided to give him a more critical and engaged post.

"Quieres un cigarro?" asked Rick, holding up his pack toward the taxi driver.

"Gracias," he replied, raising his right hand in refusal.

"You don't smoke?" asked Rick, lighting up.

"A little," said the driver. "But it's not my religion."

The problem was that Rick wasn't well connected. So he was kept off the fast track. All that mattered in the CIA was who you knew. It was as simple as that.

Sure he'd made a few mistakes, even big ones. But who hadn't? While stationed in New York, he'd left a briefcase full of important files on the subway, putting the life of a Soviet agent in jeopardy. Some Polish woman had found the case and called the FBI. He'd eaten shit for weeks behind that incident, yet here in Mexico the same thing had happened—an agent had left important papers in a taxi cab. They disappeared for good, but this guy's father-in-law was a division chief, so they'd let it slide.

"They say the pollution in Mexico City is so bad that it's already like smoking two packs of cigarettes a day," Rick told the driver with an exhale, the tobacco salving his aching throat and lungs. "So I figure a few more won't hurt me."

"*Sí, señor,*" said the driver. "A few more, a few less, it doesn't matter."

So I'm not the world's greatest recruiter. Big deal. I've had my shining moments, too. Rick had caught a Mexican mole in the embassy, who hadn't even been polygraphed by the numbnuts who'd hired him. But did that make a difference? No. The bigwigs were so humiliated by the incident that they'd just swept it under the carpet. And Bill Casey, working with less than half a brain by Rick's estimation, was so afraid of a Communist insurrection in Latin America that he allocated no money or manpower to Rick's Soviet section in Mexico. How did they expect him to make a difference?

What was the point of his job, anyway? Every rational intelligence report supported the contention that the Soviets actually provided no tangible threat to the United States. The arms race and the cold war were bullshit mechanisms to keep the military industrial complex in place, and a bunch of gray and paunchy bureaucrats in their jobs. He felt thoroughly alienated. Sitting alone in his apartment the previous night, toward the bottom of a fifth of vodka, he mused that maybe he'd quit the CIA and go to live with Rosario in Colombia.

"Let me out here," Rick said, "at the Monumento de la Revolución."

"*Servido, señor,*" said the driver after pulling to a stop

aside the enormous structure, domed atop imposing pillars. Rick paid him, left the cab, and automatically looking behind his shoulder to see if he'd been followed, walked down two blocks of a crowded side street. He made a sharp turn at the next corner and slipped inside the dimly lit, leatherette-and-chromium bar of the Hotel Diplomático.

~

"You know who killed your country?" asked Igor, swirling the last of the chilled vodka in his tumbler and then swallowing it in one gulp. He licked his front teeth noisily, savoring the taste of the liquor. "It was one man only."

"Let me guess," said Rick, reclining in his chair, his feet propped on another. He inhaled a cigarette between his lips while another forgotten one smoldered in the ashtray. Hadn't Igor and he had this conversation months ago? He was sure of it, but he'd forgotten the punchline. "Johnson in Vietnam. No, Kennedy. Or the guys who had him killed. No, wait a minute." Rick began to laugh scornfully. "You're probably going to say Truman for dropping the bomb."

Igor clucked his tongue, removing the bottle of Stolichnaya from the ice bucket and checking the sparsity of its contents before pouring himself some more. "They are little potatoes. They are angels compared to worst villain in American history." He checked Rick's glass as well, and though it was more than half full, topped it off. "It was Doctor Spock."

"Doctor Spock?" asked Rick, ash falling onto his lap, "On *Star Trek*?"

"Imbecile!" said Igor. He laughed throatily, a round-skinned, thick-fingered hand on his belly. "That's Mister Spock! Played by distinguished Russian actor, coincidentally.

I'm talking about Doctor Spock, author of notorious baby book."

Rick, doubled over, caught up in Igor's laughter, smoke spurting from his nose, asked, "What the fuck does he have to do with anything?"

"Because he is telling a generation of citizens to spoil their children," said Igor, banging a fat fist on the table. A few plates clattered. They were empty, except for one, which had a few remaining sliced cucumbers, sprinkled with lime and powdered chile. The wet red pepper made them look like someone had bled on them from a nasty shaving cut.

"The most subversive, the most heretical message in history of publishing," declaimed Igor. "It causes more harm than any book, except for maybe Bible. For forty years, all Americans are reading Doctor Spock, and they are pampering their children. Who grow up to become selfish, indulgent, greedy brats, thinking of themselves only and not of community. The children of what your people call 'the decade of me.'"

Igor, his round ruddy face growing purple, seemed to be enjoying himself immensely as he improvised. "And this army of millions of spoiled brats, my friend, will cause destruction of capitalism. When it comes time to fight, they won't know how. Blacks won't do it for you, like in Vietnam. It's the beginning of the ending. You'll see, Ricky." Igor looked behind him, searching for the waiter. He wasn't there, so Igor shouted at the top of his lungs, "MARIO! TENGO HAMBRE!" There were only a few other patrons in the bar, Mexicans in suits and ties of synthetic fabric, who averted their eyes and ignored the Russian.

A fiftyish waiter in a black jacket, his receding hair parted in the middle and slicked in place, was at the table in a moment. *"Sí, patrón, qué desea usted?"*

"We're hungry," said Igor, holding two of the empty plates in his hand. *"No podemos tomar tanto sin comer."* He spoke Spanish well, although with the same thick accent with which he spoke English, trilling all his *rs*, whether single or double-barreled.

"Sí, patrón, al instante," said Mario, grabbing the empty plates and hopping to the kitchen, where the cook had prepared a special cache of Russian-style goodies for their favored client.

"I don't think so," said Rick, lighting a fresh cigarette with the butt of the previous one. Between his sore throat and the smoke he was beginning to sound like an old lawn mower. "You know you guys are a lot more vulnerable than we are. We got more missiles than you. More bombs. More nukes. More ships, more planes, more men, more everything. And you're broke. Your system's the one that's going down. I wouldn't be surprised if the whole goddamn house of cards fell in . . ." He waved his hand, the cigarette between his fingers. "I don't give you another ten years." A look of contempt crossed Igor's eyes, but Rick mistook it for injury. "And you know I say this as a friend."

"Yes, I know you are my friend," exclaimed Igor, grabbing Rick by the scruff of his neck and rubbing his forehead together with his counterpart's. "You Americans are so sensitive!"

They sat in silence for a few moments. "You're going to miss Mexico, my friend?" asked Igor.

"You read my mind," said Rick. "I'm leaving in two weeks." Most of the hacks in the embassy complained about the pollution, the crowds, the bureaucracy, but Rick liked Mexico City. He liked the palm trees and the yellow cabs, the spicy food and the flowing booze, the servility of the men and the availability of the women—his first year here he'd had three affairs in quick succession, before he'd met Rosario. He'd also banked most of his $44,000 salary, living like a playboy off a lavish expense account, in the style of Simon Templar in *The Saint,* as he'd always dreamed a spy should live.

"I'll miss you, my friend," said Igor. Yet his look was steely, not tender.

Already forty when he'd arrived, Rick felt he'd finally come into his own in Mexico. On that first posting in Ankara he'd been scared and green, so eager to be a good Operations officer that he'd flopped completely. The tension was heightened by Nan, his wife, also a CIA officer at the time. To accompany him to Turkey, she'd had to accept a demotion, which she bitterly resented and for which she'd never forgiven him. The assignment in New York had been more entertaining, but not as much as it might have been, after Nan discovered women's lib and their marriage began to disintegrate.

In truth, they'd had little in common. Rosario, Rick's new love, was virtually Nan's opposite: passionate where Nan was detached, opinionated where she was indecisive, strong where she was fragile. Nan wasn't weak by any means, but her power had been sneaky, indirect, from a passive cover. They'd hardly talked. In contrast, Rosario, like many Latin American women, kept her feelings in the front window, never held anything back.

Mario arrived with more fortifications: pickled herring

from a jar Igor had brought, sliced and fried chorizo, beets in vinegar, and a concoction of diced potatoes, peas, carrots, and corn, swimming in mayonnaise, called *ensalada rusa*. "*Provecho, señores,*" he said.

"*Momento, Mario!*" said Igor. He held up the plate of *ensalada rusa* and casually flicked his wrist, as if ready to fling it like a Frisbee. "Are you trying to insult me, Mario? I thought you were my friend."

"*Ay, perdón, señor,*" said Mario.

Igor shoved the plate in Mario's hands. "The next time you bring me this *mierda*, Mario, I swear I'm throwing it on the floor! And I'll make you go down on all fours and eat it like a dog!"

"*Lo siento muchísimo, patrón.*"

"Boil the potatoes, mash the anchovies into a paste, and mix them with the mayonnaise!"

"*Sí, señor,*" said Mario, scurrying toward the kitchen with the offending plate.

"You know why Mexicans are so fucked?" asked Igor. "Because of the shit they are eating." Rick began to laugh. "Tortillas! Chile peppers! How dare they call that slop 'Russian salad.'" His baggy eyes betrayed deep offense. "I'm thinking of making a formal complaint to Miguel de la Madrid!"

The idea of Igor griping to the Mexican president about the name of a food caused Rick to laugh so hard the vodka spilled from his mouth. Igor jabbed at the sliced beets with a fork and stuffed a couple in his mouth. The juice dribbled onto his chin, towards his black turtleneck sweater. He poured the last of the vodka into his glass. "*MARIO! OTRA BOTELLA!*" he screamed.

A second bottle. After five hours of drinking, Rick felt woozy. He had thought he knew how to hold his liquor until he met Igor, who could put away enormous quantities for twenty-four hours at a clip, and still seem as fresh and energetic as when he'd started.

~

A thin pallid character wearing a brown toupee in the shape of a cabbage leaf had arrived an hour earlier, about nine-thirty, set up an electric organ, and begun to play the popular standards of the Latin-American repertoire: *"Frenesí," "Piel canela," "Solamente una vez."* He'd invested in an instrument with an automatic drum machine to attract a wider public, but it hadn't helped much. Aside from Rick and Igor, more than halfway through their second fifth of vodka, only a few more Mexicans in cheap suits had arrived. At the next table, four young women with teased hair and high heels, boxy but soft in their tight minidresses, sat chattering with one another, waiting for one of the men to offer to buy a drink. Igor was flirting with a chubby one, whose smile was enhanced by a gold front tooth.

"Have some vodka if you want a drink," he said, holding up the bottle.

She wrinkled her nose fetchingly. *"Es que me sabe feo sin Coca,"* she said, but nonetheless walked over with an empty glass. *"No quieres que te acompañe?"* she asked.

"Yes, of course I want you to," said Igor, pouring her a drink. "But what will my wife say?"

The girl smiled devilishly. *"Ella no tiene que saber nada."*

"She has a nose like a vulture," said Igor. "She'll smell your perfume on me a block away." He squeezed her ample behind. "Sit down with your friends, *mi amor.* My colleague and I are discussing important things."

"*Eres malo,*" she said with a smile, and returned to her table.

Rick sat smoking his forty-ninth cigarette of the day, watching with amusement as Igor trifled with the bar girl. He'd had his share of such juicy figs in the last couple of years, particularly when he first arrived. Thank God women's lib hadn't made any headway in Latin America, he thought.

Igor looked at Rick through slitted eyes. "It's going to be tough," he said.

"What?" asked Rick.

"What you are saying before. The divorce."

"Yeah, but it's for the best, in the end. Besides, I've got Rosario."

"You really love her."

"God, yes." Rick took another drink. "You know, she's the first woman I've ever met who's smarter than me. One night we talked for two hours about *The Waste Land.* The only time I ever talked with Nan about T. S. Eliot was after we saw *Cats.*"

"But what about money?"

"Oh, yeah," said Rick. "It's going to be messy. The bitch is gonna skin me alive. I'll be walking around Washington wearing a barrel."

"And Rosario's going with you?"

Just the thought made Rick feel better. "She'll be joining me in a few months. After I get the divorce sorted out."

"She's one classy lady. She won't look good in a barrel."

"We'll work it out," said Rick. His voice lacked the edge of confidence.

"I hope," said Igor gravely.

"Hey, it's not that bad."

"Rick, look at her side. She's from nice Columbian family. She's accustomed to live in big style."

"She's not rich, she's middle-class."

Igor said, "You Americans and your stinking 'middle-class!' You have noticed what Mexicans are meaning when they say 'middle-class'? They have three servants and travel abroad every year, but they can't afford a Mercedes. Same thing in Colombia. You know she is thinking she marries a rich gringo. Or 'middle-class' gringo."

"Rosario knows I haven't got a cent. I've been honest with her."

"All Latin Americans think all gringos are rich!" Igor laughed, banging a palm on the table. "And look at how you are living here! Eating in best restaurants. Flying to Acapulco for weekend. Taxis everywhere. And all on expense account, no?"

Rick smiled sheepishly. "Well . . . it's Company business."

"The Company pays your rent here, no? You aren't spending a cent of your salary. She is probably thinking it's the same thing when you are back in the States."

When Rick pictured what life would be like at Langley, he flashed on a few images: a potty little suburban apartment, small rooms with beige carpeting, a built-in kitchenette with a linoleum floor. He saw himself sitting at a Formica-topped table, writing one check for the rent, and another for Nan's place in New York—until he could come up with a fat divorce settlement, anyway. He saw a Dodge Dart with birdshit on the hood, which was probably all he could afford to drive. A crummy motel room at some beach on the Maryland coast, where they'd go for a weekend in the summer, if there was any money left over.

"Look, Ricky." Igor gulped more vodka. "You know I think of you as brother," he said matter-of-factly.

"Thanks, Igor. I feel the same way."

"What I'm saying is. If you want." He looked at Rick for a long moment and spoke very softly. "I could make you rich."

Rick felt his face flush.

"You have access to information, I could be guaranteeing you and Rosario would never have to worry about money again. And your children wouldn't either. Ever."

Years ago, Rick had been caught cheating on Nan in the most humiliating way for both of them: with his pants around his ankles in a supply closet porking another CIA officer, and not a very pretty one, either, at a company Christmas party. Nevertheless, some years later, in New York, when he began to suspect she was having an affair with another man (he never knew for sure), he felt a keen sense of sadness and disappointment, a bottomless hurt, an abysmal emptiness, that overwhelmed him.

And that was precisely what he felt right now, looking at the pleasant pudgy face of Igor, his counterpart in the KGB, trying to recruit him. Rick had thought they were above all that. They'd been having these drawn-out drinking sessions periodically throughout his tour in Mexico City. Of course it had been Rick's original intention to try to recruit Igor, but he gave up on the idea because he thought it would destroy their friendship. He was under the impression that there had been an unspoken understanding between them that neither would ever make the pitch. They had too much respect for each other.

"How much would I be worth?" asked Rick.

"Well, I can't give you exact figure," said Igor. "In the long term, millions."

Rick doubted that: the Russians were notorious cheapskates. He had imagined being a mole in the past; probably every spy did, at one time or another. He'd seen himself walking around obscure corners of nameless cities, making little chalk marks on sidewalks or mailboxes, leaving packages of documents in woodsy areas in public parks. Or exchanging them for shoe boxes full of cash, in nondescript, unfashionable restaurants. In a sense it would be more exciting and of course more lucrative than what he was doing now. He'd probably be good at it. He knew he had the balls, and he was sufficiently discreet. The latter was hardly important: the CIA was so clueless it would be easy to get away with. It would be almost worth it to show all those smartasses in the CIA how brain-dead they truly were.

"You know, Igor," he said, "I've made my share of mistakes in forty-two years. I married the wrong woman. I made some. . . miscalculations on the job. I have a hard time getting along with my bosses." His voice cracked so he paused to light another cigarette. "You've heard me bitch and moan about the Company. I think we've been doing some fucked-up things, especially under Reagan. I'm pretty disgusted with some of my government's policies right now." He leaned forward so his face was inches away from Igor's, and said in a whisper, "But I'd never sell it out. *Never.* Okay? Do I make myself clear? You can go back and tell the boys that pull your strings that *Aldrich Ames is not a traitor.*" There were tears in his eyes.

Rick stood, squinting from emotion and cigarette smoke, removed a few large bills from his wallet and threw them on the table. "Good-bye," he said and weaved out.

Igor watched him go. It was no skin off his ass either way, but he was confident the American would come around. It was just a matter of time. The Mexican girl at the next table was giving him the big eyes, the light from the candle atop her table shining on her gold tooth. *"Ven acá, chiquitita,"* he said.

ON THE ROAD
Jack Kerouac

Then we turned our faces to Mexico with bashfulness and wonder as those dozens of Mexican cats watched us from under their secret hatbrims in the night. Beyond were music and all-night restaurants with smoke pouring out of the door. "Whee," whispered Dean very softly.

"Thassall!" A Mexican official grinned. "You boys all set. Go ahead. Welcome Mehico. Have good time. Watch you money. Watch you driving. I say this to you personal, I'm Red, everybody call me Red. Ask for Red. Eat good. Don't worry. Everything fine. It not hard enjoin yourself in Mehico."

"*Yes!*" shuddered Dean and off we went across the street into Mexico on soft feet. We left the car parked, and all three of us abreast went down the Spanish street into the middle of the dull brown lights. Old men sat on chairs in the night and looked like Oriental junkies and oracles. No one was actually looking at us, yet everybody was aware of everything we did. We turned sharp left into the smoky lunchroom and went in to music of campo guitars on an American 'thirties jukebox. Shirt-sleeved Mexican cabdrivers and straw-hatted Mexican hipsters sat at stools, devouring shapeless messes of tortillas, beans, tacos, whatnot. We bought three bottles of cold beer—*cerveza* was the name of beer—for about thirty Mexican cents or ten American cents each. We bought packs of Mexican cigarettes for six cents each. We gazed and gazed at our wonderful Mexican money that went so far, and played with it and looked around and smiled at everyone. Behind us lay the whole of America and everything Dean and I had previously known about life, and life on the road. We had finally found the magic land at the end of the road and we never dreamed the extent of the magic. "*Think* of these cats staying up all hours of the night," whispered Dean. "And think of this big continent ahead of us with those enormous Sierra Madre mountains we saw in the movies, and the jungles all the way down and a whole desert plateau as big as ours and reaching clear down to Guatemala and God knows where, whoo! What'll we do? What'll we do? Let's move!" We got out and went back to the car. One last glimpse of America across the hot lights of the Rio Grande bridge, and we turned our back and fender to it and roared off.

Instantly we were out in the desert and there wasn't a light or a car for fifty miles across the flats. And just then dawn was coming over the Gulf of Mexico and we began to see the ghostly shapes of yucca cactus and organpipe on all sides. "What a wild country!" I yelped. Dean and I were completely awake. In Laredo we'd been half dead. Stan, who'd been to foreign countries before, just calmly slept in the back seat. Dean and I had the whole of Mexico before us.

"Now, Sal, we're leaving everything behind us and entering a new and unknown phase of things. All the years and troubles and kicks—and now *this!* so that we can safely think of nothing else and just go on ahead with our faces stuck out like this, you see, and *understand* the world as, really and genuinely speaking, other Americans haven't done before us—they were here, weren't they? The Mexican war. Cutting across here with cannon."

"This road," I told him, "is also the route of old American outlaws who used to skip over the border and go down to old Monterrey, so if you'll look out on that graying desert and picture the ghost of an old Tombstone hellcat making his lonely exile gallop into the unknown, you'll see further . . ."

"It's the world," said Dean. "My God!" he cried, slapping the wheel. "It's the world! We can go right on to South America if the road goes. Think of it! Son-of-a-*bitch!* Gawd-*damn!*" We rushed on. The dawn spread immediately and we began to see the white sand of the desert and occasional huts in the distance off the road. Dean slowed down to peer at them. "Real beat huts, man, the kind you only find in Death Valley and much worse. These people don't *bother* with appearances." The first town ahead that had any conse-quence on the map was called Sabinas Hidalgo. We looked forward to it eagerly. "And the road don't look any different than the American road," cried Dean, "except one mad thing and if you'll notice, right here, the mileposts are written in kilometers and they click off the distance to Mexico City. See, it's the only city in the entire land, everything points to it." There were only 767 more miles to that metropolis; in kilometers the figure was over a thousand. "Damn! I gotta go!" cried Dean. For a while I closed my eyes in utter exhaus-tion and kept hearing Dean pound the wheel with his fists and say, "Damn," and "What kicks!" and "Oh, what a land!" and "Yes!" We arrived at Sabinas Hidalgo, across the desert, at about seven o'clock in the morning. We slowed down completely to see this. We woke up Stan in the back seat. We sat up straight to dig. The main street was muddy and full of holes. On each side were dirty broken-down adobe fronts. Burros walked in the street with packs. Barefoot women watched us from dark doorways. The street was completely crowded with people on foot beginning a new day in the Mexican countryside. Old men with handlebar mustaches stared at us. The sight of three bearded, bedraggled American youths instead of the usual well-dressed tourists was of unusual interest to them. We bounced along over Main Street at ten miles an hour, taking everything in. A group of girls walked directly in front of us. As we bounced by, one of them said, "Where you going, man?"

I turned to Dean, amazed. "Did you hear what she said?"

Dean was so astounded he kept on driving slowly and saying, "Yes, I heard what she said, I certainly damn well did, oh me, oh my, I don't know what to do I'm so excited and sweetened in this morning world. We've finally got to heaven. It couldn't be cooler, it couldn't be grander, it couldn't be any-*thing.*"

"Well, let's go back and pick em up!" I said.

"Yes," said Dean and drove right on at five miles an hour. He was knocked out, he didn't have to do the usual things he would have done in America. "There's millions of them all along the road!" he said. Nevertheless he U-turned and came by the girls again. They were headed for work in the fields; they smiled at us. Dean stared at them with rocky eyes. "Damn," he said under his breath. "*Oh!* This is too great to be true. Gurls, gurls. And particularly right now in my stage and condition, Sal, I am digging the interiors of these homes as we pass them—these gone doorways and you look inside and see beds of straw and little brown kids sleeping and stirring to wake, their thoughts congealing from the empty mind of sleep, their selves rising, and the mothers cooking up breakfast in iron pots, and dig them shutters they have for windows and the old men, the *old men* are so cool and grand and not bothered by anything. There's no *suspicion* here, nothing like that. Everybody's cool, everybody looks at you with such straight brown eyes and they don't say anything, just *look,* and in that look all of the human qualities are soft and subdued and still there. Dig all the foolish stories you read about Mexico and the sleeping gringo and all that crap—and crap about greasers and so on—and all it is, people here are straight and kind and don't put down any bull. I'm so amazed by this." Schooled in the raw road night, Dean was come into the world to see it. He bent over the wheel and looked both ways and rolled along slowly. We stopped for gas the other side of Sabinas Hidalgo. Here a congregation of local straw-hatted ranchers with handlebar mustaches growled and joked in front of antique gas-pumps. Across the fields an old man plodded with a burro in front of his switch stick. The sun rose pure on pure and ancient activities of human life.

Now we resumed the road to Monterrey. The great mountains rose snow-capped before us; we bowled right for them. A gap widened and wound up a pass and we went with it. In a matter of minutes we were out of the mesquite desert and climbing among cool airs in a road with a stone wall along the precipice side and great whitewashed names of presidents on the cliffsides—ALEMAN! We met nobody on this high road. It wound among the clouds and took us to the great plateau on top. Across this plateau the big manufacturing town of Monterrey sent smoke to the blue skies with their enormous Gulf clouds written across the bowl of day like fleece. Entering Monterrey was like entering Detroit, among great long walls of factories, except for the burros that sunned in the grass before them and the sight of thick city adobe neighborhoods with thousands of shifty hipsters hanging around doorways and whores looking out of windows and strange shops that might have sold anything and narrow sidewalks crowded with Hongkong-like humanity. "Yow!" yelled Dean. "And all in that sun. Have you dug this Mexican sun, Sal? It makes you high. Whoo! I want to get on and on—this road drives *me!!*" We mentioned stopping in the excitements of Monterrey, but Dean wanted to make extra-special time to get to Mexico City, and besides he knew the road would get more interesting, especially ahead, always ahead. He drove like a fiend and never rested. Stan and I were completely bushed and gave it up and had to sleep. I looked up outside Monterrey and saw enormous weird twin peaks beyond Old Monterrey, beyond where the outlaws went.

Montemorelos was ahead, a descent again to hotter altitudes. It grew exceedingly hot and strange. Dean absolutely had to wake me up to see this. "Look, Sal, you *must* not miss." I looked. We were going through swamps and alongside the road at ragged intervals strange Mexicans in tattered rags walked along with machetes hanging from their rope belts, and some of them cut at the bushes. They all stopped to watch us without expression. Through the tangled bush we occasionally saw thatched huts with African-like bamboo walls, just stick huts. Strange young girls, dark as the moon, stared from mysterious verdant doorways. "Oh, man, I want to stop and twiddle thumbs with the little darlings," cried Dean, "but notice the old lady or the old man is always somewhere around—in the back usually, sometimes a hundred yards, gathering twigs and wood or tending animals. They're never alone. Nobody's ever alone in this country. While you've been sleeping I've been digging this road and this country, and if I could only tell you all the thoughts I've had, man!" He was sweating. His eyes were red-streaked and mad and also subdued and tender—he had found people like himself. We bowled right through the endless swamp country at a steady forty-five. "Sal, I think the country won't change for a long time. If you'll drive, I'll sleep now."

I took the wheel and drove among reveries of my own, through Linares, through hot, flat swamp country, across the steaming Rio Soto la Marina near Hidalgo, and on. A great verdant jungle valley with long fields of green crops opened before me. Groups of men watched us pass from a narrow old-fashioned bridge. The hot river flowed. Then we rose in altitude till a kind of desert country began reappearing. The city of Gregoria was ahead. The boys were sleeping, and I was alone in my eternity at the wheel, and the road ran straight as an arrow. Not like driving across Carolina, or Texas, or Arizona, or Illinois; but like driving across the world and into the places where we would finally learn ourselves among the Fellahin Indians of the world, the essential strain of the basic primitive, wailing humanity that stretches in a belt around the equatorial belly of the world from Malaya (the long fingernail of China) to India the great subcontinent to Arabia to Morocco to the selfsame deserts and jungles of Mexico and over the waves to Polynesia to mystic Siam of the Yellow Robe and on around, on around, so that

you hear the same mournful wail by the rotted walls of
Cádiz, Spain, that you hear 12,000 miles around in the
depths of Benares the Capital of the World. These people
were unmistakably Indians and were not at all like the
Pedros and Panchos of silly civilized American lore—they
had high cheekbones, and slanted eyes, and soft ways; they
were not fools, they were not clowns; they were great, grave
Indians and they were the source of mankind and the fathers
of it. The waves are Chinese, but the earth is an Indian thing.
As essential as rocks in the desert are they in the desert of
"history." And they knew this when we passed, ostensibly
self-important moneybag Americans on a lark in their land;
they knew who was the father and who was the son of
antique life on earth, and made no comment. For when
destruction comes to the world of "history" and the
Apocalypse of the Fellahin returns once more as so many
times before, people will still stare with the same eyes from
the caves of Mexico as well as from the caves of Bali, where it
all began and where Adam was suckled and taught to know.
These were my growing thoughts as I drove the car into the
hot, sunbaked town of Gregoria.

Earlier, back at San Antonio, I had promised Dean, as a
joke, that I would get him a girl. It was a bet and a challenge.
As I pulled up the car at the gas station near sunny Gregoria
a kid came across the road on tattered feet, carrying an enormous windshield-shade, and wanted to know if I'd buy. "You
like? Sixty peso. Habla *Español? Sesenta peso.* My name
Victor."

"Nah," I said jokingly, "buy señorita."

"Sure, sure!" he cried excitedly. "I get you gurls, onnytime. Too hot now," he added with distaste. "No good gurls

when hot day. Wait tonight. You like shade?"

I didn't want the shade but I wanted the girls. I woke up Dean. "Hey, man, I told you in Texas I'd get you a girl—all right, stretch your bones and wake up, boy; we've got girls waiting for us."

"What? what?" he cried, leaping up, haggard. "Where? where?"

"This boy Victor's going to show us where."

"Well, lessgo, lessgo!" Dean leaped out of the car and clasped Victor's hand. There was a group of other boys hanging around the station and grinning, half of them barefoot, all wearing floppy straw hats. "Man," said Dean to me, "ain't this a nice way to spend an afternoon. It's so much *cooler* than Denver poolhalls. Victor, you got gurls? Where? A *donde?*" he cried in Spanish. "Dig that, Sal, I'm speaking Spanish."

"Ask him if we can get any tea. Hey kid, you got ma-ree-wa-na?"

The kid nodded gravely. "Sho, onnytime, mon. Come with me."

"Hee! Whee! Hoo!" yelled Dean. He was wide awake and jumping up and down in that drowsy Mexican street. "Let's all go!" I was passing Lucky Strikes to the other boys. They were getting great pleasure out of us and especially Dean. They turned to one another with cupped hands and rattled off comments about the mad American cat. "Dig them, Sal, talking about us and digging. Oh my goodness, what a world!" Victor got in the car with us, and we lurched off. Stan Shephard had been sleeping soundly and woke up to this madness.

We drove way out to the desert the other side of town

and turned on a rutty dirt road that made the car bounce as never before. Up ahead was Victor's house. It sat on the edge of cactus flats overtopped by a few trees, just an adobe cracker-box, with a few men lounging around in the yard. "Who that?" cried Dean, all excited.

"Those my brothers. My mother there too. My sistair too. That my family. I married, I live downtown."

"What about your mother?" Dean flinched. "What she say about marijuana."

"Oh, she get it for me." And as we waited in the car Victor got out and loped over to the house and said a few words to an old lady, who promptly turned and went to the garden in back and began gathering dry fronds of marijuana that had been pulled off the plants and left to dry in the desert sun. Meanwhile Victor's brothers grinned from under a tree. They were coming over to meet us but it would take a while for them to get up and walk over. Victor came back, grinning sweetly.

"Man," said Dean, "that Victor is the sweetest, gonest, franticest little bangtail cat I've ever in all my life met. Just look at him, look at his cool slow walk. There's no need to hurry around here." A steady, insistent desert breeze blew into the car. It was very hot.

"You see how hot?" said Victor, sitting down with Dean in the front seat and pointing up at the burning roof of the Ford. "You have ma-ree-gwana and it no hot no more. You wait."

"Yes," said Dean, adjusting his dark glasses, "I wait. For sure, Victor m'boy."

Presently Victor's tall brother came ambling along with some weed piled on a page of newspaper. He dumped it on

Victor's lap and leaned casually on the door of the car to nod and smile at us and say, "Hallo." Dean nodded and smiled pleasantly at *him*. Nobody talked; it was fine. Victor proceeded to roll the biggest bomber anybody ever saw. He rolled (using brown bag paper) what amounted to a tremendous Corona cigar of tea. It was huge. Dean stared at it, popeyed. Victor casually lit it and passed it around. To drag on this thing was like leaning over a chimney and inhaling. It blew into your throat in one great blast of heat. We held our breaths and all let out just about simultaneously. Instantly we were all high. The sweat froze on our foreheads and it was suddenly like the beach at Acapulco. I looked out the back window of the car, and another and the strangest of Victor's brothers—a tall Peruvian of an Indian with a sash over his shoulder—leaned grinning on a post, too bashful to come up and shake hands. It seemed the car was surrounded by brothers, for another one appeared on Dean's side. Then the strangest thing happened. Everybody became so high that usual formalities were dispensed with and the things of immediate interest were concentrated on, and now it was the strangeness of Americans and Mexicans blasting together on the desert and, more than that, the strangeness of seeing in close proximity the faces and pores of skins and calluses of fingers and general abashed cheekbones of another world. So the Indian brothers began talking about us in low voices and commenting; you saw them look, and size, and compare mutualities of impression, or correct and modify, "Yeh, yeh"; while Dean and Stan and I commented on them in English.

"Will you d-i-g that weird brother in the back that hasn't moved from that post and hasn't by one cut hair diminished the intensity of the glad *funny* bashfulness of his smile? And

the one to my left here, older, more sure of himself but sad,
like hung-up, like a bum even maybe, in town, while Victor is
respectably married—he's like a gawddam Egyptian king, that
you see. These guys are real *cats*. Ain't never seen anything
like it. And they're talking and wondering about us, like see?
Just like we are but with a difference of their own, their interest probably resolving around how we're dressed—same as
ours, really—but the strangeness of the things we have in the
car and the strange ways that we laugh so different from
them, and maybe even the way we smell compared to them.
Nevertheless I'd give my eye-teeth to know what they're saying about us." And Dean tried. "Hey Victor, man—what you
brother say just then?"

Victor turned mournful high brown eyes on Dean. "Yeah,
yeah."

"No, you didn't understand my question. What you boys
talking about?"

"Oh," said Victor with great perturbation, "you no like
this mar-gwana?"

"Oh, yeah, yes fine! What you *talk* about?"

"Talk? Yes, we talk. How you like Mexico?" It was hard to
come around without a common language. And everybody
grew quiet and cool and high again and just enjoyed the
breeze from the desert and mused separate national and
racial and personal high-eternity thoughts.

It was time for the girls. The brothers eased back to their
station under the tree, the mother watched from her sunny
doorway, and we slowly bounced back to town.

But now the bouncing was no longer unpleasant; it was
the most pleasant and graceful billowy trip in the world, as
over a blue sea, and Dean's face was suffused with an unnat-

ural glow that was like gold as he told us to understand the springs of the car now for the first time and dig the ride. Up and down we bounced, and even Victor understood and laughed. Then he pointed left to show which way to go for the girls, and Dean, looking left with indescribable delight and leaning that way, pulled the wheel around and rolled us smoothly and surely to the goal, meanwhile listening to Victor's attempt to speak and saying grandly and magniloquently "Yes, of course! There's not a doubt in my mind! Decidedly, man! Oh, indeed! Why, pish, posh, you say the dearest things to me! Of course! Yes! Please go on!" To this Victor talked gravely and with magnificent Spanish eloquence. For a mad moment I thought Dean was understanding everything he said by sheer wild insight and sudden revelatory genius inconceivably inspired by his glowing happiness. In that moment, too, he looked so exactly like Franklin Delano Roosevelt—some delusion in my flaming eyes and floating brain—that I drew up in my seat and gasped with amazement. In myriad pricklings of heavenly radiation I had to struggle to see Dean's figure, and he looked like God. I was so high I had to lean my head back on the seat; the bouncing of the car sent shivers of ecstasy through me. The mere thought of looking out the window at Mexico—which was now something else in my mind—was like recoiling from some gloriously riddled glittering treasure-box that you're afraid to look at because of your eyes, they bend inward, the riches and the treasures are too much to take all at once. I gulped. I saw streams of gold pouring through the sky and right across the tattered roof of the poor old car, right across my eyeballs and indeed right inside them; it was everywhere. I looked out the window at the hot, sunny streets and saw a woman in a doorway and I thought she was listening to every word we said and nodding to herself—routine paranoiac visions due to tea. But the stream of gold continued. For a long time I lost consciousness in my lower mind of what we were doing and only came around sometime later when I looked up from fire and silence like waking from sleep to the world, or waking from void to a dream, and they told me we were parked outside Victor's house and he was already at the door of the car with his little baby son in his arms, showing him to us.

"You see my baby? Hees name Pérez, he six month age."

"Why," said Dean, his face still transfigured into a shower of supreme pleasure and even bliss, "he is the prettiest child I have ever seen. Look at those eyes. Now, Sal and Stan," he said turning to us with a serious and tender air, "I want you par-ti-cu-lar-ly to see the eyes of this little Mexican boy who is the son of our wonderful friend Victor, and notice how he will come to manhood with his own particular soul bespeaking itself through the windows which are his eyes, and such lovely eyes surely do prophesy and indicate the loveliest of souls." It was a beautiful speech. And it was a beautiful baby. Victor mournfully looked down at his angel. We all wished we had a little son like that. So great was our intensity over the child's soul that he sensed something and began a grimace which led to bitter tears and some unknown sorrow that we had no means to soothe because it reached too far back into innumerable mysteries and time. We tried everything; Victor smothered him in his neck and rocked, Dean cooed, I reached over and stroked the baby's little arms. His bawls grew louder. "Ah," said Dean, "I'm awfully sorry, Victor, that we've made him sad."

"He is not sad, baby cry." In the doorway in back of Victor, too bashful to come out, was his little barefoot wife, with anxious tenderness waiting for the babe to be put back in her arms so brown and soft. Victor, having shown us his child, climbed back into the car and proudly pointed to the right.

"Yes," said Dean, and swung the car over and directed it through narrow Algerian streets with faces on all sides watching us with gentle wonder. We came to the whorehouse. It was a magnificent establishment of stucco in the golden sun. In the street, and leaning on the windowsills that opened into the whorehouse, were two cops, saggy-trousered, drowsy, bored, who gave us brief interested looks as we walked in, and stayed there the entire three hours that we cavorted under their noses, until we came out at dusk and at Victor's bidding gave them the equivalent of twenty-four cents each, just for the sake of form.

And in there we found the girls. Some of them were reclining on couches across the dance floor, some of them were boozing at the long bar to the right. In the center an arch led into small cubicle shacks that looked like the places where you put on your bathing suit at public municipal beaches. These shacks were in the sun of the court. Behind the bar was the proprietor, a young fellow who instantly ran out when we told him we wanted to hear mambo music and came back with a stack of records, mostly by Pérez Prado, and put them on over the loudspeaker. In an instant all the city of Gregoria could hear the good times going on at the Sala de Baile. In the hall itself the din of the music—for this is the real way to play a jukebox and what it was originally for—was so tremendous that it shattered Dean and Stan and me for a moment in the realization that we had never dared to play music as loud as we wanted, and this was how loud we wanted. It blew and shuddered directly at us. In a few minutes half that portion of town was at the windows, watching the *Americanos* dance with the gals. They all stood, side by side with the cops, on the dirt sidewalk, leaning in with indifference and casualness. "More Mambo Jambo," "Chattanooga de Mambo," "Mambo Numero Ocho"—all these tremendous numbers resounded and flared in the golden, mysterious afternoon like the sounds you expect to hear on the last day of the world and the Second Coming. The trumpets seemed so loud I thought they could hear them clear out in the desert, where the trumpets had originated anyway. The drums were mad. The mambo beat is the conga beat from Congo, the river of Africa and the world; it's really the world beat. Oom-*ta,* ta-poo-*poom*—omm-*ta,* ta-poo-*poom*. The piano montunos showered down on us from the speaker. The cries of the leader were like great gasps in the air. The final trumpet choruses that came with drum climaxes on conga and bongo drums, on the great mad Chattanooga record, froze Dean in his tracks for a moment till he shuddered and sweated; then when the trumpets bit the drowsy air with their quivering echoes, like a cavern's or a cave's, his eyes grew large and round as though seeing the devil, and he closed them tight. I myself was shaken like a puppet by it; I heard the trumpets flail the light I had seen and trembled in my boots.

On the fast "Mambo Jambo" we danced frantically with the girls. Through our deliriums we began to discern their varying personalities. They were great girls. Strangely the wildest one was half Indian, half white, and came from

Venezuela, and only eighteen. She looked as if she came from a good family. What she was doing whoring in Mexico at that age and with that tender cheek and fair aspect, God knows. Some awful grief had driven her to it. She drank beyond all bounds. She threw down drinks when it seemed she was about to chuck up the last. She overturned glasses continually, the idea also being to make us spend as much money as possible. Wearing her flimsy housecoat in broad afternoon, she frantically danced with Dean and clung about his neck and begged and begged for everything. Dean was so stoned he didn't know what to start with, girls or mambo. They ran off to the lockers. I was set upon by a fat and uninteresting girl with a puppy dog, who got sore at me when I took a dislike to the dog because it kept trying to bite me. She compromised by putting it away in the back, but by the time she returned I had been hooked by another girl, better looking but not the best, who clung to my neck like a leech. I was trying to break loose to get at a sixteen-year-old colored girl who sat gloomily inspecting her navel through an opening in her short shirty dress across the hall. I couldn't do it. Stan had a fifteen-year-old girl with an almond-colored skin and a dress that was buttoned halfway down and halfway up. It was mad. A good twenty men leaned in that window, watching.

At one point the mother of the little colored girl—not colored, but dark—came in to hold a brief and mournful convocation with her daughter. When I saw that, I was too ashamed to try for the one I really wanted. I let the leech take me off to the back, where, as in a dream, to the din and roar of more loudspeakers inside, we made the bed bounce a half-hour. It was just a square room with wooden slats and no ceiling, ikon in a corner, a washbasin in another. All up and down the dark hall the girls were calling, *"Agua, agua caliente!"* which means "hot water." Stan and Dean were also out of sight. My girl charged thirty pesos, or about three dollars and a half, and begged for an extra ten pesos and gave a long story about something. I didn't know the value of Mexican money; for all I knew I had a million pesos. I threw money at her. We rushed back to dance. A greater crowd was gathered in the street. The cops looked as bored as usual. Dean's pretty Venezuelan dragged me through a door and into another strange bar that apparently belonged to the whorehouse. Here a young bartender was talking and wiping glasses and an old man with handlebar mustache sat discussing something earnestly. And here too the mambo roared over another loudspeaker. It seemed the whole world was turned on. Venezuela clung about my neck and begged for drinks. The bartender wouldn't give her one. She begged and begged, and when he gave it to her she spilled it and this time not on purpose, for I saw the chagrin in her poor sunken lost eyes. "Take it easy, baby," I told her. I had to support her on the stool; she kept slipping off. I've never seen a drunker woman, and only eighteen. I bought her another drink; she was tugging at my pants for mercy. She gulped it up. I didn't have the heart to try her. My own girl was about thirty and took care of herself better. With Venezuela writhing and suffering in my arms, I had a longing to take her in the back and undress her and only talk to her—this I told myself. I was delirious with want of her and the other little dark girl.

Poor Victor, all this time he stood on the brass rail of the bar with his back to the counter and jumped up and down gladly to see his three American friends cavort. We bought him drinks. His eyes gleamed for a woman but he wouldn't accept any, being faithful to his wife. Dean thrust money at him. In this welter of madness I had an opportunity to see what Dean was up to. He was so out of his mind he didn't know who I was when I peered at his face. "Yeah, yeah!" is all he said. It seemed it would never end. It was like a long, spectral Arabian dream in the afternoon in another life—Ali Baba and the alleys and the courtesans. Again I rushed off with my girl to her room; Dean and Stan switched the girls they'd had before; and we were out of sight a moment, and the spectators had to wait for the show to go on. The afternoon grew long and cool.

Soon it would be mysterious night in old gone Gregoria. The mambo never let up for a moment, it frenzied on like an endless journey in the jungle. I couldn't take my eyes off the little dark girl and the way, like a queen, she walked around and was even reduced by the sullen bartender to menial tasks such as bringing us drinks and sweeping the back. Of all the girls in there she needed the money most; maybe her mother had come to get money from her for her little infant sisters and brothers. Mexicans are poor. It never, never occurred to me just to approach her and give her some money. I have a feeling she would have taken it with a degree of scorn, and scorn from the likes of her made me flinch. In my madness I was actually in love with her for the few hours it all lasted; it was the same unmistakable ache and stab across the mind, the same sighs, the same pain, and above all the same reluctance and fear to approach. Strange that Dean and Stan also failed to approach her; her unimpeachable dignity was the thing that made her poor in a wild old whorehouse, and think of that. At one point I saw Dean leaning like a statue toward her, ready to fly, and befuddlement cross his face as she glanced coolly and imperiously his way and he stopped rubbing his belly and gaped and finally bowed his head. For she was the queen.

Now Victor suddenly clutched at our arms in the furor and made frantic signs.

"What's the matter?" He tried everything to make us understand. Then he ran to the bar and grabbed the check from the bartender, who scowled at him, and took it to us to see. The bill was over three hundred pesos, or thirty-six American dollars, which is a lot of money in any whore-house. Still we couldn't sober up and didn't want to leave, and though we were all run out we still wanted to hang around with our lovely girls in this strange Arabian paradise we had finally found at the end of the hard, hard road. But night was coming and we had to get on to the end; and Dean saw that, and began frowning and thinking and trying to straighten himself out, and finally I broached the idea of leaving once and for all. "So much ahead of us, man, it won't make any difference."

"That's right!" cried Dean, glassy-eyed, and turned to his Venezuelan. She had finally passed out and lay on a wooden bench with her white legs protruding from the silk. The gallery in the window took advantage of the show; behind them red shadows were beginning to creep, and somewhere I heard a baby wail in a sudden lull, remembering I was in Mexico after all and not in a pornographic hasheesh day-dream in heaven.

We staggered out; we had forgotten Stan; we ran back in to get him and found him charmingly bowing to the new evening whores, who had just come in for night shift. He wanted to start all over again. When he is drunk he lumbers like a man ten feet tall and when he is drunk he can't be dragged away from women. Moreover women cling to him like ivy. He insisted on staying and trying some of the newer, stranger, more proficient señoritas. Dean and I pounded him on the back and dragged him out. He waved profuse good-bys to everybody—the girls, the cops, the crowds, the children in the street outside; he blew kisses in all directions to ovations of Gregoria and staggered proudly among the gangs and tried to speak to them and communicate his joy and love of everything this fine afternoon of life. Everybody laughed; some slapped him on the back. Dean rushed over and paid the policemen the four pesos and shook hands and grinned and bowed with them. Then he jumped in the car, and the girls we had known, even Venezuela, who was wakened for the farewell, gathered around the car, huddling in their flimsy duds, and chattered good-bys and kissed us, and Venezuela even began to weep—though not for us, we knew, not altogether for us, yet enough and good enough. My dusky darling love had disappeared in the shadows inside. It was all over. We pulled out and left joys and celebrations over hundreds of pesos behind us, and it didn't seem like a bad day's work. The haunting mambo followed us a few blocks. It was all over. "Good-by, Gregoria!" cried Dean, blowing it a kiss.

Victor was proud of us and proud of himself. "Now you like bath?" he asked. Yes, we all wanted wonderful bath.

And he directed us to the strangest thing in the world: it was an ordinary American-type bathhouse one mile out of town on the highway, full of kids splashing in a pool and showers inside a stone building for a few centavos a crack, with soap and towel from the attendant. Besides this, it was also a sad kiddy park with swings and a broken-down merry-go-round, and in the fading red sun it seemed so strange and so beautiful. Stan and I got towels and jumped right into ice-cold showers inside and came out refreshed and new. Dean didn't bother with a shower, and we saw him far across the sad park, strolling arm in arm with good Victor and chatting volubly and pleasantly and even leaning excitedly toward him to make a point, and pounding his fist. Then they resumed the arm-in-arm position and strolled. The time was coming to say good-by to Victor, so Dean was taking the opportunity to have moments alone with him and to inspect the park and get his views on things in general and in all dig him as only Dean could do.

Victor was very sad now that we had to go. "You come back Gregoria, see me?"

"Sure, man!" said Dean. He even promised to take Victor back to the States if he so wished it. Victor said he would have to mull this over.

"I got wife and kid—ain't got a money—I see." His sweet polite smile glowed in the redness as we waved to him from the car. Behind him were the sad park and the children.

ONE DASH—HORSES

Stephen Crane

RICHARDSON PULLED UP HIS HORSE and looked back over the trail, where the crimson serape of his servant flamed amid the dusk of the mesquite. The hills in the west were carved into peaks, and were painted the most profound blue. Above them, the sky was of that marvelous tone of green—like still, sun-shot water—which people denounce in pictures.

José was muffled deep in his blanket, and his great toppling sombrero was drawn low over his brow. He shadowed his master along the dimming trail in the fashion of an assassin. A cold wind of the impending night swept over the wilderness of mesquite.

"Man," said Richardson, in lame Mexican, as the servant drew near, "I want eat! I want sleep! Understand—no? Quickly! Understand?"

"Si, señor," said José, nodding. He stretched one arm out of his blanket, and pointed a yellow finger into the gloom. "Over there, small village! Si, señor."

They rode forward again. Once the American's horse shied and breathed quiveringly at something which he saw or imagined in the darkness, and the rider drew a steady, patient rein and leaned over to speak tenderly, as if he were addressing a frightened woman. The sky had faded to white over the mountains, and the plain was a vast, pointless ocean of black.

Suddenly some low houses appeared squatting amid the bushes. The horsemen rode into a hollow until the houses rose against the somber sundown sky, and then up a small hillock, causing these habitations to sink like boats in the sea of shadow.

A beam of red firelight fell across the trail. Richardson sat sleepily on his horse while the servant quarreled with somebody—a mere voice in the gloom—over the price of bed and board. The houses about him were for the most part like tombs in their whiteness and silence, but there were scudding black figures that seemed interested in his arrival.

José came at last to the horses' heads, and the American slid stiffly from his seat. He muttered a greeting, as with his spurred feet he clicked into the adobe house that confronted him. The brown, stolid face of a woman shone in the light of the fire. He seated himself on the earthen floor, and blinked drowsily at the blaze. He was aware that the woman was clinking earthenware, and hieing here and everywhere in the maneuvers of the housewife. From a dark corner of the room there came the sound of two or three snores twining together.

The woman handed him a bowl of tortillas. She was a submissive creature, timid and large-eyed. She gazed at his enormous silver spurs, his large and impressive revolver, with the interest and admiration of the highly privileged cat of the adage. When he ate, she seemed transfixed off there in the gloom, her white teeth shining.

José entered, staggering under two Mexican saddles large enough for building sites. Richardson decided to smoke

Stephen Crane

a cigarette, and then changed his mind. It would be much finer to go to sleep. His blanket hung over his left shoulder, furled into a long pipe of cloth, according to a Mexican fashion. By doffing his sombrero, unfastening his spurs and his revolver belt, he made himself ready for the slow, blissful twist into the blanket. Like a cautious man, he lay close to the wall, and all his property was very near his hand.

The mesquite brush burned long. José threw two gigantic wings of shadow as he flapped his blanket about him—first across his chest under his arms, and then around his neck and across his chest again, this time over his arms, with the end tossed on his right shoulder. A Mexican thus snugly enveloped can nevertheless free his fighting arm in a beautifully brisk way, merely shrugging his shoulder as he grabs for the weapon at his belt. They always wear their serapes in this manner.

The firelight smothered the rays which, streaming from a moon as large as a drumhead, were struggling at the open door. Richardson heard from the plain the fine, rhythmical trample of the hoofs of hurried horses. He went to sleep wondering who rode so fast and so late. And in the deep silence the pale rays of the moon must have prevailed against the red spears of the fire until the room was slowly flooded to its middle with a rectangle of silver light.

Richardson was awakened by the sound of a guitar. It was badly played—in this land of Mexico, from which the romance of the instrument ascends to us like a perfume. The guitar was groaning and whining like a badgered soul. A noise of scuffling feet accompanied the music. Sometimes laughter arose, and often the voices of men saying bitter things to each other; but always the guitar cried on, the treble

197

sounding as if some one were beating iron, and the bass humming like bees.

"Damn it! they're having a dance," muttered Richardson, fretfully. He heard two men quarreling in short, sharp words like pistol shots; they were calling each other worse names than common people know in other countries.

He wondered why the noise was so loud. Raising his head from his saddle pillow, he saw, with the help of the valiant moonbeams, a blanket hanging flat against the wall at the farther end of the room. Being of the opinion that it concealed a door, and remembering that Mexican drink made men very drunk, he pulled his revolver closer to him and prepared for sudden disaster.

Richardson was dreaming of his far and beloved North.

"Well, I would kill him, then!"

"No, you must not!"

"Yes, I will kill him! Listen! I will ask this American beast for his beautiful pistol and spurs and money and saddle, and if he will not give them—you will see!"

"But these Americans—they are a strange people. Look out, señor."

Then twenty voices took part in the discussion. They rose in quivering shrillness, as from men badly drunk.

Richardson felt the skin draw tight around his mouth, and his knee joints turned to bread. He slowly came to a sitting posture, glaring at the motionless blanket at the far end of the room. This stiff and mechanical movement, accomplished entirely by the muscles of the wrist, must have looked like the rising of a corpse in the wan moonlight, which gave everything a hue of the grave.

My friend, take my advice, and never be executed by a

hangman who doesn't talk the English language. It, or anything that resembles it, is the most difficult of deaths. The tumultuous emotions of Richardson's terror destroyed that slow and careful process of thought by means of which he understood Mexican. Then he used his instinctive comprehension of the first and universal language, which is tone. Still, it is disheartening not to be able to understand the detail of threats against the blood of your body.

Suddenly the clamor of voices ceased. There was a silence—a silence of decision. The blanket was flung aside, and the red light of a torch flared into the room. It was held high by a fat, round-faced Mexican, whose little snake-like mustache was as black as his eyes, and whose eyes were black as jet. He was insane with the wild rage of a man whose liquor is dully burning at his brain. Five or six of his fellows crowded after him. The guitar, which had been thrummed doggedly during the time of the high words, now suddenly stopped.

They contemplated each other. Richardson sat very straight and still, his right hand lost in the folds of his blanket. The Mexicans jostled in the light of the torch, their eyes blinking and glittering.

The fat one posed in the manner of a grandee. Presently his hand dropped to his belt, and from his lips there spun an epithet—a hideous word which often foreshadows knife-blows, a word peculiarly of Mexico, where people have to dig deep to find an insult that has not lost its savor.

The American did not move. He was staring at the fat Mexican with a strange fixedness of gaze, not fearful, not dauntless, not anything that could be interpreted; he simply stared.

The fat Mexican must have been disconcerted, for he continued to pose as a grandee with more and more sublimity, until it would have been easy for him to fall over backward. His companions were swaying in a very drunken manner. They still blinked their beady eyes at Richardson. Ah, well, sirs, here was a mystery. At the approach of their menacing company, why did not this American cry out and turn pale, or run, or pray them mercy? The animal merely sat still, and stared, and waited for them to begin. Well, evidently he was a great fighter; or perhaps he was an idiot. Indeed, this was an embarrassing situation, for who was going forward to discover whether he was a great fighter or an idiot?

To Richardson, whose nerves were tingling and twitching like live wires, and whose heart jolted inside him, this pause was a long horror; and for these men who could so frighten him there began to swell in him a fierce hatred—a hatred that made him long to be capable of fighting all of them, a hatred that made him capable of fighting all of them. A 44-caliber revolver can make a hole large enough for little boys to shoot marbles through, and there was a certain fat Mexican, with a mustache like a snake, who came extremely near to have eaten his last tamale merely because he frightened a man too much.

José had slept the first part of the night in his fashion, his body hunched into a heap, his legs crooked, his head touching his knees. Shadows had obscured him from the sight of the invaders. At this point he arose, and began to prowl quakingly over toward Richardson, as if he meant to hide behind him.

Of a sudden the fat Mexican gave a howl of glee. José had come within the torch's circle of light. With roars of singular ferocity the whole group of Mexicans pounced on the American's servant.

He shrank shuddering away from them, beseeching by every device of word and gesture. They pushed him this way and that. They beat him with their fists. They stung him with their curses. As he groveled on his knees, the fat Mexican took him by the throat and said: "I'm going to kill you!" And continually they turned their eyes to see if they were to succeed in causing the initial demonstration by the American.

Richardson looked on impassively. Under the blanket, however, his fingers were clenched as rigidly as iron upon the handle of his revolver.

Here suddenly two brilliant clashing chords from the guitar were heard, and a woman's voice, full of laughter and confidence, cried from without: "Hello! hello! Where are you?"

The lurching company of Mexicans instantly paused and looked at the ground. One said, as he stood with his legs wide apart in order to balance himself: "It is the girls! They have come!" He screamed in answer to the question of the woman: "Here!" And without waiting he started on a pilgrimage toward the blanket-covered door. One could now hear a number of female voices giggling and chattering.

Two other Mexicans said: "Yes; it is the girls! Yes!" They also started quietly away. Even the fat Mexican's ferocity seemed to be affected. He looked uncertainly at the still immovable American. Two of his friends grasped him gaily. "Come, the girls are here! Come!" He cast another glower at Richardson. "But this—" he began. Laughing, his comrades hustled him toward the door. On its threshold, and holding back the blanket with one hand, he turned his yellow face with a last challenging glare toward the American. José, bewailing his state in little sobs of utter despair and woe, crept to Richardson and huddled near his knee. Then the cries of the Mexicans meeting the girls were heard, and the guitar burst out in joyous humming.

The moon clouded, and but a faint square of light fell through the open main door of the house. The coals of the fire were silent save for occasional sputters. Richardson did not change his position. He remained staring at the blanket which hid the strategic door in the far end. At his knees José was arguing, in a low, aggrieved tone, with the saints. Without, the Mexicans laughed and danced, and—it would appear from the sound—drank more.

In the stillness and night Richardson sat wondering if some serpent-like Mexican was sliding toward him in the darkness, and if the first thing he knew of it would be the deadly sting of the knife. "Sssh," he whispered to José. He drew his revolver from under the blanket and held it on his leg.

The blanket over the door fascinated him. It was a vague form, black and unmoving. Through the opening it shielded was to come, probably, menace, death. Sometimes he thought he saw it move.

As grim white sheets, the black and silver of coffins, all the panoply of death, affect us because of that which they hide, so this blanket, dangling before a hole in an adobe wall, was to Richardson a horrible emblem, and a horrible thing in itself. In his present mood Richardson could not have been brought to touch it with his finger.

The celebrating Mexicans occasionally howled in song. The guitarist played with speed and enthusiasm.

Richardson longed to run. But in this threatening gloom, his terror convinced him that a move on his part would be a signal for the pounce of death. José, crouching abjectly, occasionally mumbled. Slowly and ponderous as stars the minutes went.

Suddenly Richardson thrilled and started. His breath, for a moment, left him. In sleep his nerveless fingers had allowed his revolver to fall and clang upon the hard floor. He grabbed it up hastily, and his glance swept apprehensively over the room.

A chill blue light of dawn was in the place. Every outline was slowly growing; detail was following detail. The dread blanket did not move. The riotous company had gone or become silent.

Richardson felt in his blood the effect of this cold dawn. The candor of breaking day brought his nerve. He touched José. "Come," he said. His servant lifted his lined, yellow face and comprehended. Richardson buckled on his spurs and strode up; José obediently lifted the two great saddles. Richardson held two bridles and a blanket on his left arm; in his right hand he held his revolver. They sneaked toward the door.

The man who said that spurs jingled was insane. Spurs have a mellow clash—clash—clash. Walking in spurs— notably Mexican spurs—you remind yourself vaguely of a telegraphic lineman. Richardson was inexpressibly shocked when he came to walk. He sounded to himself like a pair of cymbals. He would have known of this if he had reflected; but then he was escaping, not reflecting. He made a gesture of despair, and from under the two saddles José tried to make one of hopeless horror. Richardson stooped, and with shaking fingers unfastened the spurs. Taking them in his left hand, he picked up his revolver, and they slunk on toward the door.

On the threshold Richardson looked back. In a corner he saw, watching him with large eyes, the Indian man and woman who had been his hosts. Throughout the night they had made no sign, and now they neither spoke nor moved. Yet Richardson thought he detected meek satisfaction at his departure.

The street was still and deserted. In the eastern sky there was a lemon-colored patch.

José had picketed the horses at the side of the house. As the two men came around the corner, Richardson's animal set up a whinny of welcome. The little horse had evidently heard them coming. He stood facing them, his ears cocked forward, his eyes bright with welcome.

Richardson made a frantic gesture, but the horse, in his happiness at the appearance of his friends, whinnied with enthusiasm.

The American felt at this time that he could have strangled his well-beloved steed. Upon the threshold of safety he was being betrayed by his horse, his friend. He felt the same hate for the horse that he would have felt for a dragon. And yet, as he glanced wildly about him, he could see nothing stirring in the street, nor at the doors of the tomb-like houses.

José had his own saddle girth and both bridles buckled in a moment. He curled the picket ropes with a few sweeps of his arm. The fingers of Richardson, however, were shaking so that he could hardly buckle the girth. His hands were in invisible mittens. He was wondering, calculating, hoping about his horse. He knew the little animal's willingness and courage under all circumstances up to this time, but then— here it was different. Who could tell if some wretched instance of equine perversity was not about to develop? Maybe the little fellow would not feel like smoking over the plain at express speed this morning, and so he would rebel and kick and be wicked. Maybe he would be without feeling of interest, and run listlessly. All men who have had to hurry in the saddle know what it is to be on a horse who does not understand the dramatic situation. Riding a lame sheep is bliss to it. Richardson, fumbling furiously at the girth, thought of these things.

Presently he had it fastened. He swung into the saddle, and as he did so his horse made a mad jump forward. The spurs of José scratched and tore the flanks of his great black animal, and side by side the two horses raced down the village street. The American heard his horse breathe a quivering sigh of excitement.

Those four feet skimmed. They were as light as fairy puffballs. The houses of the village glided past in a moment, and the great, clear, silent plain appeared like a pale blue sea of mist and wet bushes. Above the mountains the colors of the sunlight were like the first tones, the opening chords, of the mighty hymn of the morning.

The American looked down at his horse. He felt in his heart the first thrill of confidence. The little animal, unurged and quite tranquil, moving his ears this way and that way with an air of interest in the scenery, was nevertheless bounding into the eye of the breaking day with the speed of a frightened antelope. Richardson, looking down, saw the long, fine reach of forelimb as steady as steel machinery. As the ground reeled past, the long dried grasses hissed, and cactus plants were dull blurs. A wind whirled the horse's mane over his rider's bridle hand.

José's profile was lined against the pale sky. It was as that of a man who swims alone in an ocean. His eyes glinted like metal fastened on some unknown point ahead of him, some mystic place of safety. Occasionally his mouth puckered in a little unheard cry; and his legs, bent back, worked spasmodically as his spurred heels sliced the flanks of his charger.

Richardson consulted the gloom in the west for signs of a hard-riding, yelling cavalcade. He knew that, whereas his friends the enemy had not attacked him when he had sat still and with apparent calmness confronted them, they would certainly take furiously after him now that he had run from them—now that he had confessed to them that he was the weaker. Their valor would grow like weeds in the spring, and upon discovering his escape they would ride forth dauntless warriors.

Sometimes he was sure he saw them. Sometimes he was sure he heard them. Continually looking backward over his shoulder, he studied the purple expanses where the night was marching away. José rolled and shuddered in his saddle, persistently disturbing the stride of the black horse, fretting and worrying him until the white foam flew and the great shoulders shone like satin from the sweat.

At last Richardson drew his horse carefully down to a walk. José wished to rush insanely on, but the American spoke to him sternly. As the two paced forward side by side, Richardson's little horse thrust over his soft nose and inquired into the black's condition.

Riding with José was like riding with a corpse. His face resembled a cast in lead. Sometimes he swung forward and almost pitched from his seat. Richardson was too frightened himself to do anything but hate this man for his fear. Finally he issued a mandate which nearly caused José's eyes to slide out of his head and fall to the ground like two silver coins.

"Ride behind me—about fifty paces."

"Señor— —" stuttered the servant.

"Go!" cried the American, furiously. He glared at the other and laid his hand on his revolver. José looked at his master wildly. He made a piteous gesture. Then slowly he fell back, watching the hard face of the American for a sign of mercy.

Richardson had resolved in his rage that at any rate he was going to use the eyes and ears of extreme fear to detect the approach of danger; and so he established his servant as a sort of outpost.

As they proceeded he was obliged to watch sharply to see that the servant did not slink forward and join him. When José made beseeching circles in the air with his arm he replied by menacingly gripping his revolver.

José had a revolver, too; nevertheless it was very clear in his mind that the revolver was distinctly an American weapon. He had been educated in the Rio Grande country.

Richardson lost the trail once. He was recalled to it by the loud sobs of his servant.

Then at last José came clattering forward, gesticulating and wailing. The little horse sprang to the shoulder of the black. They were off.

Richardson, again looking backward, could see a slanting flare of dust on the whitening plain. He thought that he could detect small moving figures in it.

José's moans and cries amounted to a university course in theology. They broke continually from his quivering lips. His spurs were as motors. They forced the black horse over the plain in great headlong leaps.

But under Richardson there was a little insignificant rat-colored beast who was running apparently with almost as much effort as it requires for a bronze statute to stand still. As a matter of truth, the ground seemed merely something to be touched from time to time with hoofs that were as light as blown leaves. Occasionally Richardson lay back and pulled stoutly at his bridle to keep from abandoning his servant.

José harried at his horse's mouth, flopped around in the saddle, and made his two heels beat like flails. The black ran like a horse in despair.

Crimson serapes in the distance resemble drops of blood on the great cloth of plain.

Richardson began to dream of all possible chances. Although quite a humane man, he did not once think of his servant. José being a Mexican, it was natural that he should be killed in Mexico; but for himself, a New Yorker— —

He remembered all the tales of such races for life, and he thought them badly written.

The great black horse was growing indifferent. The jabs of José's spurs no longer caused him to bound forward in wild leaps of pain. José had at last succeeded in teaching him that spurring was to be expected, speed or no speed, and now he took the pain of it dully and stolidly, as an animal who finds that doing his best gains him no respite.

José was turned into a raving maniac. He bellowed and screamed, working his arms and his heels like one in a fit. He resembled a man on a sinking ship, who appeals to the ship. Richardson, too, cried madly to the black horse.

The spirit of the horse responded to these calls, and, quivering and breathing heavily, he made a great effort, a sort of final rush, not for himself apparently, but because he understood that his life's sacrifice, perhaps, had been invoked by these two men who cried to him in the universal tongue. Richardson had no sense of appreciation at this time—he was too frightened—but often now he remembers a certain black horse.

From the rear could be heard a yelling, and once a shot was fired—in the air, evidently. Richardson moaned as he looked back. He kept his hand on his revolver. He tried to imagine the brief tumult of his capture—the flurry of dust from the hoofs of horses pulled suddenly to their haunches, the shrill, biting curses of the men, the ring of the shots, his own last contortion. He wondered, too, if he could not somehow manage to pelt that fat Mexican, just to cure his abominable egotism.

It was José, the terror-stricken, who at last discovered safety. Suddenly he gave a howl of delight, and astonished his horse into a new burst of speed. They were on a little ridge at the time, and the American at the top of it saw his servant gallop down the slope and into the arms, so to speak, of a small column of horsemen in gray and silver clothes. In the dim light of the early morning they were as vague as shadows, but Richardson knew them at once for a detachment of rurales, that crack cavalry corps of the Mexican army which polices the plain so zealously, being of themselves the law and the arm of it—a fierce and swift-moving body that knows little of prevention, but much of vengeance. They drew up suddenly, and the rows of great silver-trimmed sombreros bobbed in surprise.

Richardson saw José throw himself from his horse and begin to jabber at the leader of the party. When he arrived he found that his servant had already outlined the entire situation, and was then engaged in describing him, Richardson, as an American señor of vast wealth, who was the friend of almost every governmental potentate within two hundred miles. This seemed to profoundly impress the officer. He bowed gravely to Richardson and smiled significantly at his men, who unslung their carbines.

The little ridge hid the pursuers from view, but the rapid thud of their horses' feet could be heard. Occasionally they yelled and called to each other.

Then at last they swept over the brow of the hill, a wild mob of almost fifty drunken horsemen. When they discerned the pale-uniformed rurales, they were sailing down the slope at top speed.

If toboggans halfway down a hill should suddenly make up their minds to turn around and go back, there would be an effect somewhat like that now produced by the drunken horsemen. Richardson saw the rurales serenely swing their carbines forward, and, peculiar-minded person that he was, felt his heart leap into his throat at the prospective volley. But the officer rode forward alone.

It appeared that the man who owned the best horse in this astonished company was the fat Mexican with the snaky mustache, and, in consequence, this gentleman was quite a distance in the van. He tried to pull up, wheel his horse, and scuttle back over the hill as some of his companions had done, but the officer called to him in a voice harsh with rage.

"——!" howled the officer. "This señor is my friend, the friend of my friends. Do you dare pursue him, — —?— —! — —!— —!— —!" These lines represent terrible names, all different, used by the officer.

The fat Mexican simply groveled on his horse's neck. His face was green; it could be seen that he expected death.

The officer stormed with magnificent intensity: "——!
——!——!"

Finally he sprang from his saddle and, running to the fat Mexican's side, yelled: "Go!" and kicked the horse in the belly with all his might. The animal gave a mighty leap into the air, and the fat Mexican, with one wretched glance at the contemplative rurales, aimed his steed for the top of the ridge. Richards again gulped in expectation of a volley, for, it is said, this is one of the favorite methods of the rurales for disposing of objectionable people. The fat, green Mexican also evidently thought that he was to be killed while on the run, from the miserable look he cast at the troops. Nevertheless, he was allowed to vanish in a cloud of yellow dust at the ridgetop.

José was exultant, defiant, and, oh! bristling with courage. The black horse was drooping sadly, his nose to the ground. Richardson's little animal, with his ears bent forward, was staring at the horses of the rurales as if in an intense study. Richardson longed for speech, but he could only bend forward and pat the shining, silken shoulders. The little horse turned his head and looked back gravely.

Under the Volcano
Malcolm Lowry

Two MOUNTAIN CHAINS TRAVERSE the republic roughly from
north to south, forming between them a number of valleys
and plateaus. Overlooking one of these valleys, which is
dominated by two volcanoes, lies, six thousand feet above
sea level, the town of Quauhnahuac. It is situated well south
of the Tropic of Cancer, to be exact on the nineteenth parallel,
in about the same latitude as the Revillagigedo Islands to the
west in the Pacific, or very much further west, the southern-
most tip of Hawaii—and as the port of Tzucox to the east on
the Atlantic seaboard of Yucatan near the border of British
Honduras, or very much further east, the town of Juggernaut,
in India, on the Bay of Bengal.

The walls of the town, which is built on a hill, are high,
the streets and lanes tortuous and broken, the roads winding. A fine American-style highway leads in from the north
but is lost in its narrow streets and comes out a goat track.
Quauhnahuac possesses eighteen churches and fifty-seven
cantinas. It also boasts a golf course and no less than four
hundred swimming pools, public and private, filled with the
water that ceaselessly pours down from the mountains, and
many splendid hotels.

The Hotel Casino de la Selva stands on a slightly higher

hill just outside the town, near the railway station. It is built far back from the main highway and surrounded by gardens and terraces which command a spacious view in every direction. Palatial, a certain air of desolate splendour pervades it. For it is no longer a Casino. You may not even dice for drinks in the bar. The ghosts of ruined gamblers haunt it. No one ever seems to swim in the magnificent Olympic pool. The springboards stand empty and mournful. Its jai-alai courts are grass-grown and deserted. Two tennis courts only are kept up in the season.

Towards sunset on the Day of the Dead in November, 1939, two men in white flannels sat on the main terrace of the Casino drinking anís. They had been playing tennis, followed by billiards, and the racquets, rainproofed, screwed in their presses—the doctor's triangular, the other's quadrangular—lay on the parapet before them. As the processions winding from the cemetery down the hillside behind the hotel came closer the plangent sounds of their chanting were borne to the two men; they turned to watch the mourners, a little later to be visible only as the melancholy lights of their candles, circling among the distant, trussed cornstalks. Dr. Arturo Díaz Vigil pushed the bottle of Anís del Mono over to M. Jacques Laruelle, who now was leaning forward intently.

Slightly to the right and below them, below the gigantic red evening, whose reflection bled away in the deserted swimming pools scattered everywhere like so many mirages, lay the peace and sweetness of the town. It seemed peaceful enough from where they were sitting. Only if one listened intently, as M. Laruelle was doing now, could one distinguish a remote confused sound—distinct yet somehow inseparable from the minute murmuring, the tintinnabulation of the mourners—as of singing, rising and falling, and a steady trampling—the bangs and cries of the fiesta that had been going on all day.

M. Laruelle poured himself another anís. He was drinking anís because it reminded him of absinthe. A deep flush had suffused his face, and his hand trembled slightly over the bottle, from whose label a florid demon brandished a pitchfork at him.

"—I meant to persuade him to go away and get dealcoholisé," Dr. Vigil was saying. He stumbled over the word in French and continued in English. "But I was so sick myself that day after the ball that I suffer, physical, really. That is very bad, for we doctors must comport ourselves like apostles. You remember, we played tennis that day too. Well, after I looked the Consul in his garden I sended a boy down to see if he would come for a few minutes and knock my door, I would appreciate it to him, if not, please write me a note, if drinking have not killed him already."

M. Laruelle smiled.

"But they have gone," the other went on, "and yes, I think to ask you too that day if you had looked him at his house."

"He was at my house when you telephoned, Arturo."

"Oh, I know, but we got so horrible drunkness that night before, so perfectamente borracho, that it seems to me, the Consul is as sick as I am." Dr. Vigil shook his head. "Sickness is not only in body, but in that part used to be call: soul. Poor your friend, he spend his money on earth in such continuous tragedies."

M. Laruelle finished his drink. He rose and went to the parapet; resting his hands one on each tennis racquet, he gazed down and around him: the abandoned jai-alai courts, their bastions covered with grass, the dead tennis courts, the fountain, quite near in the centre of the hotel avenue, where a cactus farmer had reined up his horse to drink. Two young Americans, a boy and a girl, had started a belated game of ping-pong on the verandah of the annex below. What had happened just a year ago to-day seemed already to belong in a different age. One would have thought the horrors of the present would have swallowed it up like a drop of water. It was not so. Though tragedy was in the process of becoming unreal and meaningless it seemed one was still permitted to remember the days when an individual life held some value and was not a mere misprint in a communiqué. He lit a cigarette. Far to his left, in the northeast, beyond the valley and the terraced foothills of the Sierra Madre Oriental, the two volcanoes, Popocatepetl and Ixtaccihuatl, rose clear and magnificent into the sunset. Nearer, perhaps ten miles distant, and on a lower level than the main valley, he made out the village of Tomalín, nestling behind the jungle, from which rose a thin blue scarf of illegal smoke, someone burning wood for carbon. Before him, on the other side of the American highway, spread fields and groves, through which meandered a river, and the Alcapancingo road. The watchtower of a prison rose over a wood between the river and the road which lost itself further on where the purple hills of a Doré Paradise sloped away into the distance. Over in the town the lights of Quauhnahuac's one cinema, built on an incline and standing out sharply, suddenly came on, flickered off, came on again. "No se puede vivir sin amar," M. Laruelle said . . . "As that estúpido inscribed on my house."

"Come, amigo, throw away your mind," Dr. Vigil said behind him.

"—But hombre, Yvonne came back! That's what I shall never understand. She came back to the man!" M. Laruelle returned to the table where he poured himself and drank a glass of Tehuacan mineral water. He said:

"Salud y pesetas."

"Y tiempo para gastarlas," his friend returned thoughtfully.

M. Laruelle watched the doctor leaning back in the steamer chair, yawning, the handsome, impossibly handsome, dark, imperturbable Mexican face, the kind deep brown eyes, innocent too, like the eyes of those wistful beautiful Oaxaqueñan children one saw in Tehuantepec (that ideal spot where the women did the work while the men bathed in the river all day), the slender small hands and delicate wrists, upon the back of which it was almost a shock to see the sprinkling of coarse black hair. "I threw away my mind long ago, Arturo," he said in English, withdrawing his cigarette from his mouth with refined nervous fingers on which he was aware he wore too many rings. "What I find more—" M. Laruelle noted the cigarette was out and gave himself another anís.

"Con permiso." Dr. Vigil conjured a flaring lighter out of his pocket so swiftly it seemed it must have been already ignited there, that he had drawn a flame out of himself, the gesture and the igniting one movement; he held the light for M. Laruelle. "Did you never go to the church for the bereavèd here," he asked suddenly, "where is the Virgin for those who have nobody with?"

M. Laruelle shook his head.

"Nobody go there. Only those who have nobody them with," the doctor said, slowly. He pocketed the lighter and looked at his watch, turning his wrist upwards with a neat flick. "Allon-nous-en," he added, "vámonos," and laughed yawningly with a series of nods that seemed to carry his body forward until his head was resting between his hands. Then he rose and joined M. Laruelle at the parapet, drawing deep breaths. "Ah, but this is the hour I love, with the sun coming down, when all the man began to sing and all the dogs to shark—"

M. Laruelle laughed. While they had been talking the sky had grown wild and stormy to the south; the mourners had left the slope of the hill. Sleepy vultures, high overhead, deployed downwind. "About eight-thirty then, I might go to the cine for an hour."

"Bueno. I will see you this night then, in the place where you know. Remember, I still do not believe you are leaving to-morrow." He held out his hand which M. Laruelle grasped firmly, loving him. "Try and come to-night, if not, please understand I am always interested in your health."

"Hasta la vista."

"Hasta la vista."

—Alone, standing beside the highway down which he had driven four years before on the last mile of that long, insane, beautiful journey from Los Angeles, M. Laruelle also found it hard to believe he was really going. Then the thought of to-morrow seemed well-nigh overwhelming. He had paused, undecided which way to walk home, as the little overloaded bus, Tomalín: Zócalo, jounced past him downhill toward the barranca before climbing into Quauhnahuac. He was loth to take that same direction to-night. He crossed the street, making for the station. Although he would not be traveling by train the sense of departure, of its imminence, came heavily about him again as, childishly avoiding the locked points, he picked his path over the narrow-gauge lines. Light from the setting sun glanced off the oiltanks on the grass embankment beyond. The platform slept. The tracks were vacant, the signals up. There was little to suggest any train ever arrived at this station, let alone left it:

Quauhnahuac

Yet a little less than a year ago the place had been the scene of a parting he would never forget. He had not liked the Consul's half-brother at their first encounter when he'd come with Yvonne and the Consul himself to M. Laruelle's house in the Calle Nicaragua, any more, he felt now, than Hugh had liked him. Hugh's odd appearance—though such was the overwhelming effect of meeting Yvonne again, he did not obtain even the impression of oddity so strongly that he was able later in Parián immediately to recognize him— had merely seemed to caricature the Consul's amiable half-bitter description of him. So this was the child M. Laruelle vaguely remembered hearing about years before! In half an hour he'd dismissed him as an irresponsible bore, a professional indoor Marxman, vain and self-conscious really, but affecting a romantic extroverted air. While Hugh, who for various reasons had certainly not been "prepared" by the Consul to meet M. Laruelle, doubtless saw him as an even more precious type of bore, the elderly aesthete, a confirmedly promiscuous bachelor, with a rather unctuous possessive manner toward women. But three sleepless nights later an eternity had been lived through: grief and bewilderment at an unassimilable catastrophe had drawn them together. In the hours which followed his response to Hugh's telephone call from Parián M. Laruelle learned much about Hugh: his hopes, his fears, his self-deceptions, his despairs. When Hugh left, it was as if he had lost a son.

Careless of his tennis clothes, M. Laruelle climbed the embankment. Yet he was right, he told himself, as reaching the top he paused for breath, right, after the Consul had been "discovered" (though meantime the grotesquely pathetic situation had developed where there was not, on probably the first occasion when one had been so urgently needed, a British Consul in Quauhnahuac to appeal to), right in insisting Hugh should waive all conventional scruples and take every advantage of the curious reluctance of the "police" to hold him—their anxiety, it all but appeared, to be rid of him just when it seemed highly logical they should detain him as a witness, at least in one aspect of what now at a distance one could almost refer to as the "case" —and at the earliest possible moment join that ship providentially awaiting him at Vera Cruz. M. Laruelle looked back at the station; Hugh left a gap. In a sense he had decamped with the last of his illusions. For Hugh, at twenty-nine, still dreamed, even then, of changing the world (there was no other way of saying this) through his actions—just as Laruelle, at forty-two, had still then not quite given up hope of changing it through the great films he proposed somehow to make. But to-day these dreams seemed absurd and presumptuous. After all he had made great films as great films went in the past. And so far as he knew they had not changed the world in the slightest. — However he had acquired a certain identity with Hugh. Like Hugh he was going to Vera Cruz; and like Hugh too, he did not know if his ship would ever reach port . . .

M. Laruelle's way led through half-cultivated fields bordered by narrow grass paths, trodden by cactus farmers coming home from work. It was thus far a favorite walk, though not taken since before the rains. The leaves of cacti attracted with their freshness; green trees shot by evening sunlight might have been weeping willows tossing in the gusty wind which had sprung up; a lake of yellow sunlight appeared in the distance below pretty hills like loaves. But there was something baleful now about the evening. Black clouds plunged up to the south. The sun poured molten glass on the fields. The volcanoes seemed terrifying in the wild sunset. M. Laruelle walked swiftly, in the good heavy tennis shoes he should have already packed, swinging his tennis racquet. A sense of fear had possessed him again, a sense of being, after all these years, and on his last day here, still a stranger. Four years, almost five, and he still felt like a wanderer on another planet. Not that that made it any the less hard to be leaving, even though he would soon, God willing, see Paris again. Ah well! He had few emotions about the war, save that it was bad. One side or the other would win. And in either case life would be hard. Though if the Allies lost it would be harder. And in either case one's own battle would go on.

How continually, how startlingly, the landscape changed! Now the fields were full of stones: there was a row of dead trees. An abandoned plough, silhouetted against the sky, raised its arms to heaven in mute supplication; another planet, he reflected again, a strange planet where, if you looked a little further, beyond the Tres Marías, you would find every sort of landscape at once, the Cotswolds, Windermere, New Hampshire, the meadows of the Eure-et-

Loire, even the grey dunes of Cheshire, even the Sahara, a planet upon which, in the twinkling of an eye, you could change climates, and, if you cared to think so, in the crossing of a highway, three civilizations; but beautiful, there was no denying its beauty, fatal or cleansing as it happened to be, the beauty of the Earthly Paradise itself.

Yet in the Earthly Paradise, what had he done? He had made few friends. He had acquired a Mexican mistress with whom he quarrelled, and numerous beautiful Mayan idols he would be unable to take out of the country, and he had—

M. Laruelle wondered if it was going to rain: it sometimes, though rarely, did at this time of year, as last year for instance, it rained when it should not. And those were storm clouds in the south. He imagined he could smell the rain, and it ran in his head he would enjoy nothing better than to get wet, soaked through to the skin, to walk on and on through this wild country in his clinging white flannels getting wetter and wetter and wetter. He watched the clouds: dark swift horses surging up the sky. A black storm breaking out of its season! That was what love was like, he thought; love which came too late. Only no sane calm succeeded it, as when the evening fragrance or slow sunlight and warmth returned to the surprised land! M. Laruelle hastened his steps still further. And let such love strike you dumb, blind, mad, dead—your fate would not be altered by your simile. Tonnerre de dieu . . . It slaked no thirst to say what love was like which came too late.

The town was almost directly to his right now and above him, for M. Laruelle had been walking gradually downhill since leaving the Casino de la Selva. From the field he was crossing he could see, over the trees on the slope of the hill, and beyond the dark castled shape of Cortez Palace, the slowly revolving Ferris wheel, already lit up, in the square of Quauhnahuac; he thought he could distinguish the sound of human laughter rising from its bright gondolas and, again, that faint intoxication of voices singing, diminishing, dying in the wind, inaudible finally. A despondent American tune, the St. Louis Blues, or some such, was borne across the fields to him, at times a soft windblown surge of music from which skimmed a spray of gabbling, that seemed not so much to break against as to be thumping the walls and towers of the outskirts; then with a moan it would be sucked back into the distance. He found himself in the lane that led away through the brewery to the Tomalín road. He came to the Alcapancingo road. A car was passing and as he waited, face averted, for the dust to subside, he recalled that time motoring with Yvonne and the Consul along the Mexican lake-bed, itself once the crater of a huge volcano, and saw again the horizon softened by dust, the buses whizzing past through the whirling dust, the shuddering boys standing on the backs of the lorries holding on for grim death, their faces bandaged against the dust (and there was a magnificence about this, he always felt, some symbolism for the future, for which such truly great preparation had been made by a heroic people, since all over Mexico one could see those thundering lorries with those young builders in them, standing erect, their trousers flapping hard, legs planted wide, firm) and in the sunlight, on the round hill, the lone section of dust advancing, the dust-darkened hills by the lake like islands in driving rain. The Consul, whose old house M. Laruelle now made out on the slope beyond the barranca, had seemed happy enough too then, wandering around Cholula with its three hundred and six churches and its two barber shops, the "Toilet" and the "Harem," and climbing the ruined pyramid later, which he had proudly insisted was the original Tower of Babel. How admirably he had concealed what must have been the babel of his thoughts!

Two ragged Indians were approaching M. Laruelle through the dust; they were arguing, but with the profound concentration of university professors wandering in summer twilight through the Sorbonne. Their voices, the gestures of their refined grimy hands, were unbelievably courtly, delicate. Their carriage suggested the majesty of Aztec princes, their faces obscure sculpturings on Yucatecan ruins:

"—perfectamente borracho—"

"—completamente fantástico—"

"Si, hombre, la vida impersonal—"

"Claro, hombre—"

"Positivamente!"

"Buenas noches."

"Buenas noches."

They passed into the dusk. The Ferris wheel sank from sight: the sounds of the fair, the music, instead of coming closer, had temporarily ceased. M. Laruelle looked into the west; a knight of old, with tennis racquet for shield and pocket torch for scrip, he dreamed a moment of battles the soul survived to wander there. He had intended turning down another lane to the right, that led past the model farm where the Casino de la Selva grazed its horses, directly into his street, the Calle Nicaragua. But on a sudden impulse he turned left along the road running by the prison. He felt an obscure desire on his last night to bid farewell to the ruin of Maximilian's Palace.

To the south an immense archangel, black as thunder, beat up from the Pacific. And yet, after all, the storm contained its own secret calm.

The Bum

W. Somerset Maugham

GOD KNOWS HOW OFTEN I had lamented that I had not half the time I needed to do half the things I wanted. I could not remember when last I had had a moment to myself. I had often amused my fancy with the prospect of just one week's complete idleness. Most of us when not busy working are busy playing; we ride, play tennis or golf, swim or gamble; but I saw myself doing nothing at all. I would lounge through the morning, dawdle through the afternoon and loaf through the evening. My mind would be a slate and each passing hour a sponge that wiped out the scribblings written on it by the world of sense. Time, because it is so fleeting, time, because it is beyond recall, is the most precious of human goods and to squander it is the most delicate form of dissipation in which man can indulge. Cleopatra dissolved in wine a priceless pearl, but she gave it to Antony to drink; when you waste the brief golden hours you take the beaker in which the gem is melted and dash its contents to the ground. The gesture is grand and like all grand gestures absurd. That of course is its excuse. In the week I promised myself I should naturally read, for to the habitual reader reading is a drug of which he is the slave; deprive him of printed matter and he grows nervous, moody and restless; then, like the alcoholic bereft of brandy who will drink shellac or methylated spirit, he will make do with the advertisements of a paper five years old; he will make do with a telephone directory. But the professional writer is seldom a disinterested reader. I wished my reading to be but another form of idleness. I made up my mind that if ever the happy day arrived when I could enjoy untroubled leisure I would complete an enterprise that had always tempted me, but which hitherto, like an explorer making reconnaissances into an undiscovered country, I had done little more than enter upon: I would read the entire works of Nick Carter.

But I had always fancied myself choosing my moment with surroundings to my liking, not having it forced upon me; and when I was suddenly faced with nothing to do and had to make the best of it (like a steamship acquaintance whom in the wide waste of the Pacific Ocean you have invited to stay with you in London and who turns up without warning and with all his luggage) I was not a little taken aback. I had come to Vera Cruz from Mexico City to catch one of the Ward Company's white cool ships to Yucatan; and found to my dismay that, a dock strike having been declared over-night, my ship would not put in. I was stuck in Vera Cruz. I took a room in the Hotel Diligencias overlooking the plaza, and spent the morning looking at the sights of the town. I wandered down side streets and peeped into quaint courts. I sauntered through the parish church; it is picturesque with its gargoyles and flying buttresses, and the salt wind and the blazing sun have patined its harsh and massive walls with the mellowness of age; its cupola is covered with white and blue tiles. Then I found that I had seen all that was to be seen and I sat down in the coolness of the arcade that surrounded the square and ordered a drink. The sun beat down on the plaza with a merciless splendour. The coco-palms drooped dusty and bedraggled. Great black buzzards perched on them for a moment uneasily, swooped to the ground to gather some bit of offal, and then with lumbering wings flew up to the church tower. I watched the people crossing the square; negroes, Indians, Creoles and Spanish, the motley people of the Spanish Main; and they varied in colour from ebony to ivory. As the morning wore on, the tables around me filled up, chiefly with men, who had come to have a drink before luncheon, for the most part in white ducks, but some notwithstanding the heat in the dark clothes of professional respectability. A small band, a guitarist, a blind fiddler and a harpist, played rag-time and after every other tune the guitarist came round with a plate. I had already bought the local paper and I was adamant to the newsvendors who pertinaciously sought to sell me more copies of the same sheet. I refused, oh, twenty times at least, the solicitations of grimy urchins who wanted to shine my spotless shoes; and having come to the end of my small change I could only shake my head at the beggars who importuned me. They gave one no peace. Little Indian women, in shapeless rags, each one with a baby tied in the shawl on her back, held out skinny hands and in a whimper recited a dismal screed; blind men were led up to my table by small boys; the maimed, the halt, the deformed exhibited the sores and the monstrosities with which nature or accident had afflicted them; and half naked, underfed children whined endlessly their demand for coppers. But these kept their eyes open for the fat policeman who would suddenly dart out on them with a thong and give them a sharp cut on the back or over the head. Then they would scamper, only to return again when, exhausted by the exercise of so much energy, he relapsed into lethargy.

But suddenly my attention was attracted by a beggar who, unlike the rest of them and indeed the people sitting round me, swarthy and black-haired, had hair and beard of a red so vivid that it was startling. His beard was ragged and his long mop of hair looked as though it had not been brushed for months. He wore only a pair of trousers and a cotton singlet, but they were tatters, grimy and foul, that barely held together. I have never seen anyone so thin; his legs, his naked arms were but skin and bone and through the rents of his singlet you saw every rib of his wasted body; you could count the bones of his dust-covered feet. Of that starveling band he was easily the most abject. He was not old, he could not well have been more than forty, and I could not but ask myself what had brought him to this pass. It was absurd to think that he would not have worked if work he had been able to get. He was the only one of the beggars who did not speak. The rest of them poured forth their litany of woe and if it did not bring the alms they asked continued until an impatient word from you chased them away. He said nothing. I supposed he felt that his look of destitution was all the appeal he needed. He did not even hold out his hand, he merely looked at you, but with such wretchedness in his eyes, such despair in his attitude, it was dreadful; he stood on and on, silent and immobile, gazing steadfastly, and then, if you took no notice of him, he moved slowly to the next table. If he was given nothing he showed neither disappointment nor anger. If someone offered him a coin he stepped forward a little, stretched out his claw-like hand, took it without a word of thanks and impassively went his way. I had nothing to give him and when he came to me, so that he should not wait in vain, I shook my head.

"Dispense Usted por Dios," I said, using the polite Castillian formula with which the Spaniards refuse a beggar.

But he paid no attention to what I said. He stood in front of me, for as long as he stood at the other tables, looking at me with tragic eyes. I have never seen such a wreck of humanity. There was something terrifying in his appearance. He did not look quite same. At length he passed on.

It was one o'clock and I had lunch. When I awoke from my siesta it was still very hot, but towards evening a breath of air coming in through the windows which I had at last ventured to open tempted me into the plaza. I sat down under my arcade and ordered a long drink. Presently people in greater numbers filtered into the open space from the surrounding streets, the tables in the restaurants round it filled up, and in the kiosk in the middle the band began to play. The crowd grew thicker. On the free benches people sat huddled together like dark grapes clustered on a stalk. There was a lively hum of conversation. The big black buzzards flew screeching overhead, swooping down when they saw something to pick up, or scurrying away from under the feet of the passers-by. As twilight descended they swarmed, it seemed from all parts of the town, towards the church tower; they circled heavily about it and hoarsely crying, squabbling and jangling, settled themselves uneasily to roost. And again bootblacks begged me to have my shoes cleaned, newsboys pressed dank papers upon me, beggars whined their plaintive demand for alms. I saw once more that strange, red-bearded fellow and watched him stand motionless, with the crushed and piteous air, before one table after another. He did not stop before mine. I supposed he remembered me from the morning and having failed to get anything from me then thought it useless to try again. You do not often see a red-haired Mexican, and because it was only in Russia that I had seen men of so destitute a mien I asked myself if he was by chance a Russian. It accorded well enough with the Russian fecklessness that he should have allowed himself to sink to such a depth of degradation. Yet he had not a Russian face; his emaciated features were clear-cut, and his blue eyes were not set in the head in a Russian manner; I wondered if he could be a sailor, English, Scandinavian or American, who had deserted his ship and by degrees sunk to this pitiful condition. He disappeared. Since there was nothing else to do, I stayed on till I got hungry, and when I had eaten came back. I sat on till the thinning crowd suggested it was bed-time. I confess that the day had seemed long and I wondered how many similar days I should be forced to spend there.

But I woke after a little while and could not get to sleep again. My room was stifling. I opened the shutters and looked out at the church. There was no moon, but the bright stars faintly lit its outline. The buzzards were closely packed on the cross above the cupola and on the edges of the tower, and now and then they moved a little. The effect was uncanny. And then, I have no notion why, that red scarecrow recurred to my mind and I had suddenly a strange feeling that I had seen him before. It was so vivid that it drove away from me the possibility of sleep. I felt sure that I had come across him, but when and where I could not tell. I tried to picture the surroundings in which he might take his place, but I could see no more than a dim figure against a background of fog. As the dawn approached it grew a little cooler and I was able to sleep.

I spent my second day at Vera Cruz as I had spent the first. But I watched for the coming of the red-haired beggar, and as he stood at the tables near mine I examined him with attention. I felt certain now that I had seen him somewhere. I even felt certain that I had known him and talked to him, but I still could recall none of the circumstances. Once more he passed my table without stopping and when his eyes met mine I looked in them for some gleam of recollection. Nothing. I wondered if I had made a mistake and thought I had seem him in the same way as sometimes, by some queer motion of the brain, in the act of doing something you are convinced that you are repeating an action that you have done at some past time. I could not get out of my head the impression that at some moment he had entered into my life. I racked my brains. I was sure now that he was either English or American. But I was shy of addressing him. I went over in my mind the possible occasions when I might have met him. Not to be able to place him exasperated me as it does when you try to remember a name that is on the tip of your tongue and yet eludes you. The day wore on.

Another day came, another morning, another evening. It was Sunday and the plaza was more crowded than ever. The tables under the arcade were packed. As usual the red-haired beggar came along, a terrifying figure in his silence, his threadbare rags and his pitiful distress. He was standing in front of a table only two from mine, mutely beseeching, but without a gesture. Then I saw the policeman who at intervals tried to protect the public from the importunities of all these beggars sneak round a column and give him a resounding whack with his thong. His thin body winced, but he made no protest and showed no resentment; he seemed to accept the stinging blow as in the ordinary course of things and with his slow movements slunk away into the gathering night of the plaza. But the cruel stripe had whipped my memory and suddenly I remembered.

Not his name, that escaped me still, but everything else. He must have recognized me, for I have not changed very much in twenty years, and that was why after that first morn-ing he had never paused in front of my table. Yes, it was twenty years since I had known him. I was spending a winter in Rome and every evening I used to dine in a restaurant in the Via Sistina where you got excellent macaroni and a good bottle of wine. It was frequented by a little band of English and American art students, and one or two writers; and we used to stay late into the night engaged in interminable argu-ments upon art and literature. He used to come in with a young painter who was a friend of his. He was only a boy then, he could not have been more than twenty-two; and with his blue eyes, straight nose and red hair he was pleasing to look at. I remembered that he spoke a great deal of Central America, he had had a job with the American Fruit Company, but had thrown it over because he wanted to be a writer. He was not popular among us because he was arrogant and we were none of us old enough to take the arrogance of youth with tolerance. He thought us poor fish and did not hesitate to tell us so. He would not show us his work, because our praise meant nothing to him and he despised our censure. His vanity was enormous. It irritated us; but some of us were uneasily aware that it might perhaps be justified. Was it possible that the intense consciousness of genius that he had, rested on no grounds? He had sacrificed everything to be a writer. He was so certain of himself that he infected some of his friends with his own assurance.

I recalled his high spirits, his vitality, his confidence in the future and his disinterestedness. It was impossible that it was the same man, and yet I was sure of it. I stood up, paid for my drink and went out into the plaza to find him. My thoughts were in a turmoil. I was aghast. I had thought of him now and then and idly wondered what had become of him. I could never have imagined that he was reduced to this frightful misery. There are hundreds, thousands of youths who enter upon the hard calling of the arts with extravagant hopes; but for the most part they come to terms with their mediocrity and find somewhere in life a niche where they can escape starvation. This was awful. I asked myself what had happened. What hopes deferred had broken his spirit, what disappointments shattered him and what lost illusions ground him to the dust? I asked myself if nothing could be done. I walked round the plaza. He was not in the arcades. There was no hope of finding him in the crowd that circled round the bandstand. The light was waning and I was afraid I had lost him. Then I passed the church and saw him sitting on the steps. I cannot describe what a lamentable object he looked. Life had taken him, rent him on its racks, torn him limb from limb, and then flung him, a bleeding wreck, on the stone steps of that church. I went up to him.

"Do you remember Rome?" I said.

He did not move. He did not answer. He took no more notice of me than if I were not standing before him. He did not look at me. His vacant blue eyes rested on the buzzards that were screaming and tearing at some object at the bottom of the steps. I did not know what to do. I took a yellow-backed note out of my pocket and pressed it in his hand. He did not give it a glance. But his hand moved a little, the thin claw-like fingers closed on the note and scrunched it up; he made it into a little ball and then edging it on to his thumb flicked it into the air so that it fell among the jangling buzzards. I turned my head instinctively and saw one of them seize it in his beak and fly off followed by two others screaming behind it. When I looked back the man was gone.

I stayed three more days in Vera Cruz. I never saw him again.

A Game for the Living
Patricia Highsmith

THEODORE HAD BEEN TO Guanajuato three or four times, but
for stays of only a day and a night. It was a special town to
him, a special favourite. Other Mexican towns were as old,
had abandoned silver-mines and aqueducts, but Guanajuato
was artistically all of a piece, like a well-composed painting.
When Theodore thought of Guanajuato, he imagined an aer-
ial view of a town built on hills and sheltered by gigantic
mountains, a town of exquisitely faded pinks and tans and
yellows. Once he had done an imaginary painting of his aer-
ial view, a smallish painting, because the town, though large
enough and spread out, suggested smallness when one was
in it, a size that one could grasp comfortably with the mind.
The picture had hung in Lelia's bedroom, and Theodore had
no idea what had happened to it, or whether anybody would
ever know it was his. He had not signed it, because a signa-
ture would have marred his composition.

Guanajuato lay off the main highway and had only one
good road of entry and exit, the turn-off from Silao that wriggled along the narrow Cañon de Marfil. From the bottom of
the *cañon* the road would climb to a panorama of plains and
mountains without a sign of human habitation, then drop

again in the gorge that shut out the sunlight. Mountains on the horizon were blue with distance, and like other landscapes Theodore had seen in Mexico it seemed to say with a majestic voice: "Here I am—a million million times bigger and older than you. Look at me and stop fretting over your petty troubles!" It gave the melancholy solace that Theodore felt while looking at the stars on a clear dark night. He began to relax, as if a frown had been erased from his forehead.

They passed a pair of Indian children who were leading a goat by its chin whiskers, and Theodore waved in response to their wave.

There was a curve, and two children sprang directly into the path of the car. Theodore stamped on the brake and the cat's carrier slid off the back seat on to the floor. Ramón's forehead hit the dashboard.

"Oranges, señor? They are good! A peso the box!" the little girl stuck the box all the way through the window.

"You will get yourself *killed* that way," Theodore said to her oblivious face. "The next car may not have such good brakes!" But already he was feeling for a peso, because she would hang on to the car if he didn't, and she would go on running in front of cars, which was the only sure way of stopping them, until she was old enough to be married.

The little girl dumped the oranges unceremoniously into his lap. "*Gracias,* señor. Another box?"

"No, thank you, *niña.*" Theodore was trying to get away before her little brother could poke his lizard through the window, but he was not quick enough.

"Iguana, señor! Five pesos! Make a fine belt!"

"No—no, thank you," Theodore said, leaning away from the horribly grinning face of the thing. He moved the car slowly.

"*Four* pesos!" The boy held it by its fat throat and its tail and walked along beside the car. The iguana looked straight into Theodore's eye, and, like something out of hell, it seemed to say: "Buy me and I'll fix *you*!"

"*Three* pesos!"

"I can't *use* an iguana!"

"*Two* pesos!" The boy took the lizard out of the window, but continued to run along beside the car. "Make shoes! Make belt!" He was speaking in English. The iguana suddenly twisted itself violently, but the boy kept his grip.

Theodore increased his speed.

"*One* peso!—*Ho-o-o-ombre!*" came the fading, tragic cry.

Theodore looked at Ramón. "Did you hurt your head, Ramón? I'm sorry."

"It was my nose," Ramón said, smiling.

GUANAJUATO CON RUIZ CORTINES!

said white-painted letters on a great flange of rock at the road's side. Another curve, a steep descent, and they were in the town suddenly, surrounded by pinkish buildings and houses and by boys of the streets who gripped the windows and would not let go.

"Need a hotel, mister?"

"Please don't open the doors!" Theodore yelled at them. He had to go more slowly now, and the boys kept up with him.

Theodore stopped at the lower plaza, and he and Ramón got out and locked the car. There were more boys, one a little tot of five or less who looked at Theodore with a threatening intensity as if he could hypnotise him into doing as he wished, and said:

"You want hotel with hot runnin' war-rter-r? Come with me and I show you! Hotel Santa Cecilia!"

"Ah, it's full up!" said an older boy in a cracking adolescent voice. "You gotta go to a *pensión,* mister!"

"We don't want a hotel," Theodore said good-naturedly, because it was the only way to get rid of them. "We are not staying here." He took Ramón by the arm.

The boys followed them a little way, still shouting, and then gave it up. It was about five o'clock, and the sun touched only the tops of the houses. Theodore walked slowly, enjoying the sensation, which he knew would vanish in a few moments, that the people were play-acting, and that the whole scene had been created by one mind to produce a single effect. Every moving thing he saw seemed dramatic and purposeful. They came to the other plaza, on which stood the grand old Teatro Juarez, its façade a mess of polished, pale green stone pillars and nineteenth-century ornament. Familiarity had made even this attractive.

"The Panteon is on a hill outside of town," Ramón said.

"Yes, I know." The Panteon was the cemetery where the mummies were. "It's late to go today, don't you think? I thought we might go tomorrow."

"All right," Ramón said agreeably.

Theodore asked Ramón if he had a preference as to an hotel. Ramón said he usually went to a very modest one called La Palma.

"It may not be comfortable enough for you, Teo."

"That doesn't matter. Let's try it if you like it."

They strolled back towards the plaza where the car was and where La Palma was, too. There was the smell of charcoal fires in the air, a hunger-stimulating fragrance of roasting corn and tortillas. The street lights had gone on. The evening was beginning.

The doorway of Hotel La Palma was wide, and as they waited for someone to appear behind the bleak desk, a car rolled into the tiled lobby and passed them, on the way to the enclosed garage at the back of the hotel. Only one room was available, at eighteen pesos. It was on the third floor, and there was an elevator, but it was temporarily out of order, the man told them. When Ramón hesitated, the man said brusquely:

"Every other hotel in town is filled up. If you don't believe me, just telephone and see." He pointed to his telephone.

"Very well, we'll take it," Theodore said.

They carried their own suitcases up. The room was an empty box with a plain double bed that sagged, a straight chair, a flimsy table, a pair of coat-hangers on a peg. There was not a picture on the wall, or a waste-basket or an ashtray. It amused Theodore.

"Probably their worst room," Ramón said apologetically.

"I don't mind it at all!"

Theodore took Leo down to the plaza and let him out of his carrier. The cat was used to travelling and had explored scores of plazas in Mexico and South America. Invariably, Leo attracted attention, a few people asked what kind of cat he was and were astounded when the cat came at command, like a dog. Even policemen, approaching him perhaps with an idea of doing their duty, ended by stooping to pet Leo and to marvel at his size and his blue eyes. The army of street boys in Guanajuato were very talkative. Theodore answered their questions with good humour, but he had to rescue Leo finally from some boys who wanted to pick him up. And there was a face or two among the adolescents that looked rather delinquent. The boy who tried to steal Leo would regret it, Theodore thought.

The water in the shower—there was no bath and not even a shower curtain—ran cool and was doubly unpleasant because Theodore was already chilled. He rubbed himself briskly with the undersized towel afterwards and said nothing about the water to Ramón. The single blanket on the bed was going to be inadequate, too, and Theodore made a mental note to get the steamer rug from the boot of his car.

They had dinner at a simple restaurant across the street from the hotel, a narrow place with wall booths, a juke-box, and undersized paper napkins in dispensers on the table. Afterwards they walked through the quiet streets that were lighted by round, yellowish street lamps. Theodore felt an inexplicable well-being and happiness, the openness of spirit that often came when he was pleased with a piece of work, but which now seemed to be caused by the town itself. He carried, folded into three napkins, the chicken from two of his three *enchilados suizos* to give to Leo.

Theodore did not think of the steamer rug until he started to get into bed. They had washed in cool water, and their teeth were chattering.

"I've got to ask them for another blanket, Ramón."

But of course there was no telephone in the room, and he was in his pyjamas. Theodore would have almost, but not quite, gone downstairs in his dressing-gown to his car, which was in the hotel garage, but—He looked at Ramón and laughed.

Ramón did not laugh. Perhaps his headache had begun to obsess his thoughts, or perhaps he wanted him to leave the room so that he could say his prayers in privacy.

Theodore put his suit on over his pyjamas. There was no light proper in the wide hallway, but a good deal of light came from people's open doors. Glancing with impersonal curiosity at the open or half-open doors, he saw people lying in bed, people undressing, yawning, scratching, a man in pyjamas tuning a guitar. Another man in slippers and dressing-gown was walking slowly, by himself, in the second-floor hallway. Downstairs, the desk was again deserted. Theodore asked one of the boys seated on a bench in the lobby if he might have another blanket.

"Ah, no, señor. The blankets are locked up, and the señor with the keys has gone home."

"I see. Thank you." He went on to the closed door of the garage at the back of the lobby. A padlock dangled from a chain. "Can you open this?" he said to the boys.

The key had to be searched for in cubby-holes behind the desk's counter. At last it was found, the door opened, a light switch found and turned on, and by climbing along someone's front bumper Theodore reached the boot of his car and got his blanket. His car was wedged with hardly an inch to spare on any side.

"I don't want that grey car moved by anybody but me, do you understand?" Theodore said to the boys. "If it has to be moved, call me, whatever the hour is."

"*Si* señor."

He had the keys and the brakes were set, but he had seen cars lifted or bumped out of the way if the owner were not to be found. Again he climbed the three flights, each with its stratum of humanity preparing for bed, and at the third floor turned left and walked towards his room.

~

"Want a guide, mister? You American? I speak English!"

"I got a car. You want to ride? Tour of the town! Twenty-five pesos! There is my car, señor!"

"No, we want to walk, thank you," Theodore said in English. They were on the sidewalk in front of the great bullet-scarred Alhóndiga de Granaditas, the objective of Hidalgo's attack in the Revolution, the scene of Pipila's heroic sacrifice, and the most famous building of the town.

They moved on, still dogged by two or three of the self-appointed town guides. Ramón stopped to look back at the doorway, and up at the ornamented corner, perhaps the corner where Hidalgo's head had hung for months, rotting in the sun, as a warning to all those who would revolt against the Spanish.

"You want to see the Panteon, señores?" asked an adolescent voice at Theodore's elbow. "I can take you. Mummies—"

"No, thank you," Theodore said, taking out his car keys. They were going to the Panteon at last.

The boys stood in a silent semicircle, momentarily taken aback by the car. "Many streets up there, señor!" "One-way streets! You need a guide!" "Bad roads for a car, señor. My car is only twenty pesos. I take you around the whole town."

At Ramón's instructions, Theodore took a west-bound, climbing street, zigzagged through the section of one-way streets near the beautiful Street of the Priests with its window-less pink-tan walls and windowless bridge like something out of medieval Europe, and climbed finally to a straighter, west-bound road. The town dropped behind them and a fresh, sunny wind blew through the windows. Theodore was in no mood to see the mummies, but he knew he would never be in a mood to see them, and since he had to see them during this sojourn in Guanajuato, this morning seemed as good a time as any. But the world was full of bright sunlight and green, living things. He could see the tops of trees moving miles away and he could have spent the day looking at all of it.

"There it is," said Ramón, bending low to see, because the Panteon was yet higher, on a hill to their right.

Theodore saw a very long wall, whose height he could not judge, set on a small plateau. The road took them by winds and turns inexorably towards it. On the wall was written the inscription that was on the walls of the cemetery where Lelia lay:

HUMBLE THYSELF! HERE ETERNITY BEGINS
AND HERE WORLDLY GRANDEUR IS DUST!

He drove on to a small area, indicated to him by a watchman at the gates, which on two sides dropped sheer for what looked like hundreds of feet. A boy of about sixteen ran up to the window and asked if Theodore wanted him to park for him. Theodore thanked him and said no.

"Last month a car went over the edge. I am very used to American cars," the boy said in English.

There was not room to turn around, but the boy made circular gestures with an air of authority as if this was exactly what he wanted Theodore to do—try to turn around and go over the edge. Theodore put the car into a parallel position with another car, his front bumper to the cemetery wall. On the way out, he would simply have to back to a place on the road where he could turn.

They walked through the gates and a field of graves and tombs spread before them, surrounded by the wall, that was nearly three times the height of a man and as thick as a coffin was long. The walls, every square yard of them, contained vaults and were marked off in squares, each with a name and date. The ground was yellowish and bone-dry, as Theodore remembered the ground of Lelia's cemetery, as if the feet of thousands of mourners had obliterated every blade of grass. Yet the faded pastel lavenders of the tombstones' shadows, the pale green traces of moisture in the walls and the instant-coffee and jelly jars of real and artificial flowers, fresh and wilted and dead, made it look like a picture by Seurat and relieved much of its gloom for Theodore. He wandered to an empty vault and looked in. It was lined with ordinary house bricks. A casket had evidently been removed, because on the ground, leaning against the wall, was a square of stone that had fronted the catacomb: Maria Josefina Barrera 1888–1937. R.E.P.

"They rent out the vaults," Ramón said, "and if the relatives do not pay the rent, they take the body out."

Theodore nodded. He had read it somewhere before. Some of the bodies had become the famous mummies, and some must be simply thrown away somewhere, he thought, like litter.

The Bridge in the Jungle
B. Traven

"Stick'm up, stranger!"

"?"

"Can't you hear, sap? Up with your fins. And you'd better snap into it!"

Through my sweat-soaked shirt I distinctly felt it was not his forefinger nor a pencil that was so firmly pressed against my ribs. It was the real thing all right. I could almost figure out its caliber—a .38, and a heavy one at that. The reason why I had been slow to obey his first order was that I believed it a hallucination. For two days while marching with my two pack mules through the dense jungle I had not met with a single human being, white, Indian, or mestizo. I knew I was still far away from the next rancheria, which I expected to reach about noon tomorrow. So who would hold me up? But it happened. From the way he spoke I knew he was no native. He fumbled at my belt this way and that; it was quite a job dragging my gun out of my holster, which was as hard and dry as wood. Finally he got it. I heard him back up. The way he moved his feet back on the ground told me that he was a rather tall fellow and either fairly well advanced in years or very tired.

"Oke, now. You can turn round if it pleases your lord-
ship."

Fifty feet to the right of the jungle trail along which I had
come, there was a little pond of fresh and not very muddy
water. It had glittered through the foliage, and from the
tracks of mules and horses leading to that water hole I knew
that it must be a paraje where pack trains take a rest or even
spend the night. So I drove my tired mules in to water them. I
needed a short rest myself and a good drink.

I had not seen anyone near nor had I heard anything.
Therefore I was astonished when, as if coming from a jungle
ghost, the gat was pushed between my ribs.

Now I looked at him, who, as I had rightly guessed, was
taller than I and slightly heavier. Fifty or fifty-five years. An
old-timer, judging from the way he was dressed (which was
not much different from my own get-up), cotton pants, high
boots, a dirty sweat-soaked shirt, and a wide-brimmed hat of
the cheap sort made in the republic.

He grinned at me. I could not help grinning back at him.
We did not shake nor tell our names. Telling other people
your name without being asked for it seems silly anyhow.

He told me that he was the manager of a sugar plantation
about thirty miles from where we now stood, but that he preferred to manage a cocoa plantation if he only could get such
a job. I told him that I was a free-lance explorer and also the
president, the treasurer, and the secretary of a one-man
expedition on the lookout for rare plants with a commercial
value for their medicinal or industrial properties, but that I
would take any job offered me on my way and that I hoped to
find, maybe, gold deposits or precious stones.

"I should know about them, brother, if there were any

around here. See, I'm long enough in this here part so that I know every stone and every rubber shrub and every single ebony tree you'll ever see. But then again, that goddamned beautiful jungle is so big and so rich—well, what I mean to say is, there are so many things that can bring money home to papa if you only know how to use them and how to doll them up when selling them, and besides that you may actually find not only gold but even diamonds. Only don't get tired looking for them."

I felt the irony he had not put into his words but into the corners of his nearly closed eyes while speaking.

Having watered his horse, filled his water bag, and gulped down a last drink from the pond, scooped up with a battered aluminum cup, he tightened the straps of the saddle which he had loosened so that the horse might drink with more gusto, mounted his goat, and then said: "Two hundred yards from here you can pick up your gat where I'll drop it on my way. I'm no bandit. But you see, brother, what do I know about you? You might be in some kind of new racket. You seem to be green around this section of the globe. At places like the one we have had so much pleasure together— I mean this one here—a guy that's in the know doesn't take any chances, if you get what I mean. That's the reason why I relieved you of your rusty iron for a while—just to keep you from playing with it. You might have taken me for a bum after your packs and beasts and you might have slugged me just for fear of me. I know greenies like you who get dizzy in the tropics—specially if they're trailing alone through the jungle without seeing a soul or even a mole for a week. Then they see things and hear things and they talk alone to themselves and listen to the talk of ghosts. Sure, you get what I mean. In such cases the first who has his iron out is the winner, you know. I'm always happy if I can be the winner over a greeny like you. Because it's the greenies I'm ten times more afraid of than a hungry tiger. A tiger, I know what he wants if I meet him, and maybe I can trick him, but a greeny who has been three days alone on a jungle trail, you never know what he might do when he sees you suddenly standing before him. Well, so long, brother, and good luck in discovering a new kind of rubber shrub."

I went after him and I saw him drop my gun. This done, he spurred his horse and two seconds later the jungle had swallowed him.

When I found myself once more alone with my mules, a strange sensation came over me that I had dreamed the whole intermission. I tried to think it all through and then I knew that every word I had heard him say, whether in my imagination or in reality, was a true statement of facts. You can easily fall victim to any sort of hallucination when you're traveling alone through the jungle, if you're not used to it. I decided to be on my guard against the jungle madness he had talked about. I also decided that the next time I met someone in the jungle I would do my best to be the winner— by doing exactly what that man had done to me.

~

Three months later, in an entirely different region, I was riding across the muddy plaza of an Indian village when I saw a white man standing in the portico of a palm-roofed adobe house.

"Hi, you! Hello!" he hollered at me.

"Hello yourself!"

It was Sleigh.

He invited me into his house to be introduced to his family. His wife was Indian, a very pretty woman with a soft, cream-like, yellowish skin, brown eyes, and strong, beautiful teeth. He had three kids, all boys, who easily could pass as American boys from the South. His wife was at least twenty-five years younger than he. The oldest of the kids was perhaps eight years old, the youngest three.

His wife fried me six eggs, which I ate with tortillas and baked beans. For drink I had coffee, cooked Indian fashion, with unrefined brown sugar.

On my entering the house his wife had greeted me: "Buenas tardes, señor!" accompanied by an almost unnoticeable nod of her head, which wore a crown of two thick black braids. After this short salutation, nearer to suspicion than to friendliness, I did not see her again. Neither did the children come in again, although I heard them playing and yelling outside.

The house was as poor as could be. There was practically no furniture, save one cot, a crude table, three crude chairs, and a hammock. Besides these things there were two trunks in the room, old-fashioned and besprinkled with mud. The house had two doors, one in front, the other at the back leading to a muddy and untidy yard. Yet there were no windows. The floor was of dried mud.

Sleigh, whose first name I never learned, did not invite me to stay overnight. It was not that he was ashamed that he could not offer me a bed; it was simply in accordance with a rule that a man traveling by horse or mule over the country knows best when to stay overnight and where, and therefore he is not urged to change his plans. If on the other hand the traveler were to ask whether he might stay overnight, he is sure to meet with unrestricted hospitality.

I did not ask Sleigh what he was doing here and how he made his living, nor did he by word or gesture indicate that he was curious to know what sort of business brought me through that little native village so far out of the way of regular communications.

~

One year later I was making a rather difficult trip on horseback on the way to the jungle sections of the Huayalexco River, where I hoped to get alligators, the hides of which brought a very good price at that time. My task turned out to be far tougher than I had expected.

At certain places along the river-banks the jungle was so dense that it would have taken many days of hard work with the help of natives to clear the banks sufficiently to enable me to approach the points where alligators were supposed to be found. Other parts of the region were so swampy no one could pass them to reach the banks. I then decided to ride farther down the river, expecting to locate territory easier to hunt in. Indians had told me that on my way downstream I would meet with a number of tributaries which at that time of the year were likely to abound with alligators.

One day while on this trip down the river I came to a pump-station practically hidden in the jungle. This pump-station was railroad property. It pumped the water from the river to another station many miles away, from where it was pumped on to the next railroad depot. For about a hundred miles along the railroad there was no water all the year round save during a couple of months when the rainy season was at its height. Hence the need to pump water to that depot. Part of this water served the engine. The greater part, though, was carried by train in special tanks to the various other depots and settlements along the railroad track, because all the people living there would have left the depots and the little villages if they were not provided with water during the dry season.

The pump-master, or, as he liked to be called, el maestro maquinista, was Indian. He worked with the assistance of an Indian boy, his ayudante. The boiler was fired with wood, some of it brought in from the jungle by an Indian wood-chopper on the back of a burro, the rest carried, in the form of old, discarded timber and rotten sleepers, from the depot.

The boiler looked as if it were ready to burst any minute. The pump, which looked as though it had been in use for more than a hundred years, could be heard two miles away. It shrieked, howled, whistled, spat, gurgled, and rattled at every nut, bolt, and joint—and the first day I was there I stayed a safe distance away in the fear that this overworked and mistreated dumb slave might throw off its chains and make a dash for freedom. The railroad, however, was justified in using this old pump until it broke down for good. To dismantle it, take it to the depot, and ship it to a junk yard would have cost more than half the price of a new pump. So it was cheaper to keep it where it was and let it work itself to death. Owing to the difficulties of transportation and mounting, it would have been bad economy for the railroad to bring down a new pump at this time, especially since the railroad expected that any day now an American company would strike oil near by and that this company would then take care of the water problem for a hundred miles along the track.

About seventy yards from the pump a bridge crossed the river. This bridge, built and owned by the oil company and made of crude heavy timber, was wide enough so that trucks could pass over it, but it had no railings. The oil company had considered railings an unnecessary expense. Had there been railings on the bridge, perhaps this story would never have been told.

"We have lots of alligators in that river, montones de lagartos, señor, of this you may be assured," the pump-master said to me. "Of course, you will understand, mister, they are not right here where the pump is."

I could understand this very well. No decent alligator who respects established morals would ever be able to live near that noisy pump and keep fit to face life's arrows bravely.

"You see, mister, I wouldn't like them around here, never. They would steal my pigs and chickens. And what do you think, and you may not believe it, but it's true just the same, they even steal little children if they're left alone for a while. No, around here there are very few if any and these are only very small ones, too young to waste a bullet on. Farther down and also upstream, three or four miles from here, you will find them in herds by the hundred—and bulls, dear me, I think they must be three hundred years of age, so big they are."

I nodded towards the opposite bank. "Who lives over there? I mean right there where the huts are."

"Oh, there, you mean. There is prairie, much pastura. In fact, it's sort of a cattle ranch. Not fenced in. All open. It belongs to an Americano. After you pass that prairie there's thick jungle again. If you ride still farther through that jungle about six or eight miles, you'll find an oil camp. Men are drilling there, testing holes to see if they can find oil. So far they haven't, and if you ask me, I think they never will. That's the same people what have built this bridge. You know, if they want to drill for oil they have to get all the machinery down here from the depot. Without a bridge they couldn't pass the river with such heavy loads. They tried it a few times during the dry season, but the trucks got stuck and it took them a week to get them out again. The bridge has cost them a lot of money, because the timber had to be brought fifteen hundred miles, and, believe me, mister, that cost money."

"Who lives on that ranch over there?"

"A gringo, like you."

"That's what you told me before. I mean who looks after the cattle?"

"Didn't I tell you right now? A gringo."

"Where does he live?"

"Right behind that brush."

I cross the bridge on my horse, pulling my pack mule along behind me.

Behind a thick wall of tropical shrubs and trees I found about ten of the usual Indian chozas or jacales—that is, palm-roofed huts.

Women squatting on the bare ground, smoking thick cigars, and bronze-brown children, most of them naked, a few dressed in a shirt or ragged pair of pants, were everywhere. None of the little girls, however, was naked, although only scantily covered by flimsy frocks.

From here I could see across the pasture which the pump-master had called the prairie. It was about a mile long and three-quarters of a mile wide. On all sides it was hemmed in by the jungle. The tracks where the oil company's trucks had passed over the prairie were still visible.

It was quite natural to find an Indian settlement here. The pasture was good and there was water all the year round. The Indians need no more. The pasture was not theirs, but that didn't bother them. Every family owned two or three goats, two or three lean pigs, one or two burros, and a dozen chickens, and the river provided them with fish and crabs.

The men used to cultivate the land near their huts, raising corn, beans, and chile. But since the oil company had started to exploit its leases, acquired twenty years before, many of the men had found work in the camps, from which they came home every Saturday afternoon, remaining until early Monday morning. The men who did not like the jobs, or who could not get them, made charcoal in the bush, which they put into old sacks to be transported by burro to the depot, where it was sold to the agents who came once a week to every depot on the railroad line.

Neither the women I saw nor the children paid any attention to me as I passed them. During the last two years they had become used to foreigners, because whoever went to the oil camps by truck, car, or on horseback stopped at this settlement, or at the pump-station, even if only for an hour or two, but frequently for the night if they arrived at the bridge late in the afternoon. Everyone, even the toughest truck-drivers, avoided the road through the jungle at night.

Among the huts I noted one which, although built Indian fashion, was higher and larger than the rest. It was located at the end of the settlement, and behind it there was a crudely built corral. No other hut as far as I could see had a similar corral.

So I rode up to that hut which boasted a corral and, obeying the customs of the land, halted my horse respectfully about twenty yards away to wait until one of the inhabitants would notice my presence.

Like all the other jacales, it had no door—only an opening against which, at night, a sort of network of twigs and sticks was set from the inside and tied to the posts. The walls were made of sticks tied together with strips of bast and lianas. Therefore if a visitor didn't wait some distance from the house until he was invited in he might find the inhabitants in very embarrassing situations.

I had waited only a minute before an Indian woman appeared. She looked me over, said: "Buenas tardes, señor!" and then: "Pase, señor, this humble house is yours."

I dismounted, tied horse and mule to a tree, and entered the hut. I found the Indian woman who had greeted me to be the wife of my old acquaintance Sleigh. After recognizing me she repeated her greeting more cordially. I had to sit down in a creaking old wicker chair which was obviously the pride of the house. She told me that her husband would be here any minute now. He was out on the prairie trying to catch a young steer which had to be doctored because it had been gored by an older bull and now had festering wounds.

It was not long before I heard Sleigh ordering a boy to open the gate of the corral and drive the steer in.

He came in. Without showing even the slightest surprise he shook hands with me and then dropped into a very low, crude chair.

"Haven't you got a paper with you? Damn if I've read or seen any paper for eight months, and believe me, man, I'd like to know what's going on outside."

"I've got the San Antonio *Express* with me. Sweat-soaked and crumpled. It's five weeks old."

"Five weeks? Hombre, then I call it still hot from the press. Hand it over!"

He asked his wife for his spectacles, which she pulled out of the palm leaves of the roof. He put them on in a slow, almost ceremonious manner. While he was fixing them carefully upon his ears he said: "Aurelia, get the caballero something to eat, he is hungry."

Of each page he read two lines. He then nodded as if he wished to approve what had been said in the paper. Now he folded it contemplatively as if he were still digesting the lines he had read, took off his specs, stood up, put the glasses again somewhere between the palm leaves under the roof, and finally pushed the folded paper behind a stick pressed against the wall, without saying thanks. He returned to his seat, folded his hands, and said: "Damn it, it's a real treat to read a paper again and to know what is going on in the world."

His desire for a newspaper had been fully satisfied just by looking at one, so that he could rest assured that the people back home were still printing them. Suppose he had read that half of the United States and all of Canada had disappeared from the surface of the earth, I am sure he would have said: "Gosh, now what do you make of that? I didn't feel anything here. Anyway, things like that do happen sometimes, don't they?" Most likely he would not have shown any sign of surprise. He was that kind of an individual.

"I'm here to get alligators."

"After alligators, you said? Great. There are thousands here. I wish you'd get them all. I can't get them away from my calves and my young steers. They make so damn much trouble. What's worse, the old man blames me. He tells the whole world that I'm selling his young cows and pocketing all the money, while in fact the alligators get them and the tigers and the lions, of which the jungle is packed full. I can tell you, the old man that owns this property, he is a mean one. How can I sell a cow, even a very young one, or anything else, without everybody here knowing about it. Tell me that. But he is so mean, the old man is, and so dirty in his soul, that's what he is. If I wasn't here looking out for his property, I can swear he wouldn't have a single cow left. But he himself is afraid to live here in the wilderness, because he is yellow, that's what he is."

"He must have money."

"Money, my eye. Who says money? I mean he hasn't much cash. It's all landed property and livestock. Only, you know, the trouble is there is nothing safe here any longer, no property, and cattle still less so. It's all on account of those bum agraristas, you know. Anyhow, I absolutely agree with you that you can easily shoot a hundred alligators here. Whole herds you can shoot if you go after them. There are old bulls among them that are stronger than the heaviest steer, and they are tough guys too, those giant alligator bulls. If one of them gets you, man, there isn't anything left of you to tell the tale. But, come to think of it, why don't we first go after a tasty antelope?"

"Are there many antelope here too?" I asked.

"Many isn't the right word, if you ask an old-timer. You

just go into the bush over there. After walking say three hundred feet, you just take down your gun and shoot straight ahead of you. Then you walk again a hundred feet or so in the same direction and there you'll find your antelope stone dead on the ground, and more often than not you'll find two just waiting to be carried away. That's how it is here. I'll tell you what we can do. Stay here with me for a few days. Your alligators, down the river or up it, won't run away. They will wait with pleasure a few days longer for you to come along and get them. What day is it today? Thursday. Fine. You couldn't have selected a better day. My woman will be off tomorrow with the kids for a visit to her folks. I'll take them to the depot. Day after I'll be back again. From that day on we'll be all by ourselves here, and we can do and live as we like. The whole outfit and all the house will be ours. One of the girls of the neighborhood will come over and do all the cooking and the housekeeping."

Biographies

Sherwood Anderson was born in Camden, Ohio, in 1876. He is the author of the collection of short stories *Winesburg, Ohio,* as well as novels, poetry, and essays.

Robin Beeman lived and taught in Mexico and now lives in Northern California. She is the author of *A Parallel Life and Other Stories* and *A Minus Tide: A Novella,* both from Chronicle Books. The excerpt reproduced here is from *The Lost Art of Desire,* 2000 winner of the *Texas Review* Novella Prize.

Stephen Crane, best known for his novel *The Red Badge of Courage,* was born in 1871 and died in 1900 of tuberculosis. He traveled extensively and wrote prolifically during his short life.

Harriet Doerr was born in Pasadena in 1910 and published her first novel, *Stones for Ibarra,* at the age of 74. She is also the author of *Consider This, Senora.*

Graham Greene was born in 1904 in England and wrote many novels, travel stories, essays, and reviews. He focused on Mexico in *The Power and the Glory* and *The Lawless Roads.* He died in France in 1991.

Ron Hansen is the author of *Mariette in Ecstasy, Desperados,* and *Atticus,* among other fiction. The novel excerpted here, *Atticus,* was a finalist for the 1996 National Book Award.

Patricia **Highsmith** published over two dozen mystery and suspense novels, including *The Talented Mr. Ripley, Strangers on a Train*, and *A Suspension of Mercy*. She died in 1995.

Geoffrey **Homes** was the pen name of Daniel Mainwaring, a Hollywood film noir screenwriter of the '40s. His novel *Build My Gallows High* was made into the 1946 film "Out of the Past," starring Robert Mitchum, Jane Greer, and Kirk Douglas, based on Mainwaring's own adaptation.

Jack **Kerouac**, one of the originals of the '50s "Beat Generation," was born in Lowell, Massachusetts, in 1922. Kerouac experienced seven years of rejection before his manuscript for *On the Road* was finally published in 1957. He died in 1969 at the age of 47.

David **Lida**, a writer and journalist, divides his time between New York City and Mexico. He is the author of *Travel Advisory*, a collection of short stories set in Mexico.

Malcolm **Lowry**, best known for the novel *Under the Volcano*, also wrote short stories and novellas. He lived all over the world, but spent the early 1940s in the U.S. and Mexico.

W. **Somerset Maugham** was born in 1874 in the British Embassy in Paris. Though trained as a surgeon, he gave up medicine for writing after finding success with his plays in London. His novels include *The Moon and Sixpence* and *Of Human Bondage*. He died in France in 1965.

Anaïs **Nin** is best known for her lifelong *Diary*, which she began in 1914. She also wrote short stories, erotica, and novels, including *A Spy in the House of Love* and *The Four-Chambered Heart*.

Sandra Scofield has written numerous novels, including *Beyond Deserving, Plain Seeing,* and *A Chance to See Egypt.* She lives in Oregon.

Dashka Slater's poetry and nonfiction have appeared in a variety of magazines and journals. *The Wishing Box* is her first novel.

Wallace Stegner, novelist and historian of the American West, wrote more than a dozen novels, including *The Big Rock Candy Mountain, Crossing to Safety,* and *Angle of Repose,* which won the Pulitzer Prize in 1972. He established the creative writing program at Stanford University where he taught for many years. Stegner died in 1993.

B. Traven remains a mysterious figure, and his identity is still a matter of debate. He is best known for his novel *The Treasure of the Sierra Madre,* which was adapted for the John Huston film of the same name.

Tennessee Williams was born Thomas Lanier Williams in Mississippi in 1914. Best known for his plays, including *A Streetcar Named Desire* and *Cat On a Hot Tin Roof,* both of which won the Pulitzer Prize, Williams also wrote short stories, works of short fiction, essays, and memoirs. He died in 1983.

ACKNOWLEDGMENTS

by Margerie Lowry. Reprinted by permission of HarperCollins Publishers, Inc. "The Bum" by W. Somerset Maugham. Reprinted with permission of The Estate of Elizabeth Lady Glendevon. Excerpt from *Collages* by Anaïs Nin. Copyright © 1964 by Anaïs Nin. Copyright © 1977 by the Anaïs Nin Trust (Rupert Pole, Trustee). All rights reserved. Reprinted by permission of the Author's Representative, Gunther Stuhlmann. "A Night in the Country" from *A Chance to See Egypt* by Sandra Scofield. Copyright © 1996 by Sandra Scofield. Reprinted by permission of HarperCollins Publishers, Inc. Excerpt from *The Wishing Box* by Dashka Slater. Copyright © 2000 by Dashka Slater. Reprinted by permission of the author and Chronicle Books LLC. Excerpt from *Angle of Repose* by Wallace Stegner. Copyright © 1971 by Wallace Stegner. Used by permission of Doubleday, a division of Random House, Inc. Excerpt from *The Bridge in the Jungle* by B. Traven. Copyright © 1938 by B. Traven. Copyright renewed © 1966 by B. Traven. Reprinted by permission of Hill and Wang, a division of Farrar, Straus and Giroux, LLC. Excerpt from "Night of the Iguana" by Tennessee Williams, from *The Theater of Tennessee Williams*, Vol. IV. Copyright © 1972 by University of the South. Reprinted by permission of New Directions Publishing Corp.